Magenta Rave

JANNA ZONDER

Published by Samille Press, 2013.

PUBLISHER'S NOTE: This is a work of fiction. Names, characters, places, and incidents either are the product of the author's imagination or are used fictitiously, and any resemblance to actual persons, living or dead, business establishments, events, or locales is entirely coincidental.

Cover Design by Janna Zonder

Contact the author through samillepress@gmail.com

ISBN-10: 0615834280
ISBN-13: 978-0615834283

DEDICATION

For Stu Zonder, the love of my life.

Your belief in me, and in this book, has never wavered. I am blessed by all the music, creativity, compassion, and just plain fun you bring to my life.

To the women and children around the world who suffer from physical, sexual, and emotional abuse, you are always in my thoughts. May you find peace and safety soon. A percentage of the profits from this book will be donated to organizations working to end sexual violence.

ACKNOWLEDGMENTS

This book has been years in the making. Many intelligent, book-loving friends have been kind enough to share their advice, support, and wisdom.

Thank you to Catherine Faherty, who called me from the beach with great excitement halfway through the book. You were the first (but not last) reader to do that. I treasure the memory. Michael Brophy, Connie Cronenwett, Carol Sheldon, and Lynn Rowe read early versions of the book. Their insights and enthusiasm greatly influenced my direction and inspired me to continue.

Thank you to Marla Rowe Gorosh for her advice on the medical aspects of the story, and to Katina Rodis and Sue Weaver for their help with the psychological aspects. Any inaccuracies in procedures or medications would be the result of my taking creative license.

Special thanks to author Bryan Robinson, who also advised me on psychological issues, but went way beyond that in his support of my work. Thank you to photographer and writer, Jon Michael Riley, for believing so strongly in this novel. To author and teacher, Vicki Lane, whose novels make you want to curl up on a sofa and read until your eyes are blurry. Your characters live on in my imagination.

Thank you to Justin Smith, Michelle Raese, and Rachelle Rogers for their technical advice. To Ashley Wilson, who supported my writing through her excellent life coaching skills. To David Robinson, artist and life coach, who encouraged me to get the book out the door.

Gabrielle Patterson, Julie Austin, Marty Finkelstein, and Erica Zonder read this book midway to its completion and gave me great feedback. Bridget Glenday, Susan Andresen, Debra Rowe, and Marla Rowe Gorosh read the book most recently. Their enthusiasm convinced me it was finally ready to fly. Thank you all!

Marsha Laura Johnson and Cary Savant—my sisters from another life. You both read *Magenta Rave* and held my hand from hundreds of miles away. Your advice and enthusiasm sustained me. Thank you.

The inspiration for this book came from someone I've never met: Lorena Bobbitt. While I do not condone her crime, she started me thinking about what circumstances or life experiences would cause a woman to commit such a gruesome and intimate act of violence.

Finally, my deepest gratitude to my husband Stu Zonder, who read and edited this book many, many times and never once complained.

ONE

January 14, 1997

Jake Kendrick struggled to lift his head, only to be slapped back down against the pillow by a pounding headache. Sprawling crucifixion-style in the center of the sagging double bed, he clutched the outer edges of the mattress to keep from being tossed off into the spinning room.

Fragments from the previous night floated to the surface of his mind, like snapshots ripped and shredded into half notions. He was on the shore, snagging bits as each wave heaved them a little closer. He began to piece the images together into something resembling a whole picture.

He'd picked up some old gal in a bar. She had a little age on her, but was still decent looking. A redhead with big tits. Jake loved big tits.

Big tits, little brains—ain't that how it goes?

She was easy enough. Seemed like they went back to her place. No, it was a motel. *That's right,* Jake thought, snagging the next scrap of memory that drifted ashore. *That dump over on Cascade. She drove.*

She said her name was Red. He couldn't remember if she said her last name, but what the hell did that matter? She was just the first piece of ass since prison. The first real pussy he'd had in a long time. Plenty more where that came from.

The last thing he remembered was Red handing him a drink at the bar. Some kind of sweet brandy. He didn't like it much, but drank it anyway. She was carrying on like it was the best shit in town. Said it would make him feel higher than Tequila and cocaine mixed together. What the hell.

Then, they were in a motel room that smelled like mold and old socks. *More like old sex,* he thought, chuckling. She had closed the blinds. *What were they doing open now?* He didn't remember opening them.

After closing the blinds, she had winked at him and said, "I'm gonna go in the john and put on something so sexy your whole body will get a hard on. I'll give you a night, baby, you ain't never gonna forget. Just wait and see."

Jake snorted, holding his still throbbing head. "I already forgot most of it."

He began to sense a dry stickiness between his legs and on his butt and muttered, "I must a come like a damn donkey."

His words hung in the empty room. He felt more alone than he had in ten years. At least in prison somebody was always making noise—fights, TVs blaring, the brothers cranking out that damn gangsta rap shit. Even the screams coming from the cells deep in the bowels of the prison—like that prison chaplain once said—"voices of the damned leaking up from hell," were better than silence. As long as it wasn't him screaming. He'd never blacked out before, and the idea terrified him. He shook his head. The room had stopped spinning.

He tried to sit up, but felt a searing pain that started in his cock and radiated throughout his entire pelvis. The pain chiseled its way deep into his lower back.

"OW! Shit!" he said, "What the hell is that?"

His penis felt raw. He could feel its blistered tip brushing against the blanket, like he had an enormous hard-on filled with some kind of infection. Some bug from that nasty cunt, he was sure.

What did that bitch give me? I'll kill her. I'll find her and cut them damn titties right off her—one at a time, nice and slow, he thought, and felt immediately calmer. He took a deep breath.

"It don't matter. Penicillin knocks everything out," he said to the empty room. "Plenty of time to deal with the bitch later."

Jake reached for the reassuring warmth of his cock. Whenever he was afraid or confused, it helped just to put his fingers around it. To feel its morning steel told him he was still one nasty motherfucker to be reckoned with.

He reached, but there was nothing there.

Jake frantically jerked the blanket off, tossing it high into the air before it settled on the floor. He was nude from the waist down. A small, white bandage marked the spot of his phantom erection.

Jake tore out of the bed and the last thing he heard before passing out was the sound of his own screams careening around the room, bounding off the walls, and crashing out into the motel parking lot. Screams that might wake the dead, but would do nothing for the dismembered.

TWO

Detective Simone Rosenberg stood beside the emergency room gurney, watching the slow rise and fall of Jake Kendrick's sheeted chest. When she had been summoned to Atlanta's Peachtree Memorial Hospital, the dispatcher had said, "You're not going to believe this one."

After fifteen years on the job, the last eight as a detective in the Sex Crimes Unit, Simone thought she'd seen everything. Until now, though, sex crimes involving mutilation had been against women or children. How many times had she comforted women with broken bones, slashed faces and breasts, or ruptured internal organs? How many times had she struggled to keep her composure while interviewing girls or boys, babies really, barely able to speak, with enormous sad eyes and ripped underpants? The women could have been her; the girls, her daughter. Jake Kendrick's mutilation was a first.

Her partner, Marty Sloan, who'd been across the room taking the responding officer's statement, ambled towards her, jingling his pocket change in double time as a counterpoint to the slow pace of his walk.

"Uniform says the guy's name is Jake Kendrick. He was out of his head when they got there. Raving about some redhead he met in a bar last night. Said the last thing he remembered was going to that sleazy motel over on Cascade. You know the one. The Traveler's Rest?"

Simone nodded.

"Kendrick said the redhead came out of the bathroom wearing some kind of belly dancing outfit. You know, with the veil covering her mouth? Seems him and her were about to get down and dirty when the next thing old Jake here knows is he wakes up with a nice neat bandage where his dick used to be."

"Jesum Piece! She take everything?" Simone asked.

"Nah, just the meat. She left the potatoes," Marty said.

"Grandpa told me we should've never left Jamaica. He said America is full of trash."

"Trash or not, you ain't telling me you're shocked by this. Hell, this is sanitized compared to what we usually find. No blood. No sign of a struggle. The damage wrapped up like some kind of present, for God's sake. I'm surprised she didn't tie a little red bow on it." Marty's disgust was palpable.

"Yeah, I know, Marty. It's just . . . something bothers me about this one."

"Bet it bothers me more." Marty crossed his legs and shielded his groin with both hands. Eyes opened wide, he bit down hard on his lower lip.

"Settle down, partner." Simone choked back a giggle that threatened to blossom into her signature full-throated belly laugh.

"When's he going to wake up?" Marty asked.

Simone looked around for the emergency room physician she had spoken with earlier. The area outside the cubicle where Kendrick's gurney was parked resembled a termite colony, with workers milling about methodically, dulled out, as if programmed before birth for some specific function.

"I'll find that doc we talked to earlier." Simone spoke over her shoulder as she strode out of the room.

Marty stood in the doorway watching as men and women alike made an aisle in the narrow hallway for her to pass. At the age of forty-two, Simone Pinnock Rosenberg's beauty had settled on her nearly six-foot frame in a way that reminded Marty of a retired thoroughbred. She still had the fluidity of movement, the grace and speed in action, but was no longer coltish, as she'd been when they first started working together.

She sure makes an impression, he thought.

AS SHE WALKED THROUGH THE HOSPITAL CORRIDOR, Simone deliberately ignored the buzz that thrummed around her. She'd had a lifetime of being valued for her looks, and knew it to be a hollow satisfaction. African and English on her father's side, Irish and Cherokee on her mother's, Simone had golden skin, high cheekbones, abundant curly black hair, and light green eyes that shimmered when she was amused.

She had immigrated with her family to the United States when she was four years old, but had spent many summers visiting her grandparents in Jamaica. As a child, she'd hated the staring eyes; people always trying to figure out exactly what race she was. When she lived with her mother, they assumed she was a mostly white girl, though certainly not "pure." When it was her father's turn, she was black, but usually not black enough for her darker schoolmates. She found it tedious to be drawn within such narrow lines.

Simone kicked up her pace into a full-blown lope and spotted the young intern scribbling notes a few feet ahead of her in the hallway. She called to him, and even her voice caused heads to turn. Especially his.

Simone was unfailingly polite in her dealings with the public. That, coupled with her slight Jamaican lilt, sprinkled with *patois* when she was so inclined, often left criminals wishing there had been just a little more they could have told her.

"Doc, okay if we try to wake Mr. Kendrick?" she asked.

"He should be coming around about now," he said. "You can give him a little nudge."

"By the way, Detective, I'm Jeff Saul." The doctor clinched Simone's extended hand and held her next to him in the hallway. "I know you must be as busy as I am, but . . ."

The young doctor hesitated, stammered slightly, then forged ahead. "Would you like to have dinner sometime?"

He's at least ten years younger than me, Simone thought. *Just what I need—another kid to take care of.*

"Sorry, doc, I'm already taken," she lied, and disengaged her hand from his. "But, thanks for asking."

"Figures," he said, taking one last, long, look at her. Simone heard him mumble as he walked away, head down, once again scribbling on a patient chart, "Women like you always are."

Men usually responded to Simone in one of two ways. They either fell instantly in love, more specifically, in lust, and couldn't do enough for her; or they were so intimidated that they constantly tried to prove their superiority. Either condition annoyed her.

The main reason her partnership with Marty had worked so well for over eight years was that he didn't fall into either of those categories. She'd never met anyone with more confidence than Marty. He was barely 5'8," wired like a hummingbird, with sandy blond hair, and a complexion that tended toward tomato red when he stayed too long in the sun. He'd never left his family's farm located north of Atlanta and commuted an hour or more, depending on traffic, to continue living there. He was a rarity for Simone—a happily married man.

"DOC SAY WE CAN WAKE UP sleeping beauty here?" Marty asked, when Simone had returned.

"Long as you don't expect me to kiss him to do it." Simone brushed an unruly curl off her cheek and tucked it back into her ponytail.

Marty nudged Jake Kendrick's shoulder. "Mr. Kendrick? Detective Sloan. I need to ask you a few questions."

Jake mumbled and slapped Marty's hand away.

Marty shook him harder.

"Leave me the fuck alone!" Jake growled and promptly fell back asleep.

Simone had been staring at Jake while Marty tried to rouse him. "God help us if women start acting like men."

"What are you talking about?" Marty asked.

"I figured out what bothers me so much about this crime. Think about it. Men go around killing or maiming anybody who pisses them off. Their mumsy don't love them enough, boo hoo, they go out and kill somebody else's mama. Their daddy beats them or belittles them, maybe they don't feel so much like a man, they go rape some woman . . . or twenty women. Girlfriend dumps them; they go to her job and pump a few rounds into anything that moves—people, dogs, birds. They don't care. If women start doing the same thing, I don't even want to think about the kind of trouble we're in for. Up 'til now, at least half the human race knew how to behave—most of the time, anyway."

Marty rolled his eyes and looked at her like she'd just declared Venusians would soon be taking over the world.

"Aw, it's probably some old gal got jealous or something 'cause this dream boat of a guy dumped her. Tell me you ain't gonna turn it into the whole damn civilization splittin' apart at the seams. You know what, Rosenberg? You were married to that civil rights nut too long. You see a conspiracy everywhere you look. What's that old saying? Sometimes a cigar is just a cigar."

Marty glanced ruefully in the direction of Jake Kendrick's recent loss and added, "In this case, I will admit it's a short little stogie."

Simone laughed. Marty had a point. Her former husband, Eli Rosenberg, had never learned to live peacefully with what he couldn't change. In 1964, when he had traveled South on the freedom buses and marched alongside sharecroppers and maids, risking his life for something more important than breathing, he'd expected nothing less than a metamorphosis over night. When change came slowly and at great cost, and worst of all, when the African-American community turned much of its collective anger against the Jews, his passions disintegrated into bitterness, and eventually paranoia.

Eli had been Simone's political science professor sophomore year at the University of Michigan, and she had married him shortly after graduation. Before meeting him, Simone had never given racial politics much thought. Oh, she'd experienced plenty of racism, but she refused to be held hostage to other people's insanity. They could just damn well own it for themselves. Simone had always appreciated and accepted differences in people as part of a grand pageantry of life. Her own family gatherings resembled a United Nations meeting, with skin colors that ranged from deepest ebony to caramel to cream. To hate or fear other races, she would have to think of them as fundamentally different from herself. How could she do that without hating her own family? Whenever she looked into a mirror, she saw the entire human race represented there. Europe, Africa, Asia. Her face was a perfect seamless puzzle, an amalgam of bits and pieces of every other human soul.

Eli had changed her all right. She was no longer the trusting island girl she had once been, but neither was she a woman given to irrational fears. Yet, something about this case unnerved her. Whoever committed this crime had breached the most deeply embedded cultural taboo in the world. What else might this suspect be capable of?

Simone heard Marty's dancing pocket change, just before he lightly tapped her on the shoulder.

"Hey," he said, wearing a look of utter confidence. "I'll bet you ten bucks it's some old girlfriend getting even."

"Maybe you're right," she said.

THREE

Easter Sunday, 1973

Dressed in his finest white polyester suit with matching bucks, the Reverend Clyde Graves swayed and blindly groped the primitive oak pulpit. His bony, searching hands clutched its edges like talons, locking him into place. His knees buckled, but his grip held firm. Much to his relief, he did not keel over. Instead, he gathered himself with great dignity and slowly lowered his head until his cheek rested beside the open Bible on the pulpit's crude surface.

As was his custom, he'd arisen early that morning and prayed for guidance before coming to church. In honor of the Lord's resurrection day, he had also allowed himself an extra hour for dressing. Vanity, he knew, was a sin, but on special days God would forgive him. His pompadour had to be perfect. If hair was a woman's crowning glory, then surely it was also proof of a man's virility. He'd fussed with it in his cramped bathroom, admiring himself in the steam-sweated mirror, combing it one way and then another, molding and sculpting it, until he swelled with pride. Now it hung lifeless as a fast-food mop, black and greasy, veiling his tear drenched face and soiling the Bible's gilded edge.

Despite his attempts to maintain his dignity, an insidious line of drool snaked its way towards the Bible, leaving him feeling dirty and weak. He moaned and shuddered slightly. Then, seized by a force outside himself, he jerked rigidly upright and whipped his head in a backward motion, sending spittle and tears and pomade sailing across the first two rows of the congregation. In the arc of the movement, his pale blue eyes opened and then rolled back into his head. A thick strand of hair settled and stuck on the bridge of his nose. He did not bother to remove it.

Slowly he righted himself and focused upon his flock. His head rocked slightly as it settled atop his thin neck. His weariness was palpable, but his icicle eyes daggered the congregation to their seats, paralyzing them, while he regained his composure.

"I'm talking about sin today, brethren," he said. "The sin that our precious Jesus died for."

He grunted the word "for" out in two syllables, "four-unh," pained and struggling, as if it contained the last exhalation he would ever make in this veil of tears called life. Then he solemnly, laboriously, sucked air back into his body.

Seated behind the Reverend in gray metal folding chairs, an amen semi-circle of elders erupted. These were men who had proven their loyalty to the Reverend and, therefore, to God.

"Hallelujah. Praise the Lord, Brother Clyde."

When the elders punctuated his sermons with praise and hallelujahs, Reverend Graves felt even stronger, as though God Himself had ordained a mighty cheering squad to back him on the battlefield of iniquity.

"Did Jesus die so men could mince around and not do right in their manly duties?" The Reverend curled his upper lip and tiptoed across the raised platform, effeminately swaying his hips.

"No, I say! It's an abomination!" he shouted and then sharply turned and slid across the floor on one foot, landing at the center of the amen circle. He lowered his head. Letting his arms hang limply by his side, he dangled before the congregation like a marionette manipulated by some divine, demented puppeteer. Then, lifting his arms to heaven, he strutted around the circle, occasionally stopping to pound the men on their chests and press his palm to their foreheads. In his exuberance, he even stomped hard on a couple of feet. Why not? It was nothing compared to Jesus' suffering. Besides, no matter what he did, they would still revere him. He was God's emissary.

"Amen, Brother Clyde! Oh Lord, oh Lord!" the elders shouted. They clapped their hands. They whistled and groaned. They hummed and bellowed. Their clatter wove itself around every pause in the Reverend's sermon.

More than anything, the Reverend loved the rhythms of his sermons. The rhythms transported him deep inside to the core of God's wrath, and from there, he could understand what was expected of him.

The heathens of High Point, Georgia,—meaning anyone who was not a member of his church—called him nothing but an old country "err-rah" preacher. He didn't care. They'd get theirs on Judgment Day. When his mind was vibrating to God's mighty tuning fork, there was nothing he could do but fill in the spaces between his thoughts with the rhythm that God, Himself, had put in his head.

"Did Jesus (err-rah) die so our women (err-rah) could walk the streets (err-rah) painted like the whores of Sodom (err-rah) and Gomorrah?

"No!" He answered his own question.

The congregation rippled before him. Hands reached toward heaven. Paper fans on wide popsicle-stick handles, picturing a serene blond and blue-eyed haloed Jesus on one side, and advertising for Graves funeral parlor on the other, fluttered like captive parrots. The pot-bellied stove in the corner hissed.

The mountains had not yet awakened from the death sleep of winter and were biting cold; but inside the one-room church, filled to capacity with over a hundred worshippers, the heat was alive. The heat was partner to the Reverend. It reminded the parishioners of hell.

"Satan? I said Satan? Get thee away from me and mine!"

The church sisters, in passionate embrace of the power let loose in the room, had begun to leap and stagger from the pews. Ample breasts and buttocks wrestled for space in the narrow confines of the aisles. Easter hats bobbed and floated like spring blossoms carried on a mighty wind. They shouted in tongues, a language only God understood; but the sisters felt the electricity surging through their bodies. They were the receptors of a heavenly Morse code sent from the omniscient mind of The Almighty. They were not required to understand the power that came over them. They had only to feel it, to open themselves, and let Him in. Their eyes glassed over, the light from within struggling to illuminate the darkness. Their lids shrouded. They surrendered.

The Reverend had been at it for more than an hour and had now come to his favorite moment in every sermon. With an almost imperceptible nod and a knowing smirk, the Reverend signaled the elders from the amen circle to move into the mass and catch the women as they fainted.

"God is working with us today! Praise the Lord," the elders murmured as they assisted the writhing women onto the floor.

THE REVEREND'S DAUGHTER, SIX-YEAR-OLD PATSY GAIL, had attended church every Sunday and Wednesday of her life, but the contortions and screams, the wild laughter, and the words she couldn't understand, still terrified her. Easter Sundays were the worst. She dreaded being reminded of sweet Jesus, who loved all the little children, red and yellow, black and white, tortured on a cross, with rusty nails piercing his flesh, his gentle arms dripping blood, his feet, swollen and bruised, seeping blood.

Jesus watched her from the wall above her daddy's head in the church, and from the wall in her living room, and from the calendar on the wall in the kitchen. She was petrified by the thought that anyone could rise up from a grave. God's spirit slipped into the bodies of everyone else in the church. It made them dance and shout. It filled them with happiness. She could not let Him come into her. Crying tears of blood, Jesus stood in the bushes outside her window each night, scratching against her screen, begging to be let in. Begging for comfort. But she was too afraid, and that was a sin.

Patsy Gail was small for her age. A runt, her father said. She had his startling blue eyes, but her hair was blond, a gift from a mother she could no longer remember. On a bench at the back of the church, sitting frozen beside her Uncle Ted, she resembled a tiny ice sculpture chiseled into perfect, inanimate, shape.

When the frenzy became unbearable, she slid from her seat and crawled upon the floor. Feeling her way along, her vision obscured by tears and a blinding panic, she searched for a place to hide amid the stomping feet and flailing bodies.

She managed to squeeze underneath the pew between two elderly women. Their flowered Easter dresses hung to their ankles and closed in front of her, creating a curtain. She cautiously peeked at her father through the narrow gap between the dresses and waited for the quiet that would follow the righteous storm.

THE REVEREND HAD NOT NOTICED when Patsy Gail slipped

away from his brother Ted's side. God had placed the burden of leadership upon the Reverend's solid shoulders; surely Ted could manage one small child. The Reverend would not crumble from the weight of his Almighty mandate, nor would he be bothered with trivialities.

Breathing raggedly, he mopped his forehead with a farmer's large handkerchief that had been handed to him by one of his elders. He opened his Bible. "Jesus spoke to John in Revelation, saying, 'Jezebel calleth herself a prophetess, to teach and to seduce my servants to commit fornication. I gave her space to repent and she repented not. I will kill her children with death, and I will give unto every one of you according to your works.'

"According to our works, brothers and sisters. Oh, you can try to hide, but God knows every hair on your head." As if to emphasize his point, he flipped his head sideways and the errant clump of hair that had clung steadfast to his nose slipped obediently back into place.

"Where will you hide from God? Just like he knew what Jezebel was up to, he knows what you're a-doin' and he knows what you're a-plannin' on a-doin'."

"Lord, here I am," Sister Lurleen shouted from the front pew. Her shrill voice grated against the Reverend's ears, causing him to look in her direction. Fat thighs vibrated as she felt the power of God surge through her. The movement in her body created a slight opening between her skirt and her neighbor's, revealing the Reverend's terrified daughter crouched between the two old women.

"Patsy Gail Graves!" The Reverend thundered and leapt from the pulpit. Like a striking rattlesnake, his arm shot between the women and jerked the child out by the wrist. He sensed a disjoining pop in her shoulder and with a malevolent look, dared her to cry. When she didn't, he was oddly dissatisfied.

He yanked her up, holding her high above his head like some prized trophy, and strutted back towards the pulpit. She hung limply, passively. "You can try to hide like this fool child," he said, "but God knows where you are. Don't never lie to yourself about that, brothers and sisters."

The Reverend lowered Patsy Gail to the floor, but did not release her. She stood beside him, small, forlorn, unable to look at the faces of congregational judgment. Her ruffled yellow dress, two sizes too large, hung slightly off her left shoulder. Her black patent leather shoes were scuffed. Her right calf bore a bruise, a remnant from a belt buckle that had strayed further down her body than the Reverend liked. Clyde Graves' aim was usually more accurate.

"Sinful women, look ye to God for forgiveness. Only He can cleanse you. Y'all know, good as I do, that it was Eve started this mess way back when the Lord was just trying out the idea of free will for folks.

"When Satan come to Eve in the form of a serpent, did Eve call out to Adam to help her? Did she say to Satan, 'Let me talk to my husband first?' Did she say, 'Satan, you need to talk to my husband?'

"No. Ol' Eve said, 'I don't need no man. I can talk for my own self!'"

The congregation burst into wild, knowing laughter. Every man and woman there knew the hell to pay for ignoring a husband's authority.

"Only man gets his instructions direct from God. It ain't just me saying this, children. You don't believe me? Look it up in your own Bible."

The Reverend had noticed a few fleeting scornful looks passed between women in the congregation. This inspired him to make his point even stronger.

"It's man's job to pass those instructions on to his woman and his children. The man must let his family know, in no uncertain terms, what God expects of them. And, the man must see to it that God's will is done.

"But, Eve, way back in the Garden of Eden, thought she knew better than Adam. Thought she knew better than God even, and look where it's landed us now."

Heads shook sympathetically.

"Umm, umm, umm," the people said. "Yes, Lord. Preach the word, Brother Clyde." The rhythm was full upon him now, coming from within, reflecting back, echoing from his flock.

"But Adam was just as bad. You know why?" he asked, contemptuously.

"Tell us Brother Clyde," a nasal voice from the congregation begged to know.

"Because, oh my brothers, Adam was weak. He let hisself be led like a lamb to slaughter—all because he was too afraid to take control of his woman. The woman made from his very rib! Made just for him! He knew what God wanted, but he let hisself be tempted. If Adam knew how to act like a man, we'd be living in paradise right now. And we wouldn't have no confusion about who does what to who neither. Can you hear God talking to you today?"

The distinction between individuals had blurred before the Reverend's eyes until the room appeared to be filled with the movement and emotion of one huge, many legged and armed entity, reminding him of some promised beast of the apocalypse.

"Amen. Amen. Hallelujah," the beast roared back at him. "Preach the word." It purred and slithered as it sweated out of its skin.

Patsy Gail had seen the beast too. It growled at her and wanted to eat her.

The Reverend picked her up again, this time gently cradling her and lifting her towards heaven as an offering.

He walked the length of the raised platform with Patsy Gail held firmly in his arms. Turning toward the congregation, he intoned, "As you tested Abraham and asked him to sacrifice his only child to you, Lord, I say not my will, but thine, oh Lord. Praise Jesus."

He heard a satisfying collective gasp from some of mothers in the congregation. When God did not take his child, he lowered her once again, with considerable disappointment, to a standing position.

"Do not be weak, my brothers. Do your duty as men. Yes, we are put here to be kind to them lesser than us, but don't get yourself confused over what's kindness and what's weakness. You have got to see to the discipline of your family. God gave man domination over the animals and the plants and even the mighty seas."

He paused, letting the force of his words settle into the hearts of the congregation. Then, he continued, "And over *woman.*

"Now, I know some of you ladies don't want to hear this but 'let him who has ears' harken to the voice of God. If we men do not take control of our families and follow the righteous path that God is leading us on . . ."

The Reverend struggled to maintain his composure.

"John said, 'the earth will be drunk with the wine of fornication, and woman will be drunk with the blood of saints.'

"Time is not long on this earth, brothers and sisters. Jesus said, 'behold I come quickly, and my reward is with me, to give every man according as his work shall be. I am the Alpha and Omega, the beginning and the end, the first and the last.'

"Oh my brethren, do not be found wanting on that day when Jesus comes."

The Reverend gave a final shudder and dropped to one

knee. He absently put his arm around his daughter's thin, quaking shoulders, leaning on her to keep himself from toppling over.

"Ted!" he cried, gasping. "Ted, come get this girl and keep her until I can teach her how to behave in church."

He gazed out into the congregation and slowly shook his head. A bemused smile played artfully against the background of his tear-streaked face. His eyes, now softened and washed pure, told the congregation that a beleaguered father's work was never done.

Ted, the Reverend's twin and mirror image, sauntered down the center aisle towards the pulpit. Women, who only moments before had been nearly unconscious on the floor, miraculously recovered their senses and scrambled for their seats. Despite the fact that today was the holiest day of the year, Ted Graves was dressed in tight jeans, work boots, and an old flannel work shirt. He felt nothing but contempt for his reverend brother who adorned himself like a peacock, strutting to attract some female. He hadn't met a female yet he couldn't take.

The sensuous, undulating quality of his movements caused the women, young and old, to look down at the Bibles clutched in their laps. As he strolled past each row, a heat of flushing cheeks spread to the outer edges of the room. The women fidgeted, bit their lips, and reached for their husbands' hands.

Without saying a word, Ted lifted Patsy Gail and carried her toward the back door. The Reverend slumped down to both knees when the burden of his daughter was lifted from him.

The choir director stepped forward. He gently placed his hand on the back of the kneeling Reverend and said, "Now let us sing 'Washed in the Blood of Jesus'."

As the guitarist hit the opening chord, Patsy Gail

screamed, "No! No!"

Her pleas went unanswered, swallowed by the maddening din that filled the room.

WHILE SHE WAS BEING CARRIED, Patsy Gail took control of the only part of herself that she could. She held her breath until her lips turned blue and she passed out. When she awoke, she saw the pink canopy of her bed floating above her. She had ascended into the clouds and they were tinged pink with the blood of Jesus. The blood became heavier and heavier until she began to suffocate from the weight of it. She tried to sit up, but felt a knee on each side of her hips sinking into the mattress. A coarse hand gripped her injured shoulder. A body hovered above her, blacking out the light. It wore a devil's mask, only lips, eyes, and nose showing.

"You can't hide from God, child," a voice hissed at her.

Where was the voice coming from? She couldn't tell. It enveloped her.

Hot breath, reeking of alcohol and tobacco, coated her face and seeped underneath her skin, crawling the length of her, raising goose flesh of revulsion as it traveled along her body. She didn't remember having taken her clothes off, but they were gone except for one sock. She had put the sock on inside out that morning. The lace was scratching her ankle.

A bead of sweat dripped upon her narrow chest from the dark figure above her and ran down her side. She felt it drop off her body and imagined it soaking into her new bedspread. She worried that she would be in trouble if it left a stain.

She was about to beg to be let up when she felt a ripping of the flesh between her legs, down there, in that part of herself that she was not allowed to touch or to name. He had put something inside her that seared upward through her body from that forbidden spot until she was consumed by flames. When she tried to scream, a hand covered her mouth and nose.

This must be Satan, she thought. I would not let Jesus in, so Satan has come instead. This must be the end of the world like Daddy said.

He tore and thrashed and pounded his huge body into her tiny one. His eyes roamed the length of her, but he would not look at her face. It was as if she had no face. She had a mouth that was given to her simply to be silenced. She felt herself shattering against him into a thousand tiny, blistered shards. He was made of iron, and she had turned to glass.

When he was done, he collapsed on top of her, motionless, crushing all but the last breath from her body. Her silent blood seeped from her and burned circles onto the pink comforter beneath her hips.

Flashes of light darted and swam in the darkness behind her eyelids like thousands of lightning bugs. She imagined that she could climb upon the back of one and fly away to heaven. There she would find that it was God who had entered her and not Satan. She would get her reward on the other side for bearing the suffering of God.

But the lightning bugs blinked out and left her alone, trapped in a dark distortion, trembling. She was burned beyond recognition, and would have been lost, except she heard a voice coming from somewhere deep inside her.

"I'm your friend," it said. "Don't worry. I'll take care of you."

And, nothing else lived inside her anymore. Not God, nor Satan. Not even herself. Just one small fierce voice that promised protection.

Before he got off her, he whispered, "God works in mysterious ways, runt. He'll kill you if you tell anybody."

Then, he laughed.

FOUR

January 15, 1997
Long-Lasting Effects of Childhood Sexual Abuse, 1997: A Case Study of Seven Female Survivors
Delia Whitfield, Ph.D. Clinical Psychology
Client IDs 616-01 through 616-04
Weekly Group Session

After an already exhausting day, Dr. Delia Whitfield was finishing up insurance claim forms while waiting for her regular Monday evening therapy group to arrive. *Damn insurance companies*, she thought. They made filing claims torturous in the hopes that therapists would give up, and they wouldn't have to reimburse them. They delayed compensation for months, left her on hold when she tried to phone them, and when they finally did pay, she'd already spent more hours trying to collect than the claims were worth.

"This sucks, doesn't it girl?" She slammed the paperwork down onto the desktop. Her dog, Sophie, a flop-eared brown mutt she'd rescued from an interstate median, had managed to squeeze up under the desk and was dozing on Delia's feet.

Many of her colleagues had already gone to a cash only,

full fee policy. Delia didn't blame them. She was practically working for free these days. After ten years in private practice, between compliance with state mandated requirements for continuing education, the high cost of malpractice insurance, and her pro bono clients, she barely broke even. Fortunately, her husband John had independent means and didn't care in the least how much money she made. Or didn't make. In fact, the less John knew about her practice, the happier he was.

Delia looked at her watch. It was almost time to start. With the exception of one newcomer, she had been working with the same Monday night group for almost six years. They would straggle in shortly.

Delia housed her practice in a Craftsman's bungalow she'd purchased while finishing her Ph.D. in Clinical Psychology at the University of Georgia. At the time, she was just looking for a cheap way to live and go to school. She'd had no idea the Midtown Atlanta neighborhood would one day become one of the most desirable in the city. The original homeowners, fearing the changing demographics, had flown to the burbs like white homing pigeons. Druggies, pimps and prostitutes had gradually taken control of the neighborhood.

Delia had paid thirty thousand dollars for the place when the neighborhood was at its worst. Working feverishly the first couple of weeks after moving in, she'd removed condoms, syringes and liquor bottles from the front yard. Over the next six months, after full days of teaching and writing her dissertation, she'd sanded and scraped and painted. To her great surprise, underneath the layers of filth and old wallpaper, was a lovely home with hardwood floors and a working fireplace. Her bedroom's antique beveled windows were positioned perfectly to catch the early morning light, and her small lot was covered with mature azaleas and lush flowering dogwoods. Ancient enormous oaks lined the street, giving much needed shade in the hot months of July and August. By the time she'd married John, she was too attached to sell the house.

From the first, Delia had taken great care to create a safe and nurturing environment for her clients, even though it took her years to recoup her costs from the sliding scale fees she charged. She had chosen colors that were close to nature—soft roses and greens, sunny yellows, Caribbean blues. They were heightened hues, not overpowering but significant, like the colors in a Georgia O'Keefe painting.

Exquisite sculptures of goddesses and angels stood guard like talismans against their devils. Smiling grandmother dolls and laughing baby dolls adorned tabletops. Paintings of powerful or serene women covered the walls. Her criterion for choosing art was how she felt when she looked at a piece. If she felt uplifted or empowered, or simply soothed by an image, she bought it. She was determined to create a new reality for the women, if only for the short time they were with her.

Their reality, the one in which they lived every day, their inner reality, was as bleak as a graffiti laden subway ride to hell. They had no need to be reminded during therapy of the chaos and violence in the world. Each woman had survived her own personal war, her own Vietnam, her Rwanda, where the allies and enemies looked alike and spoke the same language. It was a guerrilla war in which they found themselves, never knowing when the enemy might spring from behind the bushes or lunge at them from their own dinner tables with no warning.

Women who've been attacked never feel completely safe, but Delia had managed to create a tenuous safe haven for them in her practice. Like the over-feathered nest of a protective mother eagle, her sanctuary safeguarded the women and held them aloft, until one day they would be able to fly away from her for good.

Delia again slammed down the paperwork. She could only look at those absurd claim forms for so long before she felt fury building up inside. Why should anyone have to jump through so many damn hoops just to collect what they're owed?

"Enough of this! Let's see who's here, Sophie" Delia said.

Apparently forgetting she was under a desk, Sophie sprang up and banged her head on the way out.

"Watch it, girl," Delia said, gently patting the unfazed dog.

Delia calmed herself, putting on her best therapist's face, and strolled through the office towards the meeting room. She loved the abundant life she had created throughout the house. Jade plants, dieffenbachia, wandering Jews, fresh cut flowers in crystal vases filled every room, each plant bursting with good health.

She was especially fond of the elaborate salt-water fish tank in the waiting room that covered half a wall with color and movement. When her clients' rage and grief threatened to overwhelm her, she would gaze into the fish tank until she regained her balance. The creatures darting through the water, playing hide and seek among the swaying plants and coral reef, the sacrifice of the feeder fish swimming out their brief lives, the subculture of amphipods, shrimp, and crabs, everything working in a delicate balance, reassured her that there was purpose, or at least order, in the universe.

By the time she reached the meeting room, her clients were already seated quietly in a circle. Sophie lumbered ahead of Delia, circling among the group, collecting head pats, licking a hand here and there, until she was in her favorite spot under a tall ficus tree in the corner.

Delia seated herself in the group. "Welcome everyone. Let's begin by going inside. Check within yourself. Are all parts of each person comfortable with holding hands tonight?"

The question was essential for her clients with Dissociative Identity Disorder, a condition formerly known as multiple personality. If Delia didn't check beforehand, it never failed that one of the frightened, fragmented parts would surface and act out, ruining their centering process.

Once she had ascertained that each person could tolerate being touched—at least for the moment—she said, "Close your eyes and let's take some deep centering breaths. While you are breathing, imagine yourself surrounded by a golden healing light. This light is made up of the most perfect peace anyone could ever experience. This light fills your mind and body and pulsates around you. Feel its warmth as it flows from you to your sister. From your hand to her hand and from her hand on and on until the circle is complete, and we are bathed in a golden halo. Now feel yourself letting go of tension, feel your shoulders and neck relax, continue to breathe deeply and slowly, and be content and safe in this circle of light."

As they held hands, Delia looked around at each woman and felt stirred by love and concern as she watched their expressions slowly evolve from anxious and angry to almost peaceful. Over the course of the years, she had guided them from near incapacitation to the relatively high functioning, productive women they had become. Still, they would probably never be "cured." How does anyone ever completely get over what these women had endured? Is anyone well in a culture that winks and says, "Boys will be boys?" Is anyone well when the culture is sick?

Yet, Delia felt hopeful for her little group.

Directly to her right sat Bea Watkins, the oldest member at age seventy. A hard working, wiry countrywoman, Bea was kind and comical, with a slightly bawdy sense of humor. Her speech pattern was somewhat archaic, as if she were still living in an earlier time when the State of Georgia was isolated from the rest of the country.

Bea's only child, a daughter named Ruth, was long dead from complications caused by a botched appendectomy. As a result, she had taken the younger women in the group under her wing, mothering them the way she longed to mother her own daughter. Mothering them the way they longed to be mothered. She often brought home made cookies and butter-filled pies to share after the group meetings.

Sometimes Delia had to remind herself that this loving, funny woman had spent thirty years married to a man who beat and belittled her when he was drunk, and ignored her when he was sober.

After her daughter Ruth died, Bea lost the will to fight her husband. She prayed that he would go ahead and kill her. Her religious beliefs prevented her from leaving him or from committing suicide, so she was stuck waiting, hoping that some storm would blow through Georgia's tornado alley and kill them both in their cursed marriage bed.

When at last her tormentor died from cirrhosis of the liver, Bea's ability to feel returned slowly over time. Her emotions tingled within her like tiny pinpricks at first, as if her heart had fallen asleep, and was beginning to awaken. Then, one day without warning, the emotions ambushed her. Unrelenting waves of grief and shame coursed through her thin body. She was a proud woman whose rural background had prevented her from asking for help. Country people were supposed to be entirely self-sufficient, but after stumbling upon a lecture given by Delia at the local library, she had started therapy with her the next week, hoping to understand how she, a perfectly capable woman, could have given away her life to an ignorant tyrant.

Next to Bea sat Tina Galenski, age thirty-five, from Union City, New Jersey, the only non-native southerner in the group. Of all the women, Tina was the most reluctant to voice her feelings during the group sessions and had lately resorted to bringing poems she had written.

She'd been a quiet child, so reluctant to talk that her mother had called her Mouse. It was a name she hated. What are mice but disease carrying vermin that no one wants around? Her silence in group therapy was a deep, mysterious pit that everyone skirted, to avoid falling into a searing pain perhaps blacker than their own. But in private sessions, Tina had gradually opened up, revealing a childhood so traumatizing that Delia wondered what quality within, what tiny speck of self-esteem, had allowed her to survive. Rage, Delia had decided. Rage kept Tina going. It fed her and protected her. It made her quick and able to predict consequences.

Tina was exquisitely beautiful, with hazel eyes, honey blond hair to her shoulders, and a glittering toughness that she wore like a suit of razors. She made her living as a lingerie model for a small shop off Cascade in Southwest Atlanta called The Sultan's Palace. She didn't mind the work. Seducing men was something she was well qualified for, by both looks and experience.

Next sat Catherine O'Donnell, professional actress and group dynamo. Delia always kept a special watch during group sessions over Catherine, her only Dissociative Identity Disorder client. Tonight was no different. So far, she seemed exceptionally content. In fact, Delia had never seen Catherine's face and body posture so relaxed this early in the centering process.

Delia had identified four distinct personalities, whom Catherine referred to as the "cousins." She and Delia had worked together for more than seven years to integrate the cousins into one core personality. But Catherine feared she would be destroying the best parts of herself if she integrated them. She insisted they were to remain alive and separate.

Instead, she had created a one-woman show around them and their shared childhood sexual abuse. Each of the "cousins" performed from a particular point of view. Catherine was fully aware of what they were doing and could step in if any personality began to lose control. It was as close to integration of the personalities as she was willing to go, and Delia, for the moment, considered it a victory.

At the age of thirty-eight, Catherine was in her prime professionally. The age range of characters she could play was as broad as it ever would be. Like many people who are blond as children, Catherine's hair had darkened to a warm brown, which created a startling contrast between her alabaster skin and deep blue eyes. She was charismatic, with a keen intellect. The more Delia learned about the depravity of Catherine's abusers, the more amazed she became that Catherine could function at all. Outwardly, she appeared to be the most successful member of the group.

Delia was learning, however, that Catherine was truly the consummate actress, who could substitute an imaginary world for the real one at will. Often during their private sessions, just when they were beginning to make headway, Catherine would retreat into a fictional past she had created for herself as a child. Or, she would allow one of the most stubborn, impossible "cousins" to speak for her. Getting Catherine to confront her pain required all of Delia's skills as a therapist, and she often felt like she was slow dancing on eggshells.

Completing the circle was Janet Hobbs, a morbidly obese woman with a lovely face that was positively radiant on those rare occasions when she smiled. She weighed three hundred and fifty pounds, and at twenty-four, was the group's youngest and newest member.

Janet had been raped and beaten repeatedly as a child by

her father. She was terrified of relationships with men, but the overriding emotion Delia felt from her was a suffocating grief, as if she were in mourning for her lost childhood. Underneath the layers of fat camouflage, lay a grief as still as death.

I need to get some help with Janet. Nutritionist, exercise coach, maybe antidepressants—she's still so hostile and unable to talk. Janet's problems overwhelmed Delia at times.

The women had been holding hands and visualizing light for a couple of minutes. Delia smiled as she watched relaxation settle on each woman's face. Their frown lines softened, they sighed and yawned. Even Sophie emitted a long, heartfelt groan from her corner of the room. Delia watched as the women's faces registered Sophie's "comment" with smiles all around. The centering exercise was an effective technique for leaving the day's baggage outside.

"Now give your sister to the right a little squeeze." Delia paused as the women gently squeezed each other's hands.

"And now your sister to the left."

Again the women complied.

"When you open your eyes, take with you into the session the knowledge that we are supporting each other in this very important work tonight. When you feel ready, slowly open your eyes."

The women stretched their arms upward and rolled their heads from side to side. They shifted in their chairs and stretched their feet out in front of them. Gradually, they opened their eyes. They spread their chairs out to create the amount of personal space each one needed. Once they were settled, Delia asked, "Who wants to claim time tonight?"

Catherine O'Donnell leapt from her seat. "Me!" she said.

She held a copy of the *Atlanta Times* in front of her and walked around the room from woman to woman, making certain everyone got a good look. On the front page, Jake

Kendrick's most recent mug shot appeared with the headline, "**_Bloody Jake Assaulted._**"

In a voice that was fluid and melodious, but edged with contempt, Catherine read aloud the account of Jake's misfortune.

In a bizarre reversal of history, Jake Kendrick was the victim of a sexual assault some time after midnight last night. Kendrick, also known as "Bloody Jake," met the female assailant at The Fox's Hole, a bar located on the south side of Atlanta. Kendrick stated that he and the woman had spent the evening drinking and, afterwards, had driven to the Traveler's Rest Motel on Cascade Avenue, where the woman had rented a room for the night.

A spokesperson for the Atlanta Police Department said Kendrick was drugged at some point in the evening. When he regained consciousness the following morning, he discovered that his penis had been surgically removed.

Police describe the alleged assailant as a buxom woman with bright red hair, approximately 5'7" tall, wearing blue stretch pants, a blue denim shirt with glitter appliqués, and red cowboy boots. The woman told Kendrick her name was Red. The Police Department is working on a composite drawing, which they expect to release tomorrow.

Tamika Washington of Peachtree Memorial Hospital confirmed that Kendrick had been admitted to their emergency room at approximately 1:30 p.m. today. She stated that while Kendrick was understandably upset over the attack, he was in good condition physically and had suffered very little loss of blood. Washington further stated that the amputation appeared to be the work of someone with medical or veterinary training, but would not speculate further.

Catherine looked up from the paper. No one moved or

made a sound. *Had they forgotten how to breathe?* Each woman in the group knew Bloody Jake Kendrick from the publicity surrounding his trial. More importantly, they all knew someone enough like him from their own lives to fill them with dread.

Knowing full well the group was hanging on her every word, Catherine cleared her throat and grinned at Delia. "Shall I continue?"

Delia smiled back at her. "Let's do a check with the group. Is anyone uncomfortable with this?"

The group members turned, almost in unison, and stared at Delia as if in a trance.

Finally, Bea snapped to attention. "Come on honey, don't just leave me hanging here."

"I heard that's what Jake's dick said just before Red whacked it." Tina's eyes sparkled with wicked amusement.

Delia looked at her in amazement. A humorous remark like that was uncharacteristic for Tina. Could this be a new development in her recovery?

When the laughter had died down, Catherine opened the newspaper to the second page and began to read again.

Kendrick, dubbed "Bloody Jake" after his arrest for the 1987 rape and mutilation of a teenage girl in Nevada, was released from Redding Prison in Macon, GA, two months ago after serving eight years of a twenty-five year sentence.

At the trial, the young victim, who had been Kendrick's neighbor, testified that he had lured her into his car on the pretext that her mother was involved in an accident, and had offered to give her a ride to the hospital. After driving her to an isolated area in the desert, he raped her, severed her hands, and left her for dead.

Covered with blood and near death, the girl crawled to a nearby highway and flagged down a passing motorist. Her

testimony, along with forensic evidence in Kendrick's car and home, resulted in his conviction.

Kendrick has never admitted responsibility for the crime. He stated at his sentencing that he didn't know why the girl would want to frame him, but speculated that it might be because her family had filed complaints with the city over the way he kept his yard. In December of last year, Kendrick was given an early parole from prison for exemplary behavior.

The Atlanta Police Department would not comment further on the investigation of the attack on Kendrick, other than to state that they have no leads at this time. They are asking anyone who may have seen Kendrick, or his alleged assailant, last night at the Fox's Hole bar or at the Traveler's Rest Motel to call the CrimeStopper's Hotline at 404-577-TIPS (8477). Callers will not have to reveal their names.

Catherine paused before speaking and looked directly at each of her group mates, measuring the impact of the newspaper article. "All right!" she said, nearly squealing with delight. "Did this guy get what was coming to him, or what? I mean . . . I get so tired of feeling like we have no recourse except to put up with these violent bastards. Y'all know as well as I do that Jake Kendrick is just pure evil. Seems to me Red got herself all dolled up and said, 'Let's see what you can do to a grown woman, Jake. This ain't no teenage girl you're messing with now.'"

Catherine's mountain twang and southern grammar were in full bloom, surfacing as they always did when she was moved by something. As an actress, she'd spent her entire career suppressing that twang, changing it, or occasionally using it if the play demanded, but once her passions were aroused in real life, she felt so much more comfortable wrapping her tongue around a word the way her mama might have.

"Yep, ol' Red just probably said to herself one night, 'somebody's gotta do something about this shit.' That fool won't be raping any other young girls."

"You don't need a penis to rape somebody," Tina spoke up softly, and then moved tentatively toward Catherine, reaching for the newspaper.

Catherine handed her the paper and gently patted Tina's back, rubbing in circular motions. "I know, but that's what he's always used. It's got to take some of the pleasure out of it for him if he's forced to use a beer bottle,"

"Wonder what she done with it?" Bea asked, shaking her head in amazement.

"Me, I would've left it stuck in his mouth." The little mouse from New Jersey apparently had another roar in her. She jerked away from Catherine's touch.

Janet, an accountant, inevitably measured events in terms of financial profit or loss. "No, then some liberal asshole would sew it back on for him. He'd be free as a bird to start up again, once it was working. And, guess who'd end up paying his doctor bills? Us. Taxpayers." The big woman smiled and leaned back in the special chair Delia had ordered to accommodate her large size.

Tina studied the newspaper article a moment longer, but apparently could find no further clues to Red's identity. "Maybe she didn't even know who he was and was pissed at him for something. Or, maybe, she was trying to even the score. Women always just take this shit."

Tina turned directly to Delia. "You know it better than anyone, Delia, we take it and take it and take it, until we're too tired to fight, and all we're doing is scrambling to stay alive. She deserves a medal, if you ask me."

"She ought to cut off his hands, too," Bea said.

Delia had never seen the women so excited, but wondered if she needed to rein them in. She wasn't too concerned about Bea or Janet, but Tina had spent time in juvenile detention for attacking a boy with a knife in high school. The last thing Delia wanted was to encourage violent behavior in any of her group members. "I know this seems like justice—it does to me too at first glance—but are we safer in a society that practices an 'eye for an . . .'"

Catherine interrupted, "I'd feel a lot safer in that kind of world than I do in this one, where perverts like Kendrick can be back on the streets. How the hell do you *ever* get released from prison after cutting off a child's hands?"

FIVE

February 9, 1997

Detective Simone Rosenberg stared bleakly at the scummy coffee pot in the station house break room. She knew the hygienic move would be to scrub it thoroughly with steel wool and leave a note chiding the rest of the squad. Something to the effect of "No wonder they call us pigs." But, she just didn't have it in her this morning. Shrugging, she poured water into the pot, carefully avoiding whatever it was that clung like black moss to the rim of the reservoir. Today she would take her chances.

She'd been up until after three a.m. with Minerva who had come down with her fourth respiratory ailment in as many months. A sickly baby weighing barely four pounds when she was born prematurely, Minerva was now fourteen but her lungs were still weak and susceptible to every germ that passed within fifty feet of her. The wet, cold days of winter were the worst.

If they had been living in Jamaica, Simone would have had a host of aunts or cousins to rally around the child, but in Atlanta, she had to do what most single parents do—pay strangers, ask friends, and pray to God for warmer weather.

It hadn't helped matters that only two hours after she had collapsed into a fitful sleep, Dispatch had sent her stumbling out into the cold dawn.

The coffee spurted and splashed into the cloudy glass pot. *It doesn't look so good, but it smells like heaven.*

Marty walked into the break room, looking for a refill for his own cup. "You're not drinking that crap, are you? I thought you were on a health kick."

Simone poured herself a cup of the brown muck and quickly heaped in a spoonful of fake cream. "Ah, that golden color. Make you think it's rich with nutrition. Besides, all those chemicals probably kill the little bugs anyway."

Marty filled his cup and headed for his cubicle. Simone caught up with him just in time to see him stash a stack of files under his desk.

"Hell of a way to start the day." Marty dug the crime scene report out from under a precarious mound of papers on his desk and handed it to Simone.

"You talking about us or Anderson?"

"Like I give a doodle dam about George Anderson," Marty growled, "but I bet he got off to a worse start than we did."

GEORGE ANDERSON'S DAY HAD INDEED begun badly. Like Jake Kendrick before him, he'd awakened that morning in a strange motel with a grinding hangover, very little memory of the previous evening, and no penis.

Simone and Marty both knew Anderson from a previous arrest. A textbook child molester, he was plump and jolly, with a baby-face and a stubborn cowlick near the crown of his head. His flabby belly, which he tried to hide by stuffing himself into tight jeans, bulged and sagged over his belt.

Anderson was particularly attracted to well-developed girls around the age of twelve or thirteen. His pre-teen daughters gave him easy access to their friends, so he volunteered to coach their soccer and softball teams. He assisted in their recitals and plays. He targeted his daughters' most vulnerable friends—the ones with abusive or absent parents—and he whispered dirty jokes in their ears, making them giggle and feel important that a grown man would trust them with such sophisticated language. He gave them sips of beer and made them promise not to tell.

He spent months grooming parents, gaining their trust. Once he had insinuated himself into a family, he would often attend family gatherings, with or without his wife. Like many pedophiles, Anderson's entrée to molesting was by way of tickling. Inevitably before the day was over, George would end up on the floor or a couch, holding a girl down in full view of everyone. He would tickle the girl until she couldn't breathe and begged for mercy. His tickling often made the girls' mothers uncomfortable; his hands straying so close to their daughters' breasts. But the mothers looked aside, refusing to believe what their instincts were telling them. That was a big part of the thrill for Anderson. If he aroused the girls in front of other people, he could always pretend it was innocent.

Anderson was a patient man. Once he had the girls' loyalty, he would cry and tell them his wife was a cold bitch who didn't understand a man's needs. If only his wife would love him like they did. If only his mean wife was any fun to be around. By the time he got around to having sex with them, the naive girls were convinced he would leave his wife and run away with them. Unfortunately for Anderson, two of the girls he seduced decided to tell their mothers.

Marty despised Anderson's style of molestation almost more than the violent offenders. Anderson was a seducer who made the girls love him, before abandoning them to their trauma, confusion and guilt. When Marty thought of his own two daughters—how trusting they were, how pure and innocent—he could strangle a guy like Anderson and whistle a happy tune while he was doing it.

"What'd this guy get, the last time we caught him?" Marty plopped into his chair, splattering coffee onto Simone's shoe in the process.

"Sorry 'bout that, Rosenberg. Stick your foot up here and I'll clean you up."

Simone ignored his offer and shuffled through Anderson's file. "Pleaded no contest. Served three months."

"Damn. He didn't get off so easy this time, did he?"

Simone eased her tired frame into the chair beside Marty's desk. "Looks like our girl used the same drug to get Anderson into bed as she did Kendrick. That date rape drug, Rohypnol. Kids call it the 'forget me pill.'"

"You know what the real name is?" Marty cocked his head to the side, trying to remember. "Flunitrazepam. Try saying that fast three times."

"Wait 'til the coffee kicks in." Simone said.

"Yeah, they call it all kinds of things—Mexican Valium, roofies, trip and fall, mind erasers. Sounds like a barrel of laughs, don't it? Whatever happened to kids getting into their daddy's Jack Daniels?" Marty had just begun to wear reading glasses and was patting himself down to find the pocket that held his latest drugstore pair.

"Mon, the stuff's so cheap, anyone with an allowance can buy it. I heard it called the lunch money drug the other day. Can you believe that?" With a familiarity born of years of working together, Simone reached over and pulled Marty's glasses off the top of his head. She grinned and handed them to him. "Sure wouldn't want to be a kid today. I'm always checking my Minerva for signs. So far, she seems normal. Drives me crazy though."

Marty gave her a puzzled look.

"Talk. All the time. Soccer games, teachers, tests, new

clothes. She never stops. Girl even talks in her sleep."

"Same with my two," Marty said, shrugging his shoulders.

Simone closed the case file. "Looks like our suspect has learned her lesson well from the boys. Usually they're the ones slipping this poison into girls' drinks."

"Sounds to me like women's lib has gotten way out of control." Marty's face bore a half-repressed smirk.

"Yah mon. You better watch you-self. She be after you regular guys next!"

"The lab figure out what she's using to sedate them for surgery?" Marty asked.

"Nah. They're still working on it, but it's a puzzle. Something different."

"A new substance altogether?"

"It shares some properties with known anesthetics, but not identical." Simone yawned and stretched her long legs out in front of her. "It's got to be fast acting. The Rohypnol wouldn't leave them immobilized enough to stick in an intravenous line. Maybe some meth freak invented something in her kitchen."

Marty jumped up. His bony butt was killing him from all the sitting he'd been doing lately. He paced a few strides away from his desk and then turned back. "How 'bout a note. She leave one this time?"

"Same note. Same kind of paper."

The note found at Jake Kendrick's crime scene had been one piece of evidence the department had not released to the media. *II Samuel 13:14* was all it had said. Simone and Marty had looked up the Biblical passage after that first assault. *"Howbeit he would not hearken unto her voice: but, being stronger than she, forced her, and lay with her."*

"Looks like you owe me ten dollars, partner." Simone plopped Anderson's case file down on Marty's desktop.

"Since when?" Marty didn't part with ten bucks easily.

"Since it turns out our girl is not some nutty ex-girlfriend. She signed the note this time. Calls herself 'Magenta Rave.'"

"Hell's Bells! What kind of name is that?"

"Rave could have something to do with the drug parties kids have."

"Might could," Marty said. "But, this weirdo is no kid, that's for sure."

"Could be she's just real crazy and angry—you know that saying, 'a raving lunatic.' That's where the rave could be coming from." Simone paused. "Magenta is a color. Kind of like fuchsia."

Marty rolled his eyes. "Rosenberg, I ain't got a clue what color fuchsia is."

"Why does that not surprise me?" Simone eyed his monochromatic brown slacks and shirt. "It's a rich color. Purplish. You know, a purple red, like you see in a bruise."

Simone stood up to leave. "Got it in her head that she's doing the work of the Almighty."

"Looks that way, don't it?" Marty said.

"Worst kind a crazy," Simone said, slowly shaking her head. She turned to walk back to the break room for more coffee. This was definitely going to be a three-cup day.

SIX

The Atlanta Times, March 13, 1997

ASSAULTS AGAINST MEN MUST STOP
By Elizabeth Reed-Monroe
Staff Writer

In his annual State of the City address to business and community leaders, Mayor James Allen expressed "grave concerns" over the recent string of violent sexual assaults against men in the Atlanta area and vowed to "bring all power of the Mayor's office to bear against the perpetrator or perpetrators of these crimes." The Mayor condemned the actions and characterized the assailant(s) as "part of a lunatic fringe who are attempting to circumvent the due process of law."

The four victims allegedly were lured out of bars by women of various descriptions and taken to nearby motels where they were drugged and genitally mutilated. The men had all been recently released from prison after serving partial sentences for violent sexual offenses. Mayor Allen stated that the fact that the men themselves had been convicted of sexual crimes

43

"in no way justifies the violence that was perpetrated against them."

At a protest rally held in front of city hall this morning, Richard Wright, President of the Brotherhood of Formerly Incarcerated Men (BOFIM), a national men's rights organization dedicated to the reintegration of former prisoners into society, called for a thorough investigation of the Atlanta Police Department's handling of the assaults.

"Because the victims so far have been ex-prisoners, the police department has treated these vicious attacks like a big joke from day one. Like these men had it coming to them," Wright said.

He further stated, "BOFIM has been growing like wildfire in the last few years, and we are not willing to be treated like animals anymore. When we are released from prison, we have paid our debt to society. We're not going to pay forever. Besides, all men should be worried about these crimes. This is just one more example of the erosion of respect for men in our culture. If men were given the respect they deserve in this modern world, everybody would get along a lot better, and we wouldn't need so many prisons."

Wright demanded that a special task force composed of police, men's rights activists, and concerned citizens be appointed to assist in the apprehension of the perpetrator(s).

In a separate interview last night on CNN, Dr. Grace Gallento, psychologist and spokeswoman for the National Alliance for Women (NAW), stated that the NAW is opposed to any form of sexual assault, whether it is against women, children or men.

"The fact that these men have been found guilty of appalling crimes towards women and children in no way justifies this kind of retaliation. My strong recommendation to men living in the Atlanta area, particularly those who have reason to be concerned that they might be targeted by this serial assailant, is that they avoid going to bars alone; and that they never leave a bar with any woman they do not know quite well. They should not call attention to themselves through provocative behavior or dress. They should vary their routines daily so that, if they are being watched or followed, the predator would have a more difficult time predicting their next move."

SEVEN

March 14, 1997

Chief Glenda Jackson, Atlanta's first female police chief, was dangerously close to the boiling point from the heat she had been getting from the Mayor's office. She had spent most of the previous afternoon explaining to His Honor, a tedious, foppish, little man, whom she secretly despised, that Atlanta's finest were not "too busy complaining to the press about his administration," to pay attention to crime in Atlanta. Chief Jackson hated nothing more in this world than to be reprimanded by that corrupt career politician, a man whom she knew to be hopelessly inadequate in his own job.

To top everything off, she had been corralled outside the station house on her way in to work that morning and had spent the last half-hour listening to a group of irate citizens and opportunistic press jackals whine that she didn't take the crimes seriously enough, either because the victims were men or because, until yesterday, they all had been white.

As an African-American woman, Chief Jackson had walked a precarious tightrope in her profession, starting in her early years just out of NYU law school when she was a public defender. She had learned from experience how easily aggression could get out of control. If police officers couldn't maintain their cool in every situation, what did it matter that they were the good guys? She thought she could help with that and made the switch to police work. She'd always been cool under pressure. Her biggest challenge as chief was encouraging her officers to be aggressive, but keeping them balanced enough to know when to back off. She was tough, but she took great pains to appear unbiased, even if she sometimes couldn't actually *be* unbiased. It was okay for them to snicker behind her back that she was a ball buster. She expected that. However, she would not have them thinking she was racist or sexist.

After she had extricated herself from the mob outside, she strode past Marty and growled, "You and Rosenberg. In my office. Now."

Marty and Simone settled themselves into chairs in front of the chief's desk. Chief Jackson stared at them for a long time before speaking. Although she was fifty, her face showed little signs of aging, with the exception of a furrow that had stubbornly carved itself deeply into the bridge between her eyebrows. This morning it looked more like a crevasse.

Chief Jackson's ancestors had lived through the worst of slavery and Jim Crow without leaving the south. Her extended family still lived outside of Hattiesburg, Mississippi. She was short and plump, with a good sense of humor, but an intimidating presence. Though most of the officers under her command preferred not to deal with her directly, they tried hard to keep that fact from her. This morning she showed absolutely no sign of humor.

"What have you got for me, Rosenberg?" Chief Jackson propped her elbows upon her desk. She cupped her pounding forehead wearily between her two hands.

Sitting in front of the Chief's enormous desk, in chairs

slightly lower than hers, Simone and Marty immediately snapped to attention. They straightened their posture, stilled their shuffling feet, and looked like nine-year-olds who'd been summoned to the principal's office.

Before Simone could answer her question, the Chief said, through clenched teeth, "I have just spent the last half-hour defending this department to a cracker mob who wanted to know if we were going to do anything about the assaults now that a black man had been attacked."

"Everyone knows that's B.S., Chief." Marty slapped the case file on Chief Jackson's desk within reach of Simone.

Simone opened the file. "Other than race, the story's the same. Victim described her as a light-skinned black woman named Amber this time. Medium height. Said she was a dancer and promised to give him a private show back at the motel. She did that all right!"

Simone consulted her case notes and shrugged. "Everything's identical, Chief. The bar was crowded. Bartender said the victim was pretty much out of it when he left. Amber helps him out the door, they go to another 'stop and squirt' and the last thing he remembers is having a drink with her in the motel room."

Marty chimed in. "Door knobs were wiped clean. The phone, drawer pulls, hell, even the mirrors were wiped clean. The carpet's being checked, but we don't expect much. No sign of a struggle. Seems like she gets them in bed before they pass out. These old boys think they've found the queen of their dreams 'til they wake up *sans el dicko*."

Marty, congenitally unable to sit still anywhere, stuffed his hand in his pants pocket and began working his keys like a makeshift rosary. "We heard back from the lab this morning. She's injecting them with something after they swallow the roofie. The lab couldn't identify it exactly, but think it might be some kind of animal tranquilizer. Like on those nature shows where they take down a polar bear with a tranquilizer gun and he's just laying there with his tongue hanging out while they do any damn thing they want to him. The injection site has been different on each guy."

"She leave a note this time?" Chief Jackson wearily tented her hands in front of her face. "I can't tell you how *over* this case I am!"

"Yep, same Bible verse, same paper." Like most southerners of a certain age, Marty had been raised in the church, but he was unfamiliar with II Samuel. "The passage is about a rape. Seems King David had a beautiful, pious daughter named Tamar. She got lured into her half-brother's bedroom, where he raped her. We're trying to figure out if it has any more meaning than that." Marty paused, and shook his head. "Hell's bells—think the old gal's pissed off because of some rape that happened a few thousand years ago to somebody she don't even know?"

"Could be, partner. People don't get over that Bible stuff too quick." Simone grabbed Marty's arm to stop the incessant key jangling, which had gotten progressively more frenetic. "The paper she's using is always the same—like a kid's first grade tablet. You know, the kind with the red dotted line down the middle? I talked to that shrink over in Midtown, works with rape cases. You know the one? Dr. Whitfield. Delia Whitfield."

Simone turned to Marty. "You ever work with her?"

"Nope, never met her. I was supposed to once, but the case fell through before we ever got together. Heard she's good, though."

"She's been doing a study on sexual violence for a long time now. I worked with her once on a bad rape case, little girl, back when I was partnered with Levy. I like her. She don't look at cops like we're the enemy."

Chief Jackson shifted in her seat and pointedly cleared her

throat.

Simone pulled her attention back to the Chief. "Anyway, she's got a good rep, Chief. Helped me a lot on that case. I thought she might give us an angle on the perpetrator. She said the type of paper was a definite clue; maybe somebody stuck in her childhood. A woman seriously abused as a little kid and just can't get over it. Dr. Whitfield said the suspect's probably got a lot of unresolved rage."

Simone paused and gave Marty her best smart-aleck look. "She also said that description fits half the women in the world."

The Chief groaned at the last comment.

Simone laughed, and again consulted her notes. "I asked her if the behavior would fit into some specific psychological disorder. She looked at me funny, like, 'isn't it obvious?' But, she said lots of mental illnesses share a component of rage. People feel out of control with their lives. They've been abused. Then, she mentioned something called Dissociative Identify Disorder, or D.I.D., and immediately looked like she wished she hadn't. I asked her what it was and she became evasive. Said her next appointment was waiting, and I could check back with her sometime next week. I asked her if she had any D.I.D. clients, and she squawked about that being privileged info.

Simone continued. "After I left, I did a little research on D.I.D, because something in her manner made the little hairs stand up. You know what I mean? I know that you do, Chief. Anyway, it used to be called multiple personality disorder, but I guess they upgraded it to something a little more politically correct. People with D.I.D. sometimes have blackouts and can't remember what they've done because some aspect of their personality has acted on its own. It's called switching. You know, like that movie, *Sybil*? Worth looking into I think."

Marty rolled his eyes. "How? We supposed to subpoena every shrink from here to Shake Rag and back?" Marty hated psychology. All that internal soul-searching crap. In his mind, this was just some pissed off woman who hated men. Nothing too hard to understand about that. "That kid's paper you can get at any Wal-Mart. Not much chance of tracing it. Plus, she only uses a little piece cut into a four-inch square. And I do mean four inches. Very precisely cut. The ink's typical black ballpoint. Her printing is neat and small. No prints on the paper. So far, there's nothing much to go on, Chief. Whoever Snippy is, she ain't careless."

"Jesus, Marty, don't let the press get wind of that nickname." The Chief managed her first smile of the morning, in spite of herself. "We got ex-cons marching over at city hall and, yesterday, some neo-Nazi group was quoted on the national news. Both of them carrying on about this being more evidence of the breakdown of traditional American family values. The press is eating up that kind of garbage. The last thing I need is BOFIM and some Aryan militia group camping on my front lawn."

LATER THAT AFTERNOON, Simone and Marty walked into Imagine That, the leading Atlanta theatrical supply house for local productions. The small, freestanding brick building was crammed from floor to ceiling with wigs, Elizabethan garb, swords, monster masks and all the other accouterments necessary to create magic on the stage.

Thus far, the assailant who called herself Magenta Rave, but whom Marty had nicknamed Snippy, had been described as a large-breasted red-head, named Red, a timid, childlike girl named Tara, a boisterous blond with a diamond-studded gold tooth, named Judy Jones, and a light skinned, African American dancer named Amber. Each woman had been described as medium height, though Tara appeared to be shorter than the others. She had been casually dressed in a short denim skirt and sweater, and probably wasn't wearing heels. While the detectives couldn't be certain how many suspects were involved in the mutilations, they reasoned she might be just one clever woman—or man—in disguise. It was worth checking anyway since they had little else to go on.

"Be with you in a minute." A small woman carrying a large cardboard box yelled and ambled towards them from the back of the store. The box was filled to overflowing with colorful crepes, laces, and netting. Simone and Marty didn't get a good look at her until she set the box on the counter and turned towards them.

She was young, twenty-three at most. Her hair, shoe-polish black at the roots, had been chemically fried to neon orange on its spiked ends. Silver rings, studs and chains looped in various contortions over her face. Each ear had at least five earrings of various styles and lengths. Richly embroidered tattoos of maidens fighting dragons, daggers, a pentagram, and other religious symbols snaked up her thin arms from her wrists to her shoulders. Tiny chains of flowers were stitched around her ankles.

"Need some help?" She frowned, slightly.

Simone identified herself and showed the girl her badge. "We need to ask you a few questions, ma'am. Do you keep address and phone records on your customers?"

"Uh, not all of them." The clerk's eyes widened. "Did somebody, like, commit some kind of crime here?" When neither Simone, nor Marty responded, she continued. "Some of our larger customers, like the symphony or the big theaters, yuh know, the universities, we keep records on them 'cause we, like, run a line of credit for them. But anybody can walk in here and spend their cash. Whazzup?"

Marty ignored her question. "What about wigs. Do you sell those or rent them?"

The clerk turned her back to the detectives and began rustling through the box she'd brought from the back room. "We sell 'em. Have to. Some kind of weird health code." She pulled a large pink feathered boa out of the box.

"Do you remember anyone buying a red, blond or long straight brown wig in the last couple of months?" Simone asked.

The girl spun around to face Simone. "Whoa, you know how many people come in here all the time and buy wigs? Like, gimme a clue who you're looking for?"

Again, Marty ignored her question. "Have you sold three or four wigs to the same person in the past few months?"

"Lemme see. Renaissance Georgia did some kind of Shakespearean thing. They bought a few wigs. And . . . Oh, yeah, Emerson University. I can look it up. They did a big costume piece not too long ago.

The girl wrapped the feathered boa around her neck and sashayed over towards a file cabinet to pull the records. "Hey, did you see *Bar Fly Graduation* at Emerson? I had the coolest part. It was small, but like, I played this really demented high school teacher who gets her students to riot and take over this local bar, where everybody gets totally wasted and, like, totally out of control.

"When they first called me to come in for callbacks, I was like, 'Whoa. Are you serious?' But, then I . . . ."

Marty interrupted her. "Just give me the names and phone numbers of your contacts at any of the larger places. We'll get in touch with them."

The girl dashed off a few names on a legal pad, ripped the page out, and handed it to Marty. "We'll be back in touch," he said. "May need to look at some of your records."

"Cool," she said, enthusiastically shaking her head. Her large nose ring banged against her upper lip like a doorknocker. Midway to the front door, Marty was unable to contain himself and turned to face the young woman. "I know it's none of my business, but I got two little girls at home. Can you tell me, why on earth you would do all that to your pretty face?"

The girl's casual demeanor changed immediately. She blushed, then fixed Marty with a stony glare. "You're right, officer, it is none of your business." The girl turned and walked away.

She'd dismissed him, using a completely different accent, which Marty immediately recognized—old money South Georgia plantation trying to cover its bloody past with a veneer of gentility. It was an accent far more prized than his own red-clay, shit kicker brogue, and both Marty and the girl knew it.

EIGHT

Long-Lasting Effects of Childhood Sexual Abuse, 1997: A Case Study of Seven Female Survivors
Delia Whitfield, Ph.D. Clinical Psychology
Client ID #616-01
Primary Diagnosis: Complex Post Traumatic Stress Disorder (PTSD)
Chief Complaints: Fear of Intimacy, Compulsive Cleaning, Unresolved Rage

March 15, 1997

From the moment she entered Delia's office, Tina Galenski exhibited symptoms of extreme agitation. Before even saying hello to Delia, Tina paced through the room, picked up small objects, studied them for a moment, and then impatiently moved on. She snatched a book from the bookshelf, returned it immediately without opening it, and strode over to the window. She placed both hands against the glass and glared out into the back garden.

Delia allowed Tina's energy to dissipate before speaking. "You seem upset today, Tina. Would you like to sit down and talk about it?"

Tina flopped onto the sofa and curled up against the upholstered arm. She covered herself with an afghan. "I had a dream last night that somebody was trying to cut off my hands. A monster. He was holding me down and I couldn't scream or fight back. I woke up thinking of the first time I . . . you know."

"If this is too uncomfortable, it's okay if you want to just sit quietly for a while and not talk."

The sofa where Tina was huddling and Delia's chair were separated by a coffee table that held tissues and wrapped candies, a few small dolls, and a pen and paper.

"I wrote a poem this morning. I want to read that first, then maybe I can talk." Tina's hands were shaking as she pulled the poem from her purse.

"Here goes. It's called *Two Hands*."

Two hands
seize my throat
my hopes
lie crushed
between
that vise.
My mouth
a jagged scar,
ripped open
for nothing more
than a quickie,
a joke,
a small down payment,
on feeling good.
Two hands, my hands,
severed, stolen lumps,
flopping, ineffectual,
wringing stumps.

Two hands, his hands,
wanting, needing,
slap and punch,
twist and crunch.
No hands that gently pat.
No hands that lightly stroke.
No hands that simply touch.

Delia sat quietly, waiting to see if there was more. Tina appeared to struggle with her decision, but after a couple of minutes, she began. "It was freezing inside our apartment. Me and Jade was huddled up under this old tattered quilt that our grandma made for us. I was eleven, almost twelve, and Jade was three. We loved that old quilt. It was a patchwork thing, you know, old fashioned, with bouquets of roses in each square. I bet it was pretty when Granny first sent it, but it had gotten nasty over the years. Everything in our apartment was filthy.

"I was skinny, but developed boobs early. Not huge, but bigger than most girls my age. Already had my first period. I needed a bra. 'Course, I didn't get one since my mother was too busy getting loaded to deal with that kinda shit. We had moved for the umpteenth time and, once again, I hadn't started school for the year. It was about this time of year, I think. February or March.

"Like I said, Jade and me was squeezed up tight next to each other at one end of the couch. The other end was chewed up and shredded from the rats. The smell of rat piss floated up through the holes in the couch. Smelled like something died in there. I can see that image of us so clear. Like we was in the belly of some rotten carcass, everything dead around us. There wasn't nobody I could call for help. Not a fucking thing I could do."

Tina felt an old familiar fear rise up in her throat. Shutting her eyes against the surfacing memories, she gasped. Her airway was closing. She was suffocating.

Delia knew immediately what was happening: a panic attack. "Breathe slowly, Tina. Breathe through your nose. That's right. Good. Everything is under control here. You're safe. You can stop anytime you want to."

Tina inhaled deeply and wrapped both arms around her waist in the self-soothing posture that Delia had taught her. When she had regained her composure, she said, "Did I ever tell you Jade was my half-brother?" She didn't wait for an answer from Delia. "He was half white and half Chinese. He was the prettiest little boy. Much prettier than me. He looked like something out of a velvet painting. You know what I mean? His colors was unblended at the edges. His hair so black it gleamed, but his face like the finest white porcelain you ever saw. I thought of him as my personal, living, doll. Or, maybe, more like some exotic pet that I somehow got lucky enough to keep. He was that sweet, too. When he laughed, his eyes closed completely. He reminded me of this laughing Buddha mug my mother brought home from a Chinese restaurant. It had two tiny yellow and red umbrellas and smelled of oranges and cherries and sweet rum. I used to hold that mug and inhale, until I swear I sniffed the smell right out of it.

"When I told Mom the mug looked like Jade, she said, 'well, he's our little Buddha boy, isn't he?' The name stuck. He became my Buddha boy. Mom told me Buddha was a prince, so Jade became that too in my mind.

"I was such an ugly child, worried all the time, thin, starving really. I hated looking at myself in the mirror, especially after I started to develop." Tina shivered involuntarily and tucked the afghan tighter around her. "I had been getting looks from some of the garbage my mom slept with and I was nervous about it. That's why I loved looking at Jade. He still looked like a little kid. Innocent.

"We didn't know our fathers. Mom had a different boyfriend every month and not one of 'em worth the time it would take to learn their names. She joked that the only one she could remember was Jade's father. Hard to forget a chink, she said.

"This night I'm talking about was the worst. Mom had been gone for four days and didn't leave us nothing to eat, except stale crackers and a couple cans of soup. I gave Jade the last of the food the day before and he cried all night, until he just dropped off from exhaustion. I could see him fading, Delia. His eyes were dull. He could hardly speak. I stayed up watching him until morning, hoping my mom would walk through the door. But, of course, she didn't.

"I remember seeing the early morning sunlight creep in through the filthy window panes over the kitchen sink. Hundreds of cockroaches scurried away as soon as the light hit them. Their shiny backs made them look like spilled beans rolling around and dropping off the countertop. I tried to count 'em for a while. I don't know why they bothered to run. Nobody in that house had the energy to chase after them.

"I knew I had to do something, but I didn't know what. I patted Jade on the back. 'Wake up,' I said. 'Wake up, Buddha boy!' He stirred and managed this pathetic smile. I was afraid he would die if he didn't get something to eat soon. He was so cold. I rubbed his back and hugged him to warm him up.

"Trying to cheer him up, I said, 'Hey, when Mommy comes home, she's taking us to Coney Island and we'll eat hot dogs and cotton candy until we're so full we won't be able to walk. We'll rent one of those carriages pulled by a horse and it'll bring us home, lifting its tail, crapping and farting all the way. Those farts will be so stinky they could blow us out of the carriage. Except they won't, cause our bellies will be stuffed full. Not even a tornado could lift us.'"

Tina laughed hysterically until tears were streaming down her face. She sputtered out the rest of her story, holding her sides. "That little boy loved stories about poops and farts. The more the better. But, he was so weak, he couldn't laugh. His little body shook, but no sound came out."

She shook her head, tears streaming. "My poor baby Buddha."

"He said, 'Teenie, when's Mommy coming home?' I said soon. 'Liar, liar, pants on fire' he whispered, and closed his eyes. I tried to tell him some other stories, but every one I could think of had food in it. Good King Jade, the greatest king in all of China, having a victory celebration feast with French fries and hamburgers and banana pudding. What kind of story is that to tell a starving child?"

"You were a child yourself, Tina." Delia handed Tina a tissue.

"Yeah." Tina shot Delia a look that said *that's no excuse!* "I tried watching TV, but the commercials made me hungry. Finally, I couldn't stand it no more. I said to Jade, 'I'm going for help.' We both knew what that meant. Gangs roamed the hallways. I'd been threatened a couple of times already. Jade tried to stop me, but he was too weak."

Tina stood up, abruptly, tossing the afghan to the floor in the process. She forcefully kicked it under the sofa and stomped over to the window. She audibly whacked her forehead against the cool glass. Then, she did it again.

Delia edged forward in her seat and was preparing to sprint to the window if necessary to prevent Tina from hurting herself. "You don't have to go on if you are too uncomfortable."

Tina lifted her head from the window and wiped off the smudge she had left on the glass with the sleeve of her sweater. She wearily returned to the sofa and folded herself into it. The last thing she wanted was to tell this story, but tell it she would. She was tired of keeping it inside.

"See, once before, the superintendent of the building had given me a sucker and asked me to come inside his apartment. He gave me the creeps so I didn't go in. There was something about him, you know, I hadda feeling. I didn't have the words for it then, but I knew from instinct. But, this time, I didn't have no choice. I couldn't go to none of the women in the building, 'cause my mom had slept with their men or tried to sell dope to their kids. They hated her.

"I opened the door, looked both ways down the hall, and slipped into the stairwell. The stairs were dark. I could barely make out the steps. Smelled like piss. Neighborhood bums would come in there and pee right on the walls. Human piss or rat piss, I couldn't escape it. It was fuckin' everywhere. Gang symbols on the walls, like some pack of wild dogs had already marked this territory. But, I didn't have no choice. You understand that? I'd be damned if me and Jade were going to starve to death.

"When I got to the Super's door, I couldn't knock. My hand was shaking so hard. Somehow, I finally managed a little tap and when he opened the door, the heat blasted me in the face. I remember thinking, *so that's where all the heat in the building goes.*

"He was tall and skinny with these long, elegant, fingers—like a piano player's fingers. He kept raking them through his greasy shoulder-length hair. Had on a white undershirt, one of those old fashioned ones like in the movies—I think they call them wife beater shirts. Skin tight jeans and he was so skinny that his legs looked like they were only distantly related to each other."

Tina and Delia shared a small laugh.

"I said, 'Me and Jade are hungry. Can we borrow some

food until my mom comes home?' That's what I said to him. Can you believe that? I wanted to sound so grown-up. Like one neighbor calling on another. Civilized, you know? Like on TV

"He didn't say nuthin'. He just sorta grinned and pulled me through the door. Dirty clothes were piled everywhere. His place smelled like a ghetto thrift store. Moldy shoes and old appliances. You know that smell? Depression stink. I hate that smell.

"He walked me over to the fridge and opened the door. God, Delia, it was full of food. Leftover fried chicken, pie, beer, orange pop—I started to reach for something, anything, and he slammed the door. Almost crushed my hand. 'Where's that sexy momma of yours?' he said.

"I didn't say nuthin, so he says, 'Me and your ma have a deal. Betcha didn't know that. See, I help her and she helps me. She does me little favors and I don't kick her sorry ass out when she's late on the rent. You and me could work out the same kind a deal. Like, I give you some food and you don't even have to pay me back, if you'll do one little thing for me. Hell, I'll even give you some money. Betcha'd like that, huh?'

"*I'd like that just fine*, I thought. But I was scared and it showed on my face.

"He says, 'Don't worry. It won't hurt. You'll like it.'

"Sit down, he says, and pushes me into a kitchen chair. I was sittin' eye level to his zipper. He starts unzipping and I hear each tooth of it click, unlocking whatever was in his pants. Some time bomb's about to explode, I'm thinking. Tick. Tick. Tick. Tick. It was all in slow motion, you know, how they say death comes to you. There's me sitting, bug eyed—like some bizarre cartoon character—and any second my stupid head was going to be charred off.

"I was dizzy from hunger. This might sound strange, since

I was so young, but I had a realization sitting there in that slowed down time. I knew nobody—no knight, or king, or superman, certainly not my own mother—was ever coming to help me. I was on my own.

"When his thing popped out, I looked away from it and up into his hard eyes. They were cold as death. I looked back at his penis. The only other one I had seen was Jade's. This thing was angry and huge. I started to move away and he pulled me by the back of my head. 'Suck it,' he said. Then he rammed it into my mouth and I couldn't breathe. I fought like hell, scratching and slapping at his hands, but it was like a rabbit fighting with a bear.

"I was smothering and choking. Panic spread throughout my body and I started to shake uncontrollably. I thought I was dying. Every place he touched hurt—my shoulders, my neck, my throat. I couldn't breathe. I couldn't scream.

"Then, my mind went somewhere that was empty. You know? Like a void. This calmness came over me and some instinct made me relax my throat. Every few thrusts I could get a breath. I stopped fighting him and closed my eyes."

Tina paused. She regulated her breathing, the way Delia had taught her, until she was taking slow, deep breaths. Breathing in through her nose for a count of four and breathing out through her mouth for a count of eight.

When Tina's breathing normalized, Delia said, "I know this is really difficult for you. Are you okay to go on?"

"It's weird. After a little while, I wasn't feeling nuthin. It was more like I wasn't there. I always had a good imagination, so I pictured me and Jade holding hands, flying high over Union City. We landed on Coney Island. We were riding the merry-go-round and going up and down, whirling around in space. We were giggling and before I knew it, I felt this warm liquid in my mouth. I swallowed it and smiled across the aisle at Jade. 'Aren't these horses pretty?' I said.

He nodded back at me and laughed out loud.

Tina paused and looked quizzically at Delia.

"How could I do that, Delia? How could I be riding on a merry-go-round in my mind while I'm being sodomized? I must a been one crazy kid."

"You weren't crazy, Tina. You were brave and smart. What you did is a form of dissociation. Everyone dissociates from time to time. For instance, when you're in a boring meeting, or a boss is criticizing you, your mind will wander so that you don't have to hear or see what's going on. In everyday situations, your mind doesn't have to completely dissociate, just enough to tune out the unwanted information.

"In the event of sexual assault, particularly with children, the dissociation is more complete. Dissociation is the best way we have of living through those horrible moments. Your mind did exactly what it needed to do in order to protect you."

"Oh, so long as I'm not crazy." Tina rolled her eyes at Delia in perfect imitation of a silent movie lunatic.

"I stayed on that merry-go-round and I didn't come back into that stinking room until I heard his toilet flush." Tina struggled, but took a deep breath and continued. "So, I kinda come to and I look towards the bathroom. The Super is washing his hands. I see him zip up. Then he walks into the kitchen and opens the refrigerator door. He starts pulling out bread and bologna, some orange pop, and he puts them into a brown grocery bag. I say, "How about some of that pie? You promised me money, too."

"He says, 'You drive a hard bargain, little lady.' He was smiling like we're the best fuckin' friends in the world. So, he wraps up the pie and hands me the food. He drops a couple of quarters into my jacket pocket.

"He says, 'Don't tell nobody and every time you come to see me, I'll give you something to eat. You surprised me today. I can give you better stuff once we really get to know each other, like candy bars and potato chips and hamburgers. Bethcha'd like that, wouldn't you, sexy?'"

Tina's voice caught. "Next, he touches my cheek. So gentle, like he's my long-lost daddy or something. 'You're a very special young lady,' he says. 'Now, you're in my club for beautiful ladies. Hell, you're the queen of the club. I might have to get rid of the others. I'll take good care of you, baby, but it has to be our secret. Okay?'

"It was the first time in my life anybody said I was special or beautiful. First time I could remember anybody giving me anything. I felt so ashamed of what I did. It hurt and it scared me; but at the same time, I was proud of myself. Is that the sickest shit you ever heard of, or what?" Tina began to shiver violently.

Delia fished the afghan out from under the sofa and gently tucked it around Tina. "It's a perfectly reasonable reaction, considering the situation you were in. Tell me, if that had happened to Jade instead of you, would you blame Jade or think less of him."

"Nah, course not. He was a baby."

"So were you, Tina."

"I guess. Anyway, I told him I wouldn't tell.

"So he grins at me like a fucking hyena and hands me two more quarters. To seal the deal, huh? Then, he grabs me really hard, squeezing until those long fingers of his are almost doubled around my skinny arm, until I cried out. He shakes me and says, 'You tell anybody, you little bitch, and the state will come and take that precious brother of yours off to foster care. And, if they don't, I'll make fucking won-ton soup out of him. You hear me? You won't never see him again. You understand? You'll be sitting your ass in prison with your junkie ma.

"You know why you'll go to prison? Cause what you just

done was love a grown man. The law says you can't do that 'til you're grown. So, you just broke the law, little girl. It's a bad law, I know, cause what we just done felt wonderful, didn't it? But, they will throw your ass under the jail for it.'

"Then, he lightens up on the pressure on my arm and, my God, Delia, he starts acting like the sweetest lover you could ever find. He says, 'I'll teach you everything you need to know to get out of this hell hole, baby.' He runs his hand up under my skirt and strokes my vagina. He rubs my breasts. I feel myself getting wet. I want him to touch me more. I'm so ashamed 'cause it feels good. He's looking right into my eyes. It feels like happiness to me. I never felt that way before. I forget the physical pain from a few minutes ago, but I'm experiencing every other jumbled up emotion. I don't know what to do or say. I look up at him and he leans down and French kisses me. My first kiss and it's from a greasy bastard old enough to be my father.

"Swear you won't tell, he says.

"I swear, I say, and he hands me my bag of food and pushes me out the door. I'm outside his apartment, waiting, trying to figure out what to do next. I look down at the bag of food and its like somebody else's hand is holding it, you know?"

Delia nodded.

"I hear him turn on his stereo and that breaks the spell, I guess. I start crying—quietly to myself—and then I remember Jade's upstairs, and the gangs in the halls, so I make one foot go in front of the other, like a zombie. I'm Frankenstein's monster now, stiff legged, holding on to the pissy walls, creeping up the stairs and by the time I get to the top, I'm not crying anymore.

"I open the door to our apartment and there sits the fucking mother of the year, half-nodded out. She's holding Jade on her lap and they're like some Good Housekeeping picture of domestic bliss, Madonna and child, except Jade looks more like a war orphan. He's got his skinny arms wrapped around Mommy's neck.

"Where you been, Mom? I say, and she says, breezy as a prom queen, 'Been visiting friends, Mousie darlin'. Where you been?'

"My mom was from Georgia. Usually she tried to sound like she was from New York 'cause so many people made fun of her accent. But, when she was really high, she had this habit of reverting to southern belle. She was so fucking loaded that she was having a hard time staying upright. 'What you got in the bag?' she says.

"Food," I say.

"Where the hell you get food?

"I stole it.

"Mom popped up from the chair and dumped Jade on the floor like he was a cat who could land on four feet. He fell like a stone on his side and I could tell it hurt. He whimpered, you know? Then, she wheels around and slaps me as hard as she can. Nearly exhausts herself with the effort.

"'What the hell are you trying to do, Mouse? Bring the law down on us?' she says to me, like she's some kind a model for behavior.

"I don't say nuthin.

"She says, 'Give some of that shit to Jade. Don't let me catch you stealing no more.' Then she goes shuffling off, slack-jawed, to bed, like her mothering duties have been handled for the day.

"I'm telling ya, I coulda killed her. She's letting her own baby starve and . . . me having to take up the slack by sucking some pervert's dick. I started to go after her. I couldn't stand the sight of her stringy head. I was gonna whack her. If I could find a hammer, she'd be dead, but I saw Jade out the corner of my eye and he was looking at the food so hungry that it broke my heart.

"I spread that old quilt out on the floor, wiped out a couple of plates, and poured the pop into two glasses. You shoulda seen Jade's eyes when I plopped those four quarters down.

"Buddha boy, I said, we're through being hungry. We can get food and money when we need it, but you can't tell Mommy. You can't tell nobody, okay?

"Raise up your glass, I said. I lifted my glass and said, in my grandest voice, 'To my brother Jade, the richest boy in Union City.' See, we saw that movie, *It's a Wonderful Life*, and I thought maybe I could make something wonderful happen for us. Course, I didn't have a clue what I was getting myself into.

"Even hungry as we were, we both ate real slow—stretching that meal out. I remember trying to smile at him like I was Donna Reed from that movie. You know, a calm and pretty mother.

"Donna was so wise. I wanted to be smart like her more than anything in the world. If I was smart, I could take care of us. I became Jade's mother that day. I didn't know what else to do.

"Five minutes after I finished my damn meal that I had worked so hard for, I ran to the toilet and puked everything up. After that night, I just drifted from our apartment down to the Super whenever we got desperate. Course, he escalated his demands, and . . ."

The afghan wrapped tightly around her shoulders, Tina stopped talking and walked back to the window. The light had softened outside and now she could see her own image reflected in the glass. *I'm a fucking ghost*, she thought.

With her back still turned to Delia, she said, "I'm glad I told you more of the story. Now, you can understand why I'm so fucked up, right?"

Delia quickly dabbed away her own tears and cleared her throat. "Tina, you are a spectacular woman who is recovering from horrible abuse. I've seen so much progress. You *are* getting better."

Tina turned away from her own reflection to look at Delia. "I'm glad you think so. Seems to me, I'm spinning my wheels in mud most of the time."

Delia rose from her chair and faced Tina. "What happened to you wasn't fair. At the time it seemed you were choosing to go to the Super, but you really had no choice. You were a child, trying to survive and keep your little brother alive. What an incredibly brave, compassionate little girl you were, Tina! Do you know that?"

Tina looked away. "Yeah, I guess. Not that it meant anything in the end."

Delia waited until Tina reestablished eye contact with her again, and said, "You survived, Tina. That means everything."

NINE

April 13, 1997

Precariously balanced against the wall in a mold-streaked plastic chair, Magenta Rave propped her feet on the railing outside her second floor room. The motel, a small mom and pop operation recently acquired by Pakistani immigrants, had the appearance of an Alpine doll house, and looked to be just that flimsy, but it had a million-dollar view of the Blue Ridge Mountains. She had come here often to reflect and pray, to plan, and to savor the perfection of her mission. It was here on this balcony that God had first spoken to her.

She stretched contentedly and leaned back against the wall. Before her eyes, crimson light slowly filled in the edge of the world, backlighting the mountains, as if by magic, pulling them out of the black dawn. The winter morning was crisp, but not overly cold. She was two hours north of Atlanta and had already removed her make up, showered, and was luxuriating in the softness of her bath robe. She loved the early morning music of the awakening mountains.

After reviewing the events of the night before, she was satisfied that she had made no mistakes. Everything went exactly as planned. Jack's Place was typical of the bars she had been frequenting lately, only this time located in a run down neighborhood on the north side of Atlanta. The cigarette smoke inside had been revolting, like walking into a fumigation chamber. *Self-administered Raid*, she had thought. *Dim Wits*!

The man she had chosen, Jeffrey Gaines, was a perfect candidate for redemption, and his transformation would be her gift to his victims. She had studied his case thoroughly. Gaines had been released from prison after serving less than seven years of a fifteen-year sentence for the rape of an eighty-year-old woman at knifepoint in her own bedroom. He had not been hard to find and follow. He'd moved back into the family home after the death of his father.

Magenta Rave had known exactly what kind of woman Gaines would like and had dressed the part perfectly. She'd worn skinny leg jeans, a black tee shirt and a denim jacket. Her long brown wig hung board-straight like a veil on either side of her face. Thick bangs rested on the frame of her large, dark-rimmed glasses. She'd squinted constantly to give her eyes a beady appearance.

She had appeared plain and insecure, the kind of woman most men do not even see. She had reasoned that Jeffrey Gaines could not be seduced by beauty. He could be seduced only by weakness. He had been arrested in the past for fondling a young boy, so she reasoned that he would like a boyish woman. She bound her breasts tightly against her body and applied subtle make up that gave her the appearance that she was not wearing any. In fact, she was wearing a comically large prosthetic nose. She wanted Gaines to have a source of power against her, something he could ridicule. She knew it was the only way he would ever leave the bar with her. And, it had worked.

She had watched him intently, yet discreetly, for a while and when he noticed her, she smiled shyly. He beckoned her over to his table with a crook of his finger. She responded by shuffling over with her head down, as if she didn't normally do that sort of thing.

"What's your name?" Gaines had asked after she awkwardly sat down across from him.

"Candy," she had replied.

"That's a sweet name." Gaines ordered a Jack and coke for himself. "What'll you have?"

She giggled nervously and looked down at her hands folded demurely in her lap. "Just a plain coke."

Gaines slugged down the booze and Magenta Rave, calling herself Candy this time, sat quietly, listening while he talked about himself until he was thoroughly drunk. Around 1:30 a.m. when the bartender announced last call, she said, stuttering slightly, "I...I...I should be going now." The stutter was not entirely intentional—Magenta Rave did occasionally stutter—but it had worked to emphasize her naiveté.

Gaines leaned across the table and grabbed her arm. "Wait a minute. You can't just leave me here. I know this great place that's open late. Ain't nothing but fags there, but we can smoke some dope or get some good rock in the bathroom."

"I don't think so." Candy hesitated slightly, as if trying to come to terms with something she knew she shouldn't do. "Maybe you could come to my room. It's not far from here and I got a bottle of what you been drinking, good old Jack Daniels. It's not a fancy hotel, but I got cable. We could watch a movie."

Gaines had agreed immediately.

Magenta Rave had allowed him to hold onto her arm, as if he were helping her, when in fact she—as the simple girl Candy—was leading him out to her car and into the Promised Land. Her Promised Land, anyway. "I'll drive. I been just drinking co-cola all night. I promise I'll bring you back to your car whenever you want."

"What if I want it to be in the morning?" He lurched in her direction, leering.

A smile tickled the corners of Magenta's mouth. "Who knows where the morning will find us." She winked.

Gaines had begun to feel the effects of the Rohypnol she had slipped into his last drink. Her timing couldn't have been more perfect. At that moment, he would have ridden off with Genghis Khan for a love tryst.

Magenta Rave had first heard of Rohypnol, the date rape drug, after the daughter of an acquaintance had been raped. Her first reaction was outrage, but after much prayer, she realized that the drug was from God. It simply had not been put to its proper use. In her slingshot, it would be used to fell Goliath.

Some of the more beneficial effects of Rohypnol, at least for her purposes, were blackouts, amnesia, and incapacitation. While she didn't depend on it to anesthetize her redemption candidates during surgery, the drug was perfect for getting them into bed. It leveled the playing field by taking away the natural strength advantage men have over women.

Not without a struggle, she got him out the door and into her car. She buckled him in, and by the time she got him into the motel room, he was as obedient as a nun to Jesus.

"Man, I must a drunk too much. The damn room is spinning." Jeffrey Gaines wobbled forward from the motel room door and flopped onto the bed.

Magenta Rave peeked out at the parking lot, double-checked that the shades were completely drawn, and then turned on the bedside lamp. "I'll get you a glass of water."

Even in his drugged and drunken condition, Gaines leered at her as she left the room to fill the water glass. When she returned, he was out, snoring slightly, and occasionally groaning. *He's the easiest one yet*, she had thought at the time. No seduction required. No dance. Nothing.

She removed a pre-filled syringe from her bag, swabbed his arm with alcohol, and pumped 20 milligrams of her own special concoction into his muscle. Within fifteen seconds, he was paralyzed and would remain that way for about two hours; at which time he would slowly regain function, and then nod off to sleep until late morning.

From that point on, it had been easy. She removed his shoes and socks and then pulled off his pants and underwear. She washed her hands, donned surgical gloves and, with an ordinary disposable razor, shaved the area immediately surrounding his penis. She swabbed the shaved area with a Betadine solution. With a sure and steady hand, she then deftly removed his penis with four carefully placed, steady strokes from her scalpel. She lightly sutured the area, packed it with cotton, and placed a standard surgical bandage over the wound.

The operation had taken less than twenty minutes and once she was sure that he was in no danger of bleeding, she placed her still-gloved hand on his forehead. "If thy right eye offend thee, pluck it out, and cast it from thee. And if thy right hand offend thee, cut it off, and cast it from thee: for it is profitable for thee that one of thy members should perish, and not that thy whole body should be cast into hell."

"I offer this offending member to thee, Father, as restitution for the atrocities committed by this man and pray that he will now be acceptable in thy sight. Amen."

She quickly removed the surgical gloves and donned household cleaning gloves. She placed the telephone on the nightstand within Jeffrey Gaines' reach. Next, she carefully gathered the scalpel and waste, making sure that nothing had fallen beside the bed or been kicked under it, and placed it, along with his water glass, into a plastic bag, which she then stuffed into a large purse. She wiped her fingerprints from the doors and doorknobs, from the bathroom faucet and mirror, carefully avoiding her own image. When she was sure she had cleared the room of any trace of herself, she left a note that said "II Samuel 13:14 - Magenta Rave."

Rave checked Gaines' blood pressure and pulse before leaving. She glanced back just once before quietly closing the door behind her. She wanted to remember the peaceful look on his face, and imagined that it would be the last moment of real peace he would have in this life. That thought filled her with joy. She could breathe deeply for the first time in days, though her heart pounded as if it would explode.

The punishment must be appropriate to the crime, she'd thought. *Else, how will they ever learn? It's not enough to open the doors of heaven for them; they must first suffer here on earth. Suffering was the fire that would cauterize their diseased souls.* She had done what she could for the body. Only through suffering would they be cleansed and ready to join the Kingdom of God. And then, only if they repented and begged for forgiveness. That part was up to them.

She was sweating from her exertions and the claustrophobic weight of the long wig, but she carefully pulled her collar up and draped the hair so that it covered all but the narrowest sliver of her face. The door to the motel room opened directly into the parking lot. She glanced discreetly from side to side to make sure no one was about. She smiled, remembering her appearance when she had rented the room that afternoon. The front desk clerk would later describe her to police as a boisterous, heavyset blonde with big blue eyes, smelling of cheap perfume.

She headed northeast on I-85 in the direction of the mountains. She had one stop to make before she could rest. The severed penis, wrapped in gauze and plastic, was stuffed into her purse with the other debris. She knew exactly where she would dispose of it. Years before, someone she loved had been abducted from a church parking lot, raped, and murdered. Afterwards, the assailant had thrown her body into a deep ravine where the local rednecks dumped old sofas, washing machines and other garbage. That girl had been Magenta's only true friend and she had loved her deeply.

After about an hour of driving, Rave arrived in the small farming community of Langford. She parked the car on a deserted dirt road and began walking through a pine forest toward the ravine where her friend's body had been found. Ancient spirits moaned through the pines, creaking in their restless death, calling for retribution. She heard them and moaned in reply, for she too was restless. A full moon lit the cloudless, crisp night so brightly that she knew God was personally lighting her path. She found the ravine quickly and effortlessly, like she was pulled to it. It yawned before her, bottomless and black, capable of devouring all things, both innocent and evil. For a moment, she faltered and swayed at the edge of the precipice. It would be so easy to jump in. She wanted to cease mourning and be free, but the spirits, the angels, all the forces of heaven set up such a racket through the trees and inside her head that she was held there, firmly.

She removed the gauze-covered penis from its plastic bag and held it for a moment. How inconsequential it is, she thought. So small. So light. How can anything this insignificant be the source of so much devastation?

"My dear Lana, I whisper your name in this unholy place to free it. Is your spirit trapped here, trying to find its way home? Were you still alive when that monster threw you away, sacked up like garbage?"

She was crying now and shuddered, as she once again felt

the deep chasm's pull on her, like the devil's own mouth trying to suck her through the gates of hell. She braced herself against the onslaught. "I offer this sacrifice in your memory and in memory of millions of women and children throughout time who have been sacrificial lambs to the depravity of men."

She lifted the severed penis in one hand, palm up, as an offering. She bowed her head, and humbly and silently prayed for God to show her the error of her ways. Was she wrong in what she was doing? Her answer came, immediately, and with omnipotent perfection.

A joyful noise from the spirit choir—her accomplices— rose to rapturous heights, filling her with pure, radiant light. She felt the music in every cell of her body. The pine forest began to sway; yet there was no noticeable breeze. Just the tops of the trees moving and creaking to an otherworldly rhythm. The moon swelled until it filled the sky. She looked up and the man in the moon was benevolent, smiling. She knew, now more than ever, that God didn't merely condone what she was doing, but had actually chosen her for the job. She was his avenging angel.

She heaved the penis as far and as high as she could. She listened carefully, but was unable to hear the sound of it hitting the bottom of the ravine. She liked the idea of hearing it hit bottom. *Next time*, she thought, *and that time will be soon, I'll weight it with a rock.*

TEN

April 17, 1997

Contrary to Delia's policy of keeping a professional distance from her clients, she had invited her Monday night group to attend Catherine O'Donnell's show. They gathered at the office and then excitedly packed into Janet Hobb's van for the short trip to the theater. While Delia frequently attended plays, this was the first evening she had taken one of her therapy groups. Barreling through the city streets and into the Midtown theater district, laughing and chattering along the way, they spilled out into the Phoenix Theater parking lot minutes before the curtain was due to go up.

The Phoenix was housed in a small building that had once been a full-service garage. The renovation had been done by earnest volunteers with questionable carpentry skills and by ambitious acting interns hoping to score a few points with the director. Rusted rebar from the old pump station jutted up through the concrete out front. An avant-garde faux fence covered with plastic trinkets surrounded the leftover debris making it look like an abandoned bombsite. Inside the lobby, cheaply framed posters of previous productions hung strategically over cracks in the painted brick walls. Catherine

O'Donnell's headshot was displayed prominently in the center wall, along with a resume of her work. A tiny concession stand sold cheap wine and Godiva chocolates prior to the show and during intermission.

A hundred or so salvaged movie seats, with small rips and faded armrests, were squeezed uncomfortably close together in the auditorium. A subtle, but persistent, smell of mildew tinged the air and Delia dreaded the sneezing jag it might trigger. She needed to keep her wits about her. This evening had the potential for disaster, should any of her clients decompensate.

A few seconds after the group had settled handbags and jackets, and their excited chatter had died down, the lights dimmed until there was only a small spotlight directed in the corner of the minuscule bare stage. In complete silence, a slightly overweight cop with a bulbous nose and bushy mustache appeared from behind a black curtain and strutted across the stage. The spotlight followed him, illuminating his face, which was fixed in an authoritarian stare directed towards the audience.

"Women ask for it," he growled.

His gaze was harsh and unwavering, staring into the eyes of audience members until Delia sensed a growing unease within herself and around her. At the exact moment when the level of discomfort seemed intolerable to her, he smiled and began to slowly tap dance—a soft shoe routine reminiscent of Vaudeville. In a voice that was pure soprano, but had been pitched as low as it would go, he sang, "If rape is your fate, why hesitate. You tempted the boy. Lay back and enjoy. Enjoy. Enjoy. Enjoy."

Oh my God, that's Catherine. Delia hadn't been sure until she heard her sing. That realization spread down the row as smiling group members jostled to turn in surprise to each other.

The song continued on in the same vein, extolling the virtues of submission and the joys of rape, if a woman could just get over her inhibitions. The absurd song actually became funny, eliciting nervous, embarrassed laughter from the audience. When it reached a crescendo, darker, disembodied voices gradually superimposed over the cop's voice. He danced faster and faster. The voices assaulted him.

"Bitch. Whore. Who do you think you are?"

"You can run, but you can't hide, bitch."

"You women are all the same. Fucking cockteaser."

"You know you want it, bitch."

"You see this knife, girl? You see this gun?"

"If you didn't want it, why'd you speak to me?"

"If you didn't want it, why'd you go out with me?"

"If you didn't want it, why'd you invite me in?"

"I'll bitch slap you across the room."

"I'll beat the hell out of you, whore. I'll kill those little bastards of yours, too."

"You're mine, bitch. I married you. A husband can't rape his wife. Didn't you know that?"

Eventually, the cop could tap dance no longer. Fear and exhaustion caused him to stumble and his invisible assailants overcame him.

"Mercy," he cried. "Please don't do this. Why are you doing this?"

His answer from the disembodied voice was a litany of epithets. "Bitch, whore, cunt, witch, nag, piece, shrew, tease, cow, hag, slut, tramp, hussy, ho, cat, sow, harridan, baggage, slattern, wench, skirt, pussy, slit, harlot, strumpet, crone, biddy, spinster."

"Help. God help me," he cried.

There was no help. His words impotently ricocheted off the back walls of the theater and spent themselves. The lights abruptly went out and only his agonizing screams pierced the darkness.

The stage lights came back up on the empty stage and for a few moments, the audience sat in stunned silence. Then a low rumble started in the survivor group aisle and after the applause died down, everyone was discussing the scene.

Within a few minutes, Catherine was back on the stage. This time she was a little girl, no older than ten. Delia knew this was the cousin who called herself Patsy Gail. Her face was scrubbed clean of makeup and her hair hung in two long braids that framed her face. She wore patched jeans and a faded Mickey Mouse tee shirt.

Delia realized, for the first time, how incredibly young Catherine looked; nothing like the well-coifed, sophisticated woman who sat before her every Wednesday morning. She found it hard to concentrate on the performance. How different Catherine was in this scene. *Do I know this woman at all?*

The child before her on the stage was trying to make some sense of her father's incest and the only protection she could think of was to make herself as gross as possible so her father would not find her attractive. Before the audience's eyes, as she kept a steady stream of dialogue going, she somehow managed to deteriorate. Her clothes became disheveled. Her hair seemed to spring, unaided, from her braids.

"Daddy doesn't love Momma. He says she's dirty. He calls her lard ass, 'cause she's too fat. So I stopped taking my bath at night and I tried to eat until I was as big as her, so he won't love me either. But, I can't. I can't eat that much, no matter how hard I try, 'cause I just throw it up.

"I know, I'll never eat again! I'll get so teeny tiny, like a bug, he won't see me. Daddy hates bugs. I'll crawl up in the corners of the ceiling and wait in a spider web. I'll drop down the back of his shirt. He'll slap and grab and try to get me out. He'll run and jump in the lake to wash me off of him.

But, I'll hold on. I'll bite him hard. I'll turn his blood into poison soup just before I drown."

The scene continued with the fragmented part called Patsy Gail revealing more details of the incest, while willing herself to get smaller and smaller, until she lay in a fetal position on the stage. Unable to become small enough to fool her father, she simply disappeared altogether in the slowly dying spotlight. A recording of her singing in a child's voice faded along with her. "His blood is turned to poison soup. Poison from a spider bite. The little spider is awfully cute. The little spider knows how to fight." Softer and softer the song became until the theater was haunted by her loss of innocence.

When the house lights came up, the low buzz of conversation gradually built into excited chatter and continued while the patrons, mostly women, waited in line for wine and chocolates.

The second act of the show proved to be equally compelling. Catherine's first character was a buxom, vulgar woman named Tanya who made her living giving blow jobs to strangers. She was under the misguided notion that if she only went so far, she wasn't really a prostitute, since "any fool knows a blow job ain't really sex."

She thought she was safe from AIDS if blowing the bastards was all she was willing to do. Tanya was specific about the exact details of her work.

"Men are like cows," she said. "You got to milk 'em on a regular basis. I provide a public service, see? The penis is directly connected to the brain. You milk 'em to drain the pressure so their heads don't blow up. Them other organs in between? They're just for show."

Catherine had the audience laughing so hard for the first fifteen minutes that nobody saw the painful ending that was approaching. "Sometimes when I can stand to look up from my milking chores, I see they're looking at the top of my head real hard, like they trying to figure out what it is got a holt of 'em. They got this weak pitiful look on their face like a little possum that knows it's been caught by a wolf, you know? And, I want to yell, 'it's me. Tanya!' But, then I start to feel like that's a damn lie if I ever heard one. Who the hell is Tanya? She ain't no more real than them cows I'm milking. She don't count for a hill a beans. So, when I finish up for the night, I take me a couple pills to go to sleep. I wash 'em down with some good Johnny Red and when I wake up in the morning, ain't no telling who's gone be staring back at me from the mirror."

Delia recognized the fourth and final character immediately. Although in therapy Catherine despised discussing him, he was perfectly embodied on the tiny stage now. Catherine had transformed herself into a lanky, hell-fire and damnation preacher; her father, Clyde Graves. While his voice sometimes menaced the audience, it more often seduced them, creating a sexual undercurrent that was both exciting and frightening.

The character of Clyde Graves preached the gospel of Woman's original sin. His eyes burned with the passion of one possessed by righteousness. Delia was not surprised by Catherine's knowledge of the Bible. Before meeting Catherine, Delia had not realized how many passages in the Bible referred to Woman as the cause of the downfall of Man. Woman, unclean, bloody from giving birth, from menstruation, worked her evil machinations over the souls of Man. Woman, the whore, the temptress.

Though she believed in the wisdom of some Biblical passages, Delia knew it was a document that had been prepared, interpreted and abused by men who, as they jockeyed for power, crushed anyone who got in their way with a fully rationalized explanation of why God was on their side.

The contempt and hatred for women still puzzled her, though. Why? Control of women's fertility? A desire to amass harems? Patriarchy rights? Inheritance rights? *Follow the money*, she thought. You can usually find the answer there.

One thing she knew for sure was that God did not hate the gender He designed for giving birth and caring for the young, the most important job in life. No. God did not hate women, nor find them dirty.

Nor would He find children dirty. Delia would never buy the idea of original sin. That we are born sinful. What a laugh! To hold a newborn, inhale its sweet fragrance—how could anyone see a child as anything other than pure joy and innocence? Sin is something we make for ourselves. She was sure of that.

It seemed to Delia that half the men in the world have such a limited understanding of compassion that they have been forced to create a Bible, a Koran, a Torah, or other holy books, to control their behavior. *Their holy books are nothing more than rules for war,* she thought. *God's chosen get the spoils. God's UN-chosen get rape, torture, murder. They get hell.*

But why blame women? Were men in such denial about the havoc they wreak in the world that they have to find somewhere to place the blame? Some excuse for their own behavior. The devil makes them do it. The devil in the red dress and the little "come fuck me" shoes. Who better to blame than the people who love them and scare them the most? Women.

"I COULD NEVER do that in a million years." Janet's face was flushed from exertion.

"What, cut off some guy's dick or get up on stage in front

of a crowd?" Tina had been interrupted in the middle of telling Bea the latest news about Jeffrey Gaines.

"Get up on stage and act, of course!"

The therapy group was seated near the back of the InTown Café, a local restaurant popular with the after-theater crowd in Atlanta. Their table was partially hidden by tall potted plants and they were keeping an eye out for Catherine, who had not yet arrived. She would join them as soon as she got out of costume and make-up.

Janet sipped delicately from her glass of Merlot. "I can't believe how she could change herself so incredibly. I didn't recognize her when she walked out as the preacher."

Tina, who never drank alcohol, was enthusiastically munching on crudités and dip. "I know! Can you believe someone as feminine as Catherine could look so much like a man? What did she do with those boobs of hers? That's what I'd like to know."

The women laughed. Delia was pleased to see them so comfortable together, sharing hors d'oeuvres and wine. It wasn't often they had a moment to simply be together; not have to "work" on themselves.

"I was really touched by the kid. She brought up a lot of stuff for me." Janet was still slightly breathless from the effort of walking from the parking lot to their table, although they had been sitting for at least ten minutes.

"Yeah, the girl really nailed it, didn't she?" Bea was shuffling through her purse for glasses to read the menu. "You know why girl babies have a harder time being born than boy babies? We get stuck in the birth canal by that big old sign on our backs that says, 'It's all my fault.' Y'all heard that preacher tonight? One of our kind caused the downfall of the whole human race. That must have been some sweet apple Eve got a hold of."

The women nodded in agreement. Delia was thrilled to

hear Bea laughing at the absurd aspect of Christian indoctrination that had kept her prisoner in a cruel marriage for so long. If nothing else came of their trip to Catherine's play, that would be enough.

"The whole thing reminded me too much of my daddy. I don't know how you can sit here and laugh. It's disgusting." Janet was in the habit of wearing heavy make-up with a ghostly white foundation. Mascara laden tears had carved gray furrows down the front of her face. She looked like a broken china doll, badly used, cracked, and discarded by the little girl who owned her.

"You either laugh or you cry. Tonight, I'm laughing, honey." Bea dabbed Janet's face with a cocktail napkin, trying to make a few minor repairs.

Just at that moment, Catherine walked through the front door of the packed restaurant. The support group burst into spontaneous applause, causing the other diners to strain to see if Catherine was somebody they should know. Catherine made a royal curtsy when she reached the table. She now appeared the way Delia knew her—hair in a perfect French braid, simple makeup, a black dress, and matching pearl teardrop necklace and earrings.

"Thank you, thank you, my loyal fans," Catherine rose from her curtsy and gave the Queen Elizabeth wave to the restaurant customers, as if they were her subjects.

"That was remarkable, Catherine." Delia motioned for Catherine to sit. "We're dumbfounded over your ability to change yourself. We hardly recognized you."

"It's called acting, my darlings." Catherine remained standing, but her exaggerated theatrical voice broke halfway through, and she giggled. "You really liked it, huh? It means the world to me that you came."

"The fact that you wrote the play . . . it just blows me away." Delia's pride in Catherine showed on her face. She was proud of everyone in the group.

"My life wrote the play, Delia. You know that better than anyone. I just transcribed the notes." Catherine looked down at the table for a moment. Then her eyes lingered on each woman's face for a brief moment and she said, "My life and your lives wrote this play."

"Sit over here next to me, honey." Bea brushed crumbs off the empty chair with her napkin. "What are you going to do with the play from here?"

Catherine lowered herself with a dancer's grace into the chair next to Bea. "I want to tour it to college campuses, but I'm not sure how to get started. What I really need is an agent who could help me manage the business end of things."

"I could be your agent." Bea appeared embarrassed by her own suggestion. "I don't know nothing about how to do it, but I could learn. Everbody ought to see this, honey."

Catherine hugged Bea tightly. "Mama Bea," she whispered. "The job is yours if you want it."

Bea stroked Catherine's hair. "I'm just wishing there was something, anything, I could do. That poor little girl up on that stage tonight. Could be my Ruth before she died. How do I know what he done to her? I was so blind trying to keep him from killing me, I could've missed something. That's the honest-to-God truth."

While continuing to gently stroke Catherine's hair, Bea abruptly smacked the table with her free hand. "What's it going to take to change men, to make them see what's happening? All the women and kids that get killed or raped in this world. Why? Why does the congress put up with it? Judges and lawyers and police. Just let it go on so much that nobody even sees it no more. Till it happens to somebody rich. Then they set up and take notice! Like it's some kind of rare disaster."

"I know somebody who's doing something about it." Tina, the little New Jersey mouse, spoke quietly and with conviction.

"Who?" Delia asked.

"That woman. You know, the one who's been cutting off dicks? I heard she got another one."

"Well, I can't go along with that kind a thinking." Bea took a long sip of her iced tea before continuing. "Revenge done made a mess of this world already. People everwhere acting like they got the power of God and any kind of meanness is just fine."

"Yeah, but listen." Tina dipped a celery stick into the ranch dressing. "There's nothing you can really do to stop these guys. They'll be even meaner when it's over 'cause they'll be so pissed off about not having their dicks. But Red, or whatever she's calling herself now, confiscated their weapons. She's disarmed them. That's the biggest problem we have in this country . . . idiots with no self control running around armed with guns, knives, bombs or their dicks. I think we should 'disarm' every convicted rapist in the world."

At the word "disarm," Tina made a crude gesture near her crotch that made Janet laugh so hard she choked on her Merlot.

Delia was thrilled to hear the women talk about fighting back. For so many abused women, fighting back was impossible. She felt uncomfortable, though, and looked over her shoulder to make sure their conversation wasn't carrying to the tables around them. "I know you're having fun, but vengeance doesn't solve anything, does it? Maybe if we had more treatment programs, if we could intervene with boys earlier . . . ."

Catherine's blue eyes flashed angrily. "Sure, that's the way we'd like to do it. That's the intelligent way, but look where it gets us. You think too much like a woman, Delia. Men have never respected the turned cheek. They just slap the other one. The problem with women is we have horrible things happen to us and we end up feeling guilty."

Her passionate voice rising, Catherine continued. "Whoever this woman is, she's aiming her fury out, turning it against the criminals. She's not going around cutting off just any man's penis. She's cutting off the dicks of these monsters who've destroyed our lives and then been allowed to go on as if nothing important happened. Maybe if they get it into their pea brains that somebody is going to do something about it, they'll change. Personally, I wouldn't give a damn if men start looking over their shoulders every time they walk down a street, every time they hear some high heels click-clacking behind them in a parking garage. Or, how about if they had to ask themselves every single time they had a date for dinner or a movie, 'Is this somebody who will hurt me?' If their fuckin' social lives were a game of Russian roulette like ours, you'd see how fast the laws would change."

Catherine slumped back into her seat, her arms folded across her chest. She was still fired up. At that precise moment, the charming and solicitous young waiter returned to their table and looked at Catherine. "May I take your order, ma'am?"

Bea peered over her reading glasses at him. "I'm not sure you really want to take *her* order, young man."

LATER AT HOME, Delia held a capful of lavender oil under the running bathtub faucet and inhaled the sweet steam that rose. Her discarded bra and panties lay on the floor at her feet, the last articles of clothing in a long line that stretched directly from her front door.

The theater outing had been a stroke of inspiration. For the first time, she'd caught a glimpse of what her group would be like if they were simply her friends. Although their traumas had left them with a debilitating fear and anger towards men, she liked the women. She marveled at their humor, admired their courage.

But she was cold, achy and indescribably sad, nonetheless. It's this awful weather, she thought. I've never been able to keep my mood up when it gets like this. For the most part, Atlanta weather couldn't be beat. Sunny days going up to seventy could happen right in the middle of a freezing February month, and spring came early, like an indulgent God's gift, with its soft pastel palette. But days like today, when the sky couldn't decide whether to snow or sleet, but mostly settled on a bitter drizzle that chilled to the core, always got her thinking of California or Arizona. Didn't they need therapists there too? It didn't help matters either that the heater in her 1968 Mustang convertible groaned and rattled most of the way home before it finally warmed up.

Her hand shook as she swirled in a cup of bath salts that the manufacturer claimed were mined from the Dead Sea. *I really should get rid of that old car.* But it made her feel young, free to flirt with life, as she tooled around the city when the dogwoods were in bloom. She loved taking off with John on the spur of the moment and driving north to Amicalola Falls or south to Savannah. She drove with the top down for most of three seasons and when she felt the wind in her face, she was reminded of a time when she believed, in spite of much evidence to the contrary, that all good things were possible.

She had made a down payment on the six-year-old car with her first paycheck after graduating from college in 1974. She paid fifty bucks a month until she owned it. Over the years, the car had been rebuilt so many times she had lost count. New engines, new upholstery, paint jobs, bodywork, and the usual brakes and belts—it really was ridiculous. Her friends, her husband, even her clients teased her about owning only one car in her lifetime, but Delia's attachments to things or people were not easily broken.

She still had the same shade tree mechanic, her old high school buddy Amos, a true artist with a socket wrench and an engineering degree from Georgia Tech. His eyesight was going. His back couldn't always be counted on, but he loved Delia and he loved Mustangs. He spent hours talking with other Mustang freaks, going to meetings, and searching for the best parts for Delia's car and his own two old beauties. Original parts were getting harder to find, but he would keep trying—if only to have a reason for calling Delia.

Delia loved Amos too, just like she loved her car, her dog, the family heirlooms, and the other people and things she counted on to remind her who she was and what was important about her life. She needed their structure to hold her in a world that moved too fast for her tastes. She jokingly referred to herself as the "Amish" therapist. She'd balked over buying a fax, refused to send emails, and hated leaving messages on answering machines. *Much too cold and impersonal.* She had been this way her entire life. While she had no desire to pound her laundry on a boulder or shoot her own supper, she strongly felt that technology had made physical existence too easy. Humans were forgetting how to depend upon each other.

She stepped gingerly into the nearly scalding water. *I'll take the car back to Amos one more time and see if he can replace the heater.* Her feet immediately turned the color of boiled shrimp. The blush traveled rapidly up her body as she cautiously lowered herself until she was covered, except for the tips of her breasts, which floated just above the surface.

Damn tub has never been deep enough. It was the same thought she had every time she took a bath. She dampened a hand towel and spread it over her chest for warmth. The water, only slightly disturbed by her descent, lapped gently at her chin.

The bath was her nightly ritual. Her life had become filled with rituals and remedies, though she couldn't remember exactly when they started. The lavender oil was meant to help her relax so that she could sleep. St. John's Wort capsules daily for depression, tonics and purges for the chronic ache in her gut, teas, elixirs and tinctures. None of them worked for long. She would return again and again to a state of anxiety, humming like an electric wire, shoulders and head aching. Strenuous exercise helped to relieve some of the tension, but nothing lasted.

When Delia had first started out in the work, she had assumed it would get easier with time and experience. That had turned out to be only partially true. She had gotten better over time. She knew what she was doing, knew what to expect, but she had never hardened herself to the graphic horror stories she was subjected to daily. She pasted a calm expression on her face while she listened and choked back her own tears, stuffing herself with memories and rage that didn't belong to her, but that she owned by squatters rights nonetheless. She was the protective, understanding mother they had never known. She fervently wished to give them new childhoods, new memories, but that was impossible. The best she could do was to help them locate the strength within to bring about healing.

She submerged her head under the water, shivered with pleasure, and sat up. Thank God, she was finally warm. She heard a scuffling noise in the hall outside the bathroom. Sophie's glossy black nose nudged the door open and for a moment, the nose was all Delia could see poking through the tiny crack. She laughed.

"Right on time, as usual, girl. Are you hungry?"

Sophie entered the room, panting and grinning, her whole

body twisting with the thwack, thwack, rhythm of her tail as it beat against the now wide-open door. "Be out in a minute, Soph."

Shining beads of water dripped from Delia's hair, followed the curves of her cheekbones, and plopped silently into the water around her slim waist. Despite her stressful life, she was still a pretty woman, with thick auburn hair and light brown eyes, much younger looking than her years. She stood up and glanced at the bathroom mirror. *Not bad for forty-three.*

Maybe I'm like that guy in The Picture of Dorian Gray. Somewhere there's this oil painting of me that grows more grotesque by the minute, reflecting the misery that I listen to all day long. Didn't someone say "you are what you eat?" Maybe you are what you hear too.

After drying herself, she stepped out of the tub and pulled on her ancient chenille bathrobe. She wanted to be presentable by the time John got home, maybe seduce him; but tonight, like most nights lately, she was just too tired.

ELEVEN

Police Headquarters
April 18, 1997

Detective Marty Sloan tried his best to ignore the ringing phone. It was 5:00 p.m. on a Friday and he was ready to go home. Reluctantly, he snatched the receiver. "Detective Sloan."

"Hey, Marty. I need to see you right away, man."

Marty recognized his cousin Cledith Waycross immediately. "What's up, Cledith?"

The phone was silent for a moment, as if Cledith were weighing his options. "I can't talk about it over the phone. Can you meet me out at Billy's tonight?"

Marty groaned and rolled his eyes. *Cledith's paranoia is still working, even if he ain't.* "Cledith, it's Friday and I'm exhausted. I need . . . "

Cledith interrupted, "It's important, man! You know I wouldn't call you if it wasn't. It's about one of your cases. I can help you."

Not likely, Marty thought, but he agreed to meet Cledith later in the evening.

AFTER SUPPER MARTY plopped his two daughters into a sudsy bubble bath, gave Lyn a quick peck on the cheek as she knelt beside the tub with soap up to her elbows, and headed over to Captain Billy's Seafood House, a local fried fish and hushpuppies joint with the never empty jumbo glass of sweet tea. Located a few miles from Marty's farm on the outskirts of Holden County, the restaurant was owned by one of Cledith's high school buddies. Five minutes inside the place and you'd come out reeking from the rancid grease that coated the air ducts.

The night was clear and cool with a gentle breeze melding the sweet scent of springtime and newly turned fields. Marty zipped along in his Chevy Silverado pickup and was enjoying the short ride through the country, despite the fact that he dreaded spending time with Cledith. They had been good friends for while growing up, sharing dreams and secrets as only children can, but had drifted apart in high school.

Cledith had been slower than the other boys. Marty often found himself standing between Cledith and some childhood tormentor. But, there was one bully Marty couldn't protect him from and that was Cledith's dad, the notorious racist Little Bill Waycross. Like most boys, Cledith craved his dad's approval. What he got instead, usually, was a whack upside the head.

Marty had grown up being fed the same racist soup du jour of the south as Cledith—swimming in it, in fact—but Marty had been lucky. His parents, particularly his mother, had insisted that he treat everyone with respect. For his mother it was a simple choice—all people belonged to God.

Not that she would have been thrilled had any of her children married outside their race or religion. She would have been frightened for them. But that idea was so foreign in Georgia at the time, it never occurred to her. She taught

Marty that hate destroys everyone it touches. Neither she, nor his father, would have it in their home.

Her family, and especially her brother, Little Bill Waycross, held opposite views for reasons Marty had never been able to fathom. No black man had ever done anything to Little Bill, other than be born, but that was enough. He hated them all. He didn't limit himself to African-Americans, though. He hated Jews, Asians, Arabs, Indians, and anyone else who might be lining up to squat in his little patch of the world.

When Marty was fifteen, he'd had a brief, flirtatious friendship with a black girl. It was innocent. Neither of them expected the relationship to go anywhere, but they enjoyed talking to each other during study halls and sometimes sat together as part of a larger group at football games.

Little Bill got wind of the friendship and cornered Marty in an empty bedroom at a family Christmas gathering. He pinned Marty's shoulders up against the wall.

"What's this I hear 'bout you making goo-goo eyes with a jungle bunny?" Little Bill's dead eyes had bored into his.

Marty was too frightened to say anything, so he squared his shoulders and returned the best cold stare he could muster. His uncle's rank breath layered itself permanently into his consciousness.

"What is it, boy? She a good piece of ass? You getting yourself some good chocolate pussy? Hell, boy, ain't nothing wrong with that! It's a damn family tradition, just between you and me. But, you just ain't gone be stupid enough to hold hands out in public with 'em.

"You gone get that girl in trouble. White men see you talking to her and they figure she's a ripe little melon ready fer pickin'. Might just get 'em a little taste. Now, you wouldn't want that, would you boy?"

Marty shook his head. He was trembling with both fear

and outrage. He somehow mustered enough courage to say, "Anybody hurts any of my friends, I'll kill 'em."

A look passed over Little Bill's face that chilled Marty to his core. He had gone too far. Uncle Bill was going to beat the hell out of him right there in his mother's bedroom. Then Bill had laughed, if you can call a wheezing, malevolent bark a laugh. He squeezed Marty's shoulder hard enough to make him wince.

"You mix my blood with that bitch and make yerself some little pickaninnies and see what kind of hell breaks loose, boy."

Marty had torn himself away from Bill's grip and walked as calmly and deliberately from the room as he could, but the encounter had left him badly shaken. He ended his friendship with the girl the next day, making some lame excuse about how he needed to concentrate on his studies. Marty was haunted to this day by the look in her eyes, but it was a price he was willing to pay. Better for her to be safe. He couldn't bring himself to tell her what Little Bill had said. He didn't want to scare her, but more than that, he couldn't bear the shame of her knowing he was related to such evil.

Marty shook his head and cranked up the radio, trying to drown out the memory of that ugly evening. *Poor old Cledith wasn't able to walk away from that bastard.* His feelings for his cousin were an odd mixture of sadness, pity, and loathing.

Uncle Bill had beaten his racist philosophy into his two daughters and only son, Cledith, filling them, until they overflowed like a backed up sewer, spilling their bitter bile on anyone in their way.

Marty pulled into the parking lot of Captain Billy's, and turned off the motor. He was as tired as he could ever remember being. The job had been taking a toll on him, what with trying to find that nut Magenta Rave, on top of the other usual scumbags.

I just need to jump on the John Deere tomorrow and break ground for the garden. Nothing relaxed him more than plowing that old red clay farm that he loved so much—just like his daddy and granddaddy before him. Marty hadn't realized until he started on the job in Atlanta how universally despised country people are. It had always puzzled him. Just because a man is white and has a country accent doesn't mean he's an ignorant yokel who sets off bombs to kill little children in churches. In Marty's mind, farming and feeding your country was a noble thing to do.

Unfortunately, men like Cledith and Bill Waycross, the living, breathing models for the stereotypical redneck, made it nearly impossible for the South to completely heal and move forward. These clowns were still fighting the civil war, for God's sake!

Marty shrugged and opened the car door. *Hell's Bells, might as well get it over with.* He walked through the nearly deserted parking lot toward the front door. Cledith was repulsive, but Marty couldn't ignore him. Since the high school encounter with Little Bill, Marty had made it a point to keep an eye on the whole family. Never knew what kind of meanness they might be up to.

Cledith was sitting in a booth as far away from the front door as possible with his back to the wall. Marty casually strolled towards him, nodding to the only other people in the room along the way, a couple of guys he recognized from high school, cronies of Cledith's. Undoubtedly, they were here for backup if Cledith needed it.

"Hey, man, how you been?" Cledith asked as soon as Marty sat down.

"Good, Cledith." Marty gave him a perfunctory handshake. "What's going on?"

The vein on Cledith's forehead swelled and pulsed visibly.

"Just like that, huh? No, how's your mama or nothing?"

"Sorry, man, I'm in a hurry. I've got to go back to work. Night shift." Marty lied.

"Well, I'll get right down to it then. Wouldn't want you to miss a night in lovely downtown *niagaraville.*"

When Marty looked confused over the word niagaraville, Cledith said, "I'm just trying to be sensitive, man. Wouldn't want to use the N-word. Might hurt the little N-ies feelings. Can't have that. Course, nobody gives a shit about my feelings. Take the flag my great granddaddy died defending and throw it in the damn gutter and piss on it.

"Don't you get sick a seeing all them *African Americans* shuffling down the street, looking for a handout?" Cledith screwed up his face and spat out the words "African Americans" as if he had tasted something vile.

Marty waited and said nothing. No point in trying to change Cledith Waycross. Hatred had been carved upon Cledith's soul, and the best Marty could hope for was that the bitterness and cruelty would die with Cledith. However, that was not likely. His three sons were being carefully fed the same lies.

"Y'all got any idea who this bitch is that's been going around cutting off cocks?"

"Not yet," Marty said.

"Well, today's yer lucky day. I'm on set you straight on something you need to know. You ever hear of a feller named J. Hubert Hargrove?" Cledith didn't wait for a reply. "Hargrove wrote a book 'bout ten year ago that folks in the freedom movement take mighty serious. I'm on tell you something you probably ain't gone believe, but it's the damn truth whether you believe it or not."

"Cledith, I got no time for your government conspiracy . . ."

Cledith interrupted, "Now, hear me out, boy. Lots of

people don't believe it when they first hear it. Hargrove has proved that the U.S. guvment started a program long about 1969 when them hippies and draft dodgers took over—they was led by Jews, you know. They aimed to stop the growth of the Christian white population. In particular, they wanted to weaken or destroy the white man, so to make room for all them dirt races, like the niggers and spics. See them Jews is smart. They know mud men better than us. Hell, you give any of 'em a little crack cocaine or some cheap liquor and a handgun, they'll spend their time getting high and shooting each other. And when that happens, the Jews get full control of the guvment, easy."

Marty waited, impassively.

"Well, anyway, Colonel Hargrove found out about this mess and he wrote a manual on how to fight it called, *The Patriot's Duty*. See, what Hargrove says is that the government has a three-pronged attack that is going on right now against the white race. First, drugs is being put into the drinking water in the white neighborhoods to make white people sterile."

Marty's jaw dropped. His eyes rolled toward the ceiling, but before he could say anything, Cledith said, "You can take that damn look off your face. You ever read any statistics about how hard it is now for white people to reproduce theirselves? That's why all them Hollywood celebrities have to send off to China or Russia for babies"

Marty felt the beginnings of a facial tic and fought the urge to tell Cledith to fuck off.

"You watch any of them talk shows or the evening news. Everbody rich is getting that in-vitro stuff, having their babies made in test tubes, or paying some poor woman to carry their babies for them. Like I said before, you got white people sending away to China and Russia, and even damn Korea, countries that are sworn enemies of the United States, cause they can't make no babies for theirselves. That's cause the damn government has been putting anti-fertile drugs in the white man's neighborhoods for twenty or thirty years. Gonna have us all shooting blanks before it's over with.

"Then, the next prong of the attack against white people is to supply drugs to the *so-called* minority communities. Some of the drugs go in the drinking water, but most of it just goes up for sale on the street corners. Hell, them people will swaller or shoot up about anything anyway. Now, the drugs THEY'RE getting makes 'em fertile as your daddy's farm used to be. Makes 'em want to fuck like bunnies all the time."

"Sounds like I'm living in the wrong neighborhood," Marty said.

Cledith glared. "You gonna listen or make smartass comments?"

"I'd prefer the smartass comments, but go on."

"The final and most lethal prong of their attack is just out and out cutting off dicks. Some are gone be done in hospitals, you know, like it's a necessary health procedure. White men will go in for some routine thing, maybe just a check up, and them Jew doctors will inject 'em with some kind of germ or something that'll cause their dicks to get infected and have to be amputated, or else they'll die. That's one way.

"The other way, and Hargrove really spells this out, is that all those old gals—he calls 'em feministas—you know, those college cunts that get excited over nothing, are just gone track us down and whack 'em off. It's what they've wanted all along. Take down the power source, meaning white men. You cut off a man's dick and you got rid of his power, that's for damn sure.

"Me and my group, we been in touch with Hargrove and he says that whoever's doing this cutting in Atlanta, is part of the conspiracy. Don't you get it, Marty? This is just the beginning for those old gals who can't get a man and wouldn't know what to do with him if they had one. If y'all don't get this one off the streets, it'll give these other crazy sluts an excuse to act up."

Cledith paused and waited expectantly for a response from Marty. When he didn't get one, he said, "What I'm getting around to, Marty, is if the Atlanta police don't get on the ball soon, we gone be out in force looking for her. If we find her before you do, she might wake up the next morning with a few well-placed slices herself. I'm putting you on notice. We're trying to help you here."

Marty was beyond flabbergasted. In all his years on the force listening to liars trying to cover their asses, he had never heard such a mouthful of farfetched crap.

"Cledith, I swear to God, if I get any evidence that you or any of your buddies are up to vigilante justice, I'll throw you so far under the jail you'll have to dig to China to get out. I could arrest you right now for making terroristic threats and planning to obstruct a police investigation.

"We are doing everything in our power to catch whoever's doing this and we don't need the help of some Neanderthal militia group, led by that crackpot Hargrove. I don't know why in hell I wasted my time coming to meet with you."

Marty had raised his voice and noticed the other men staring at him. He lowered it to just above a whisper. "Man, get some help before you do something crazy. Your kids are going to end up orphans if you're not careful."

The vein on Cledith's forehead looked ready to pop. "Daddy said you wadn't nothing but a worthless, coon-loving mama's boy. I guess he was right about that."

Marty stared at Cledith for a long moment, getting his anger in check, and then shook his head. "I feel sorry for you, man."

"Yeah, well take your pity and shove it up your ass, Marty."

ON THE DRIVE HOME that evening, Marty thought about how different his mother and uncle were. How could two children from the same family turn out to be diametrically opposed in their thinking? *Hate is so easy. Doesn't require any self-control. Makes you feel powerful when you're caught up in it. If two people with the same blood could be so different, what hope does the world have of ever getting along? To love your neighbor—especially when they annoy the crap out of you—that takes work!*

He'd have to keep a watch over Cledith—for damn certain. No telling what that nut was capable of. *Hell's bells, one nut on the loose makes the rest of them come rolling out of the can every time.*

That night he kissed his small daughters while they were sleeping and whispered, "Love, babies. Only love," singing it like a soft lullaby he hoped would seep into their dreams.

TWELVE

Study on Long-Lasting Effects of Childhood Sexual Abuse, 1997
Delia Whitfield, Ph.D. Clinical Psychology
Client ID #616-01
Primary Diagnosis: Complex Post Traumatic Stress Disorder (PTSD)
Chief Complaints: Fear of Intimacy, Compulsive Cleaning, Unresolved Rage

Dr. Delia Whitfield was delighted to see that Tina appeared relaxed and comfortable for her regularly scheduled weekly session. They had been making great progress and Delia was hopeful that they would be able to continue. "Do you want to take up where we left off the last time, Tina?"

Tina slowly nodded her head. "Yes."

"What happened after you first went looking for food from the superintendent?"

Tina's voice was quiet, but firm. "About a month later, me and Jade were hungry again. I was lonely and scared. I started going down there. You know, whenever I needed something. I let him fuck me. I was only thirteen, but nothing mattered to me anymore. He could take my body, and I would go off in my head somewhere. Like I was sleeping through my life and as long as I didn't look too close at nothing, I could deal with it.

"Course, after awhile, the neighborhood creeps zeroed in on me, like a pack of wild dogs after a wounded rabbit. How do they know, Delia? Was it something in the way I walked, or maybe I gave off some smell? Anyway, I'd been turned out and they knew it. I guess the Super put the word out that I'd do most anything for a little money or a new dress, maybe some shoes for Jade. I got good at it. I learned to be paid up front and keep my eyes open. Started to do drugs. You know, a little pot, some beer. I never did much else because of my mom's addiction."

Tina paused and looked defiantly at Delia. "I never had no pimp neither!"

"Even when you were that young, you found a way to take care of yourself." Delia said.

"Damn right!" Tina squared her shoulders and sat up straight on the sofa. "I was thirteen, supporting me and Jade. I did the best I could. I spent the money for things we needed, like food and clothes. Didn't blow it on useless crap for me. I treated Jade good, not like he was a burden. That's pretty smart, don't you think?"

"Yes, I do." Delia struggled to keep her own sadness from showing. "Smart and brave."

Tina continued. "Then, when I was almost fourteen, Mommy died of a heroin overdose. Just like I thought she would, laid up half naked in the back bedroom of a stranger's apartment. I didn't feel nothing. I was numb by then. The state came and took Jade away."

Tina paused. "All these years, and I've never stopped missing him. All these long years."

Delia waited for Tina to compose herself.

"After that, I drifted in and out of foster homes for a

couple of years. Kept getting my ass thrown out for *inappropriate* behavior." Tina laughed, as she exaggerated the word inappropriate.

"You know, somebody would look at me the wrong way and I'd pull a knife on them or smack them in the face. God, I got hauled into court at least once every couple of months for fighting, prostitution, public indecency. Judges saying 'Miss Galenski, you better straighten up!' But, they kept on pawning me off onto these poor foster families, who didn't know what the hell they were getting into. Most of them thought they'd just make an easy buck taking me in.

"I had nothing anymore, Delia. Without Jade, I was alone. He was the only thing that gave my life any meaning. I hated myself. Tried a half-assed suicide attempt once. Then, when I was sixteen, like right after my birthday—a total surprise—my grandmother called. Said she'd been looking for us for years. She wanted me and Jade both, but it was too late for him. He'd already been adopted."

Delia could barely contain her excitement. Tina was finally opening up about her grandmother!

"I left Jersey on a southbound Greyhound one gray June morning. The perfect ugly send off from Union City. Nobody but a frazzled social worker came to the station with me, frumpin' and lumpin' along, glasses dangling off the end of her nose, telling me everything hadda work out. Don't worry, Lisa, she says.

"I say, my name's Tina, and she scrambles to look at the name on her clipboard like I couldn't possibly know my own name, and she's sending the wrong delinquent off to Georgia. I feel like spitting on her, but I sashay on board the bus carrying everything I owned in a black plastic garbage bag. Now that's *appropriate* behavior!

"I didn't know what to expect, but I figured if the Granny Clamplett thing in Georgia didn't work out, I'd at least be close to Florida and could hitch on down there. All I knew about Georgia was that it was some hick place. Nobody was gonna like me since they hated Yankees. Everybody married their cousins. Nobody ever wore shoes. Plus, I'd heard they all had sex with farm animals. At least I'd never done that! I was ready to kick ass if any of those hillbillies messed with me!

"Granny lived in this tiny place south of Atlanta called Lovejoy. How about that? I never had any love, except from Jade, and I certainly had no idea what joy felt like. And here I was going to live with some old lady who couldn't have picked me out of a lineup in a place called Lovejoy."

"How was the bus trip?" Delia asked.

Tina pulled an afghan off the end of the sofa and wrapped it around her shoulders. "You know something? It was great. About halfway down, I started to see signs for places I read about in history books. Harrisburg, Baltimore, Roanoke. It started to dawn on me that life outside of my ugly little world really existed. When I caught sight of the Blue Ridge Mountains, they took my fucking breath away. This is gonna sound so stupid, but I wanted to reach out and hug them. Can you imagine? Thinking you could hug a mountain, but it was like this gut feeling. I've never stopped loving them either.

"When we finally rolled into Georgia, everywhere I looked was this enormous forest. Much more than now, since the developers cut everything down. I hadda keep blinking my eyes. So much green! I know now that it was kudzu taking over, making these weird shapes. I wrote a poem on the bus. You wanna hear it? I was only sixteen, remember. It's not very good."

Delia nodded and gave her a little smile.

Ropes of emerald green
smother tree limbs, bound,
like kneeling girls,
praying for breath.
Collapsed barns shout,
with hoarse rooftop voices,
SEE ROCK CITY!
Or, what? I say,
spinning into Oz,
looking for a heart.

"That's powerful, Tina," Delia said. "I love your poems so much."

Obviously pleased, Tina blushed slightly and lowered her eyes. "Yeah—well finally, we get to Lovejoy. It looks like an old cowboy town, or some country town out of a movie. You know, a ragged line of stores with uneven roofs, peeling and blistering in the hot sun; the train hauling ass through it every couple of hours. Like any minute, Billy the Kid is gonna come out of the bank and shoot up the place. I try to see inside the stores, but it's impossible because of the glare on the windows. These leathery looking old farmers wearing overalls are sitting on benches outside, spitting their *terbackey* and scowling at the bus.

"The heat is scorching! People on the street move like they're wading through swamp muck, and heat waves simmer up through the asphalt like hell's burning awfully close to the surface in Georgia. And, I think *what have I gotten myself into*?

"By the time we got to Lovejoy, I was the only white person left on the bus. Everybody had been so friendly to me on the ride down. I figured black people in the south were just friendlier, but I couldn't understand why. With their history and all. Of course, I later found out that white southerners were friendlier too. Go figure.

"Anyway, we finally start to unload. I'm dragging my garbage bag through the aisle of the bus, bending and straining out every window, hoping to catch a glimpse of my grandmother. If I didn't like what I saw, I was planning to stay on the bus. Ride it down to Pensacola, Florida.

"I couldn't find her, so I stepped off into this sea of smiling people, hugging each other and babbling in deep south accents I couldn't begin to decipher; all of them black and looking for anybody but me. I felt so out of place with my white skin and my empty little life. Then, I felt this soft tap on my back.

"Are you Tina?" somebody asked me.

"I turned around and saw my grandmother. She was so tall I hadda look up at her. She had my hazel eyes—the exact same color—and, jeez, was she sturdy looking. Like an old swamp cypress, gnarled and settled against the sky. She had thick white hair pinched up into a topknot. Strands of it fell around her face. She wore overalls and a work shirt with long sleeves rolled up to the elbows. Her forehead was damp with sweat. I liked her looks right away. She made steady eye contact with me. She was a lot older than I expected. Maybe seventy.

"She said, 'I'll swan, honey, you look just like your mama. I been looking for you for a long time. I'm so glad to see you.' Then she tilted my chin up and stared at me long enough to make me real uncomfortable and said, 'My name is Elizabeth Barnes. Everbody calls me Lib. I'm your grandmother, honey. You can call me Grandma, Granny, or Lib, whichever one feels most comfortable to you.'"

"Nothin' feels right," I said.

"Granny laughed, but it was more like a choke than a real laugh. Her sadness seemed to fill her body, clear down to her feet. 'You'll get used to it. Why don't you call me Granny?'

"I said okay and then Granny scooped up the pathetic plastic garbage bag that had everything I owned in it and she put her arm around my shoulder. I stiffened up when she did that. I wasn't used to being touched without somebody wanting something for it, ya know? I wasn't about to be some old woman's slave or nuthin like that."

"Was there anything about the touch that felt good?" Delia asked.

"Yeah. It was kinda sweet. Like I belonged to her. But, I wasn't close to being able to trust nobody at that point. I just went along with the touching, like I always had with everything, and pretended not to notice.

"She kept her hand on my back and guided me over to this rattled old Chevy pick up. Looked so rusted it might shake apart on a bumpy road. She says, 'Here's our chariot! It don't look like much, but it'll get us home.'

"I had a couple of foster people say Welcome Home, Tina! Like I could just relax and make myself at home. Forget who I was, 'cause they really wanted me there. They were just in it for the money. Granny, pulls up to this old farmhouse out in the middle of thirty acres. She had a vegetable garden in the front yard and chickens were pecking around everywhere. I figured she wasn't getting no money for keeping me because the state don't pay family members, usually.

"She said my grandpa died a few years back, but before that the farm had been a successful commercial operation with hired help and everything. They had livestock and killed their own fresh meat—hogs, cows, chickens. Grew their own vegetables. I couldn't even imagine doing that! After Grandpa died, Granny sold most of the land and lived on the profit from the sale. She wasn't rich, but she got by, managed to live on the interest and social security.

"We walked into the kitchen and she said 'You hungry,

baby?' I hadda weigh maybe ninety pounds back then. I later found out she had big plans to fatten me up. When I didn't answer her, she said, 'Let's get you set up in your room, and we'll eat in a little while.'

"Even with no air conditioning, the old house was cool inside because of the high ceilings and these gigantic pecan and hickory trees that surrounded it. I followed her down a dark hall into a wood paneled bedroom. I remember the details of that room like I just left it. It needed a paint job, but overall, was clean and cheerful. Big ole antique oak bed with a mattress so high off the floor you hadda jump to get on it. That makes you feel like a little kid. You ever notice that?"

Delia smiled along with Tina and nodded. "I've got one in my house right now."

Tina continued excitedly. "Oh, this hand-made quilt spread over it, was just like the one Jade and I used to cuddle up under! The one with flowers and ribbons? That, more than anything, gave me hope, like maybe I was home finally. At least, I was related to Granny. I could see that. Antique perfume bottles and a silver brush and comb set spread out on the matching oak dresser."

Tina's eyes glowed as she described the bedroom to Delia. "An old-fashioned framed oval mirror hung on the wall above the dresser. In one corner stood a basket filled with magazines from the fifties. On the walls were pictures of long-dead relatives wearing high-collared suits and derby hats, handlebar mustaches, serious expressions, like taking a picture was the most serious thing in the world. A high school photo of my mom surrounded by other girls in evening gowns had this inscription, *The Queen and her Court*. Mom really was a fucking homecoming queen! Go figure.

"Yellowed photos cut out from old teen magazines of

Fabian, Frankie Avalon and Elvis, were thumb-tacked to one corner of the wall near the bed, like my mom was still this 1950's teenager dreaming of a greaser heart throb. Like she could walk back in the door any minute.

"The room had a small closet that was to be all mine. With shelves and a bar for hanging clothes. I know it don't seem like much, but I never had that before. Never had a room that belonged to me alone.

"I was just standing there, with my mouth hanging open and Granny said, 'This was your mama's room. I've kept it pretty much the way she left it. She was always such a neat little thing. She'd read those magazines over there at night and brush her hair a hundred strokes. Wanted to be just like Sandra Dee. That girl wanted glamour more than anybody I've ever known. She was so fussy about her hygiene, honey, you just wouldn't believe it! Used to camp out in the bathroom every morning before she could get off to school. Put her make-up on one way, then decide it wasn't right. She'd take it off and start all over again. She's always trying new hairstyles. Teasing and spraying to beat the band.

'Your grandpa would get puffed like a bullfrog, swear up and down, pacing in the kitchen that he was going to put a stop to it. I thought he'd pop a blood vessel. See, she was keeping him from getting out into the fields to work. Bless his heart, he never said a word to her about it. He'd just get up earlier and beat her in there. Couldn't stand to hurt her feelings!

'Your mama'd look up at him and say, "Why, Daddy, you know I have to look my best." She'd bat those long eyelashes and he'd just melt. I used to tell him he was a damn fool for that girl. But, I was too. Maybe we spoiled her. She was our only baby that lived. I lost a couple of babies before her . . ."'

Tina paused, seemingly lost in reverie.

After a short while, knowing how important Tina's

relationship with her grandmother was, Delia prompted her. "You do a beautiful imitation of your grandmother's dialect, Tina. And you remember so much detail from that time."

Tina slipped her shoes off and tucked her feet up under the afghan. "I kept a journal and still read it from time to time. It's the most precious thing I own. Isn't that funny? You'd think somebody like me wouldn't have nothing worth writing down. I started it even before I moved to Georgia. I wanted to remember everything in case one day somebody might take up my cause. Course, I've written poems about her, about that time in my life. She was the only one who knew my mom before she went nuts. Besides, Granny liked me. I could tell that from the start.

"After she told me about losing the babies, her voice trailed off and she stood in the middle of the room looking lost. I had a impulse to hug her. Imagine that! Me wanting to touch anybody.

"Finally, she started talking again. Her voice was shaking. She said, 'Your mother was a pretty girl, like you, honey. And smart as a whip! I can't for the life of me figure out what happened to her. She just couldn't stand being in Lovejoy after high school. She broke up with her high school sweetheart. Near as I could tell, he was a good boy. I think it tore him up pretty bad.

'We thought after college that maybe she'd move to Atlanta, and we'd at least see her on the weekends. She got a few modeling jobs there. Got her picture in the Atlanta Times modeling for Rich's Department Store. I have that picture in an album I can show you later. Me and Sheldon—that's your granddaddy's name—was so proud. Bought about twenty copies and mailed them to every cousin we could think of.

'But, no. She had to go up north where nobody could find her and help her. Got hooked on that damn heroin. Poor little thing. She was too ashamed to tell us. It broke your granddaddy's heart. Mine too. We would a done anything under the sun to save her.

'Did you know that the last time I heard from her, you were just a little bitty thing? Around one or two. Jade wasn't even born yet. I sent y'all a quilt where she was living, do you remember? Nah, you were too young. It was up in Kentucky, round Lexington, and me and her daddy—that's a picture of him over there next to the closet door—was planning a trip up to see you.'

"I walked over and studied that picture of my grandpa. He was young and handsome with dark curly hair, wearing a suit that looked a size too small. Granny said, 'Rachel sent me a picture of you.'

"She opened this large heart locket she was wearing. On one side I saw a picture of my mom in a cap and gown, looking young and just a little bit plump. On the other side was my baby picture.

"Granny said, 'I thought you were the sweetest little thing God ever put on this earth and I just couldn't wait to get my hands on you. Lord, I probably would a kissed the shine right off your little face. The next thing we knew, Rachel moved and we couldn't find y'all. Your granddaddy died broken-hearted over that, honey. I swear he did. We looked and looked for y'all. I hope you believe that.'"

Tina appeared to get agitated. She shifted on the sofa; her facial color deepened. "I didn't know how much longer I could stand there and listen. It was too much to take in. So many years of not knowing anything about Mom or family of any kind, and now this old woman was drowning me in information. I felt myself getting mad.

"So this was Mom's room, I say, with the contempt of a sixteen year old—and you know that's a lot. I slouch over to the homecoming court picture and I say, Huh! And I thought she was just a junkie. Here she was some kinda queen. That explains a lot.

"This is making Granny real uncomfortable. I can tell. She says, trying to lighten up the mood, 'I didn't know what your favorite colors were. You decide on the paint and we'll fix up this room any way you want. We can take down the pictures. I debated whether I ought to go ahead and clean it out before you got here. I thought it might be fun for you to see Rachel the way I remember her.'

"I say, I never heard nobody call her Rachel before. She went by the name Rocky. Don't ask me why. I couldn't tell ya. She acted like she was one tough bitch.

"Boy was I sorry when I said that! Granny's face grew dark and I thought she might belt me. Nobody ever called her little girl a bitch before! Not to her face anyway. I was afraid I already blew it. I hadda go and get myself thrown out before I even unpacked the garbage bag.

"Granny gets herself under control and says, 'Don't let me hear you use language like that anymore.' She says, 'I wish you had a chance to know Rachel the way I knew her, they way she really was. She was so tender. Just a tender little girl. I couldn't have asked for a better daughter while she lived at home. I know you're mad at her, but she's still your mama and she deserves respect. Lord knows, I'm mad at her too. I don't know what all you been through, baby. I 'spect it's been mighty rough. If I could take those years away, I would.'

"Granny was the first person who recognized that my life had been awful. I felt so grateful for that. For the rest of the summer, I worked hard on that farm. Out in the sun chopping weeds and fertilizing, feeding the chickens, repairing fences, picking vegetables, canning stuff. Sounds hard now, but it made me feel good, cause at the end of the day I was exhausted and I would sleep like I'm dead. No nightmares.

"For the first time in my life, I belonged to someone. We were so much alike. Granny was quiet, too, like me. But, we were not mice, like Mom called me. No more Mouse! Tina laughed. We were fierce lions in the jungle. We were Amazons! We stalked our prey and tilled our own land and nobody could say anything about what we did. We weren't dependant on men to feed or clothe us, to make demands on dirty mattresses at the end of the day. Granny spoon-fed me my first taste of freedom.

"Noise and chaos always followed my mom every fucking place she went. If Mom was quiet, it just meant her drug had kicked in. But Granny—oh, she would sometimes offer help or suggestions, you know? But, she never made me feel like I didn't have a choice about anything important.

"I worked hard all summer and at times I even amazed myself with how quickly I learned. Work seemed to ease this ache that had been with me for as long as I could remember. I learned to drive her truck, which was no easy feat, believe me. Those gears squawked with the slightest mistake. Granny would cackle with delight whenever I ground that thing into second or third. You know how that goes. Sometimes I would scratch off and fishtail in first gear trying to find the rhythm I needed to get that old wreck moving. I think that's why I'm such a good driver today. If I could drive that thing, I could drive anything."

Delia smiled. It was rare for Tina to say she was good at anything.

"She fixed three huge meals a day, like she was feeding a troop of farm hands. I gained ten pounds over the summer from the fresh corn, fried chicken, country cured ham, potato salad, peach cobblers. Umm! Have you ever had tomatoes fresh off the vine, Delia?

Delia nodded. She certainly had and she knew what Tina was talking about.

Tina continued, animated. "I had tomatoes before, but they were these tired, bland little knots that traveled from who knows where to our ghetto grocery store in New Jersey. Homegrown tomatoes left on the vine under a hot sun until they're just bursting with juice? Straight out of heaven and something I couldn't imagine before I tasted one.

"I used to feel like I wasn't never gonna be able to eat enough, although that summer, I gave it my best shot. I kept canned goods packed away in an old suitcase Granny gave me, in case I had to leave in a hurry. Bags of candy and cookies in a drawer in my bedroom. Me and Granny sat out under the wisteria arbor and split open ripe watermelons. We'd eat 'em; the juice running down our chins. We had these seed spitting contests, which Granny would almost always win 'cause she kept changing the rules. First, it would be who could spit the farthest? Next, she would say 'not the farthest, but who can come closest to that rock over there without going past it?' Then, 'who can put the highest arch on the seed?' Oh, she made me work for every win.

"We had contests to see who could pick the most muscadines and scuppernongs. I was soon able to pick twice as many as Granny. I loved that. Blackberries grew wild around the perimeter of the farm and I would eat them straight from the vine, until my tongue and lips were black.

One afternoon after picking blackberries, I said, 'Why you looking at me like that, Granny?' My hands were torn up from these ferocious briars on the bushes and my fingernails were filthy. I had seeds stuck between my teeth, and oh, the smell coming from my armpits was rank. Granny was standing in the doorway of our house, smiling, as I came walking up. I thought maybe she was laughing at me. I didn't know how to recognize love. I hadn't seen it too much before.

'I believe you've gained a little, honey. That's all,' Granny says.

"We painted my bedroom lilac and white. We removed the old photographs except the one of Mom with her homecoming court. I liked looking at that picture and imagining her as an innocent young woman, instead of the manipulating, pitiful whore she became. I didn't know it at the time, but I was creating a new history for myself. What is the truth anyway for any of us? Was my history that I had lived on a farm, the daughter of a former beauty queen? Or, was my history that I was a child whore from a ghetto in New Jersey? Which would you choose? Both were true, but not the full story.

"I was a year behind in school, but I tested into my own grade level and Granny persuaded the principal to allow me to enter tenth grade. For three months in the summer and then for four more during my first year at Lovejoy Consolidated High, I lived out a dream I had never dared to believe in before. I passed for a normal teenager. Made me nervous as hell. I felt like a pretender in my own life. No one suspected my past. No one knew the evil I had lived through in Jersey. The kids at school thought I was cute. They wanted me to come to their parties. Said I should try out for cheerleading.

"Of course, their parents remembered my mom and were curious about what had happened to her. Me and Granny told everybody that Rachel had been a secretary in New Jersey and that she died from a burst appendix. Explaining my missing father was not hard. He died in a car wreck right after I was born. We didn't talk about my brother Jade. No need to borrow trouble, Granny said.

"I started to trust. Maybe my life could turn out after all. My nightmares went away for a while. Granny threw a Christmas party and some friends from school came. That was an absolute first for me! Friends visiting my house. I met some of Mom's cousins and my great aunts and uncles.

"When Granny found out that I never got any presents from Santa Claus, she said, "Lord, honey, he just couldn't find you up in New Jersey. I already talked to him and he's coming this year."

"She asks me, 'Do you know how it works?'

"I say, 'Not really.'

"Well, she says, her eyes dancing like a kid's, he sneaks into the house while you're sleeping and leaves all kinds of goodies under the tree. Why, he's been coming to Lovejoy for years. Never misses a Christmas.

"I laughed and said, 'I haven't been too good, Granny.'

"She says, 'I been good enough for the both of us. He'll be here.'

"Christmas morning was just like something out of a movie. I woke up and stumbled half-asleep into the living room. I could smell coffee and pancakes and sausage cooking in the kitchen. Underneath the tree was a huge pile of presents, just for me. I tore into them like I was six years old! I could feel Granny's eyes on me. She was standing in the kitchen doorway, smiling, with tears running down her face. Santa brought me new blouses and skirts, sweaters, jeans, an antique doll, even a guitar!

"A note from Santa was taped to the guitar. 'Sorry about the missed years, Tina. Sometimes old Santa just messes up. I hope you can forgive me.'

"Granny wrote it, of course. I ran into the kitchen and hugged her. You asked me once if I ever felt safe, Delia, and I didn't answer you. That day was the only time in my life when I felt not only safe, but special and . . . what's the right word? Beloved? Yeah, that's it. Beloved. It wasn't the presents. It was that anyone cared enough to want me to be happy."

Delia nodded. "You didn't have to do anything to win her love. You didn't have to perform. She just loved you."

Tina smiled. "I wonder why some people get a lifetime of that feeling and some get only a moment. Or not even that."

"It's one of those unanswerable questions, Tina—we'll never know why." Delia's sadness rose up in her in a visceral way. Her voice caught and she turned her head away in an effort to hide what must have shown on her face. "At least not in this lifetime."

Delia could see the tension moving from Tina's tightly clasped hands up to her shoulders. Her jaw muscles were twitching. She apparently did not want to move on in her story. Delia saw her take several deep breaths in and slowly release them, in an effort to self-soothe.

After Tina regained her composure, keeping her eyes closed with a tear leaking from one corner, she whispered, "Three days later, with no warning, Granny had a heart attack and died in her sleep. I was alone in the house with her and found her body in the morning. Her face was twisted into a grimace as if she was trying to say something and had frozen in mid-sentence. The coroner said she had died peacefully, but she didn't look at peace to me. She looked like it took her by surprise and she wasn't anywhere near ready to go. Just because she was still under the covers didn't mean she hadn't tried to get up and get help.

"If only I heard something. Maybe she cried out to me. But no, I was sleeping like a big fat baby with my granny looking out for me."

Tina's breathing was labored and loud. "Why did she have to die then? Nothing in life makes any sense to me. Granny was old, but the day before she'd been fine. She had more energy than the fucking high school cheering squad. With my mom, I could see the end coming. Mom was killing herself every day. But Granny was so happy to be alive, so involved with her life. We just found each other. It wasn't fair. Not a damn thing in my life has ever been fair. Nothing.

"The next days were a blur. A funeral service with at least a hundred people there. I wore my new Christmas cardigan. Questions were coming at me from everywhere. What will you do Tina? Do you have any relatives on your father's side you can stay with? I wish we could take you in, but our house is full.

Somebody dragged this couple of oddballs over and said, "Meet the Clarks, Tina. They're from a girls' home called Balm in Gilead."

I said, "What the hell does that mean?"

"Balm in Gilead means to give comfort. They'll take care of you. It's for troubled girls, Tina. Or girls who don't have any family."

"But I have family, I say, and I have this farm. I could stay here.

"Didn't do no good. Somebody from Granny's family signed some papers and, before I could say kiss my ass, I was being hauled up into the mountains by Robert and Jean Clark, driving to a dormitory in another podunk place called High Point, Georgia.

"Before I left, I asked them, what'll happen to the farm? I could stay here and run it. I'm almost seventeen. I already know everything that needs to be done. What about my stuff? What about Granny's stuff?

"Then this old dragon, said she was Granny's youngest sister, says, you're too young, Tina. The law wouldn't let you. Lib didn't leave a will. Too many debts. There's nothing left. You have to go with the Reverend and Jean. It's a court order. You're lucky to have the Clarks, Tina. They're good folks. They'll see that you get through high school."

Tina smiled through her tears at Delia and said with a shrug, "Then it was good luck Tina—get your skanky ass out of here.

"I didn't find out until years later that one of granny's

nieces had cheated me out of my rightful inheritance. Granny had changed her will to leave everything to me, but the niece pulled some strings with a judge, or Granny's lawyer exchanged the old will for the new. I was never sure exactly what happened. The lawyer was an old family friend and no one wanted some northern bitch to walk away with what was left of Lib and Sheldon's small fortune. It was easy enough to do. By the time I figured it out, years later, the niece had blown the money or hidden it somehow. I couldn't even get any family photos. They cleaned out Granny's house. There was nothing to do about it, but move on."

"That must have been so hard, Tina." Delia handed Tina a box of tissues. "Do you want to go on?"

Tina had begun sobbing, but she shook her head yes.

Delia waited until Tina's crying subsided before asking, "Was there Balm in Gilead for you, Tina? Did you find comfort there?"

"I was in shock when I got there. The Clarks led me to a dormitory and pointed out a single bed. It was one of about twenty in a large room filled with identical iron frame beds. A white metal cabinet was on the wall next to it. Small high windows on the walls. I wasn't allowed to bring anything with me except my clothes and they were put in storage. We were issued uniforms. Ankle-length black skirts, white high-collared blouses, and rubber soled black shoes. We were forbidden to cut or color our hair.

"My pretty presents, Delia. My Christmas doll, photographs of me and Granny together, the picture of Mom as homecoming queen, my guitar—all that priceless stuff. I hadda leave it behind. See, the Clarks' big idea for the rehabilitation of us incorrigibles was to cut any ties to our old lives. Our possessions might remind us. Besides, over-attachment to possessions was considered ungodly. Get rid of the possessions; you get rid of the sin.

"Never mind that those two hypocrites lived in some big ass Tara-looking monstrosity overlooking the school and probably kept everything they confiscated. I read a couple of months back that some ex-inmates have sued the State of Georgia over their treatment at dear old Balm in Gilead. It wasn't so bad for me, once I accepted that I was stuck there until I turned eighteen. I tried to learn what I could, finish high school. I didn't make any waves, but I was empty inside. An empty vessel don't make waves; it just floats around on them.

"Having no men around was good, or I probably woulda left before I turned eighteen. I didn't make friends with any of the other girls. Didn't want to get close to anybody ever again. I don't quite know how to say this . . . at the end of each day, I closed my eyes and tried to forget my life. Erase it while it's happening, like intentional amnesia, you know?

Tina straightened up and blew her nose. "Delia, I hadda fight my whole life. By the time I got there, I was tired. I didn't do nothing to get myself sent there. I was behaving like a nice girl. Making good grades. I went on a couple of dates when I was living with Granny and didn't even kiss those boys goodnight at the door. What more could I do?"

Delia shifted in her seat. Their session was coming to an end. There never seemed to be enough time. "Sometimes we do everything right, Tina, and life still hands us pain. You had no control over any of this and none of it was your fault. That's the most important thing to remember. You were still a child, in the eyes of the law, and there was nothing you could have done. The only power we ever have is how we react in the present. I'm so proud of you for the courage it has taken you to talk about this very sad time in your life."

Tina's expression was hopeful. "At Balm in Gilead, I started thinking maybe God made my life especially hard for a reason. I thought if there was a reason, I could accept it better. They taught us so much Bible stuff. We had morning prayers. Bible quotes over lunch. We recited walking prayers on hikes, and after dinner, we'd sing prayers for an hour in the evening. Every time you turned around, somebody was quoting something from the Bible.

"The teachers there were big on the suffering of Job. You know, how suffering is supposed to make you stronger and how Job remained faithful to God no matter how many hardships came his way. I remember this one passage they quoted whenever any of us complained about the work or the accommodations. This passage—Job 5, Verse 17—went something like, *Happy is the man whom God corrects. Therefore, despise not the punishment of the Almighty.* So, anyway, I started thinking maybe God had some special plan for me. Else, why would I be punished so much?"

Delia asked, "Have you figured out what that plan is?"

Delia noticed an immediate change in Tina's appearance. In an instant, she had become wild-eyed and appeared panicked. She groaned, hastily stuffed her feet back into her sneakers, and started towards the door.

Delia jumped up, but stopped Tina with her voice. "Breathe, Tina. Slowly inhale through your nose. Count to four. Now, a slow release. Count to eight. That's good Tina. You're safe. Keep breathing. You are completely safe. No one here will hurt you."

Delia continued talking until she saw that Tina had relaxed and was breathing normally. "Would you like to sit down again?"

Tina moved woodenly towards the sofa and sat on the edge.

Delia returned to her own seat. "Can you tell me what came up for you just now?"

With a flat affect, Tina said, "No. I'm through. I won't talk about this anymore. You understand? I can't."

Delia knew she'd gone as far as possible with Tina and was delighted with the progress they had made. "Of course. You did great work today, Tina. I'm proud of you. Keep breathing. You are a wonderful, brave woman. Keep breathing."

When it was apparent that Tina had her emotions under control, Delia said, "Are you okay to leave now?"

"Yeah, I'm okay," Tina said.

As Tina was preparing to leave, Delia glanced at her session notes. Something was playing in her mind and she couldn't quite figure out what. "Balm in Gilead was in High Point, Georgia. Isn't that where Catherine's from? Did you know her when you lived there?"

Tina appeared uncomfortable with the question. She wouldn't make eye contact with Delia. Delia made a mental note to follow this line of questioning in a future session.

"Tina? Did you know Catherine in High Point?"

"Nah," Tina said. "Her old man used to come out as a guest preacher from time to time and rant and rave at us, but me and Catherine didn't meet until group with you. Strange, huh? What are the odds of that?"

THIRTEEN

Detective Simone Rosenberg was exhausted after a long frustrating day and the dry heat of the sauna was leeching out what little energy she had left. The sheer volume of cases was becoming overwhelming for her and Marty, and none of them seemed to be going well, least of all the latest adventures of Magenta Rave, Avenging Angel and self-appointed Savior of the World.

After working a full ten-hour day, Simone had forced herself over to Mack's Gym, her favorite no-frills club, in the hopes of working off some stress. She applied the same discipline to her daily workouts that she had used to get herself through college and onto the police force. She was consistent and methodical. She kept her mind focused on the desired outcome, and gave little thought to any interim discomfort. She had already sweated through the treadmill, rowing machine, free weights, and her mandatory two hundred crunches. Now, she sat on the sauna's hard, hot bench with only a thin towel between her and toasted buns. Across from her on the opposite side of the narrow bench sat a beautiful woman with shimmering blond hair and hazel eyes. Simone had noticed her on several occasions before, but not just because of her striking beauty. The woman did one of the most intense workouts Simone had ever witnessed.

"How'd it go today?" Simone asked, mostly out of

politeness, since it seemed to her nude people should at least say hello to each other.

"Crappy. Wasn't in the mood."

"Me neither. I had to force myself over here, and call myself names the whole time I was working out, just to get the job done." She extended her hand. "I'm Simone."

"Tina Galenski," the woman replied, firmly grasping Simone's hand.

In college, Simone had been attracted to other women. In fact, she'd had a couple of very satisfying sexual experiences with two different women, but she hadn't loved either of them. When she did fall hard for her ex-husband, Eli, it had been the infatuation of a young woman for her much older, more sophisticated professor. She'd admired his keen mind and passion for justice more than any physical attraction. She had thought she loved him, but once she outgrew her awe of him, very little emotion of any kind remained. Still, she'd repressed her desire for other women, assuming it to be a passing fancy, something a young woman might go through on her way to sexual maturity. Now, for the first time since then, she felt uneasy, excited, and slightly breathless in the presence of this woman. Their handshake generated almost as much heat within her as the sauna.

"Been coming here long?" Tina was lounging against the cedar walls of the sauna with a large, immaculately clean white towel underneath her on the bench and wrapped around her back and shoulders.

"About two years. It's close to home." Simone struggled to be conversational and actually found herself rattling on like the kind of woman she despised, filling in the silence with empty chatter. "It's such a practical little place, you know? I like it. Not like one of those clubs where everybody's prancing around in front of the picture window overlooking some hot club district in Buckhead. Wearing their latest outfits from Neiman Markup. I hate those places."

Simone was feeling a prickly kind of magic going on inside of her, like when she was a teenager. "How bout you?" She struggled to keep her voice as level and dispassionate as possible.

Tina wiped her face with the corner of her towel. "Seems like I'm always here, rain or shine, for five years now. Maybe I need to get a life!" She paused for a moment. "I've seen you before."

How had she meant that? Simone needed to know. *Was it an innocent statement, or was this beautiful woman actually attracted to her? How does one go about finding out these things? She could just ask her straight out. Are you gay? Would you like to go out for lunch? How about just kissing me one time? Would you lean across the bench right this minute and let me . . ."*

"Hey. You okay? You look a little flushed," Tina said.

"Me? I'm fine. I like the heat. Just like Jamaica, only drier."

Thank God Simone's skin tone hid most of the blush she felt creeping into her face. If she were only a shade or two lighter, like her daughter Minerva, her glow would be lighting up the entire sauna.

Now was definitely not the time to be direct with Tina, she thought. *What could be more threatening for a woman, especially if Tina were not gay, than to have a naked, six foot tall Amazon come on to her?*

In social situations, Simone usually avoided asking people what they did for a living, especially anyone she was interested in romantically. That line of dialogue would inevitably cause them to reciprocate and ask her what she did. Most people, men and women, got that deer in the headlights look the minute she said she was a detective. Law-abiding citizens started behaving as if they were guilty of something. After pleasantries, they would extricate themselves as politely, and as quickly, as possible. But she couldn't think of anything else to say and besides, she wanted to know this woman. If Tina were going to reject her, she might as well get it over with now.

"What kind of work do you do?" Simone asked.

Tina hesitated before speaking. "I'm assistant to a children's book author. I help prepare his manuscripts, do personal chores, research, that sort of thing." Tina stood up and methodically dried the sweat from her glistening body.

Something isn't right. She's not telling the whole truth. So what, just look at her! She can lie to me anytime. Simone decided to stop thinking like a detective. This woman didn't owe her anything. "Anybody I might know? I used to read every night to Minerva, my daughter—before she became a teenager and decided I was too weird to hang with."

Tina wrapped a small towel around her hair. "Probably not. He's young and just getting started. What do you do?"

Yep, there it is, Simone thought. *Never fails. Well, goodbye me irie queen. Me passionate hope 'bout to go up in steam on them rocks over there.*

Simone braced herself. "I'm a detective with the Atlanta P.D." She searched Tina's face for the twitches, the dull glazed-over look, the fearful curiosity. Nothing. In fact, Tina relaxed visibly, stretched and sighed.

"I've never met a cop before," she said, with no trace of the lie on her face.

IT HAD NOT BEEN HARD FOR SIMONE to convince Tina to go out with her. Before they'd finished their saunas, Simone had simply asked, "Would you like to have dinner?"

"Sure," Tina had answered, and had also given Simone's knee a little pat before leaving the room. This was all the encouragement Simone had required. Her love life was a desert and even if Tina were a mirage, she was just the oasis, the sweet drink of water, Simone needed.

Simone had made a mad dash home and quickly prepared daughter Minerva's supper, then dropped her at a friend's house for a sleepover.

Breathless and slightly disheveled, she'd arrived at the Italian restaurant they'd agreed upon and found Tina calmly waiting for her at a small table near the back. Tina was dressed in a simple, but body hugging, black dress and no jewelry except for a small pair of pearl earrings.

"Have you been waiting long?" Simone asked.

"All my life." Tina paused and raised her eyebrows in mock-seduction. She laughed and motioned for Simone to sit. "I'm just kidding."

After Simone ordered a glass of wine, she found she had very little to say. Tina had her completely tongue-tied. So, she opened with what she knew.

"Do you have any kids?"

"No. You?"

"One daughter. Minerva." Simone reached into her purse and pulled out a picture of Minerva sitting in front of the piano in their living room.

Tina casually studied Minerva's picture. "She's beautiful. Looks to be about sixteen."

Simone made a face of horror. "Don't tell her that. She's fourteen, and already wanting to date the seniors at school. She keeps telling me she's more mature, and if it weren't for me, blah, blah, blah. If she thought she could pass for sixteen, there'd be no peace in my house!"

"My lips are sealed." Tina solemnly pulled her perfectly manicured thumb and forefinger across her lips, as if zipping them closed. "Does she play that piano?"

It took a moment for Simone to reply as her gaze had followed Tina's hand in its perfect movement across her full lips, and the effect had mesmerized her. "What? Oh. Yeah, she used to play beautifully before the hormones kicked in. I'm hoping she'll get back to it someday."

"You seem nervous, Detective." The playful look in Tina's eyes captivated Simone.

"Me? I'm . . ."

The waiter appeared seemingly out of nowhere and placed a shared appetizer of fried calamari in front of the two women. Tina waited until he had left and said, "You're not afraid of me, are you Detective?"

Simone dipped the calamari into a spicy red sauce. "Mmm. You should try this. It's delicious."

Tina threw her head back and laughed. "Answer the question."

Simone wiped the corners of her mouth with a napkin. "I'm not afraid of anyone. I'm a cop, remember?"

Tina pretended to be shocked. "What do you think I'm looking for tonight? We're just two new friends out having dinner, aren't we?" Tina paused again as the waiter refilled their water glasses. "Now, where was I? Oh, I know. What you think we're doing here."

"Are you making fun of me?" Simone stopped compulsively eating the calamari and stared at Tina, trying her best to look stern.

Tina reached across the table and took Simone's hand. "I never make fun of people who carry loaded weapons."

Simone struggled to contain her attraction and excitement. "I'm not afraid of you, Tina. I'm just . . . rusty. I've been out of circulation for a long time."

Tina smiled. "Don't worry. It'll come back to you. It's just like riding a bike."

AFTER THEIR MEAL, THEY DROVE TO Tina's apartment, which was meticulously clean and furnished with antique white Swedish furniture, accented throughout by soft blue and yellow fabrics. Her white kitchen cabinetry, appliances, and walls gleamed. Pastel rugs and light beige carpeting covered the floors. Upon entering the apartment, she'd instructed Simone to remove her shoes and place them in cubbyholes designed and built for that purpose just inside the front door. Her bedroom was sparsely, but romantically, furnished with a white-canopied bed, piled high with lace-edged, pastel pillows. A large freestanding oval mirror with a carved, light oak frame stood near the end of the bed against the wall. An overstuffed yellow armchair sat in one corner. A framed Monet reproduction of Water Lilies hung on the light blue wall behind the bed. On the nightstand sat a framed 5 by 7 card that said, simply, "No man knoweth the day nor the hour."

Simone and Tina were lying on their sides in the big bed facing each other. They'd spent most of the evening after dinner talking, touching, and finally making love. Simone gently looped her leg over Tina's waist and pulled her tighter to her. Tina moaned.

"Did you ever read a fairy tale when you were a kid about Snow White and Rose Red?" Tina asked sleepily. "That's what we look like together."

Simone gazed past Tina's body at their reflection in the

mirror. She could see her own curves rising behind Tina's smaller body like a shadowing mountain range. Never had she felt more a part of the earth, of all that was natural, than at this moment in the arms of this incredible woman. She couldn't remember having read the fairy tale, but the descriptive names pleased her. Snow and roses. In the mirror, she saw their hair blending at their shoulders and flowing together like two rivers joining to carry snow and roses far away and out to sea. Their arms and legs were branches from a birch tree, dark and light merged, but still separate and distinct. They were the visual manifestation of night and day, a polarity as central to survival as anything in the universe. Simone could feel the rightness of it.

She noticed the small framed poster beside the bed, and asked, "What does that mean—No man knoweth the day nor the hour?"

"It's from Matthew. One of the many, many, *many* Bible lessons from this school I went to." Tina frowned slightly, then grinned, and planted a feathery kiss on Simone's forehead. "It's no big deal, really. I keep it there to remind me that time is limited. You know 'Seize the Day,' or as the locals might say, 'make hay while the sun shines.' That's all."

"You're kind of young to be worrying about time running out, aren't you?" Simone lightly stroked Tina's back and was still a bit awestruck by the vision in the mirror. She had never known anyone more beautiful.

"You can run out of time while you're still alive." Tina yawned and turned to face in the same direction as Simone. She pulled Simone's arm tighter around her. "You get too old and tired to change. You forget the things you're meant to do. I've taken a lot of wrong turns in my life. Got to make up for it somehow."

Simone kissed the back of Tina's neck. "Whatever turns you took, likkle biscuit, were perfect. They brought you to me."

FOURTEEN

Bloated and soppy with pride, Cledith Waycross stared bug-eyed at Colonel Hargrove's shadow dancing against the huge American flag hanging on the basement wall. Hargrove's silhouette flamed upward one moment and then ducked discreetly behind him the next, alternately bounding across the ceiling of the room and then hiding like a shy child.

For this important occasion, Cledith's wife, Lula, had lit the basement with candles and lanterns that now greedily sucked what little oxygen was available in the damp room. Still, despite the stuffy conditions, Cledith preferred the electricity off. He liked the spooky feeling he got from the burning firelight.

Such an honor to have Colonel J. Hubert Hargrove in his own home! Lula had spent the previous week obsessively cleaning and decorating and, Cledith had to admit, she'd done a great job. In each corner of the basement, she'd placed large, freestanding confederate battle flags. Current U.S. flags were draped over display tables that stood in front of the confederate flags. Each table displayed Nazi paraphernalia and current neo-Nazi literature. Each table also held a framed photograph of martyrs: Tim McVeigh, the Oklahoma City bomber, Branch Davidian David Koresh, Randy Weaver, who lost both his wife and daughter to the World Government forces, and of course, in a position of prominence and special honor, Adolph Hitler.

Near the speaker's podium on the family dining table were books, tapes and videos for sale, which were written and produced by Col. Hargrove. While Cledith thought this a little brazen for such a solemn and historic occasion, he understood that the money went to support The Cause and for that, ceremony would have to accommodate. He also understood that money was tight for the struggling Patriots, as it was for most Americans. Except the Jews. Everybody knew they were the puppet masters behind Uncle Sam's hand, which was firmly stuck in the common man's pocket.

The most popular video on the table—*Bio Chip Madness: Is Your Neighbor Who He Says He Is?*—had already become a classic of neo-Nazi literature. The theory presented in the video was that the New World Order government had implanted computer chip listening devices into the bodies of unsuspecting citizens, thus allowing the government to keep track of their activities. This information was being fed into a data bank and eventually, after the public had been completely processed, white citizens, or trouble makers of any stripe, would be arrested and either executed or "re-educated" through various brain washing techniques. The video also presented "evidence" of the most popular current theory, that being the reason for the evening meeting: the sterilization or other procreative destruction of all white Christian males.

After his unsuccessful meeting with Marty, in which Cledith had volunteered the services of the Patriots and had been rudely dismissed as a nut, he vowed he would never again try to work within the system. The conspiracy reached all levels of government and if he were going to have any success, it would have to be through the resources of the true Patriots. He was prepared to die if necessary, but hoped it wouldn't come to that.

Ten men, the trusted core group out of approximately fifty members of the Southeastern Regiment of Patriots for the Defense of Constitutional Government, were gathered for the important task of determining what action, if any, should be taken. Standing in a tight bunch before Col. Hargrove, they opened the meeting with an enthusiastic recitation of the

Pledge of Allegiance and the Lord's Prayer. Afterwards, they sat down on dilapidated rumpus room chairs and sofas and turned earnestly towards the distinguished looking man who had commanded their presence.

As Col. Hargrove waited for the men to settle down, his wife straightened up the sale table and replenished the supplies for the after-meeting sale.

"Fellow Patriots, lend me your ears." Although the Colonel was almost seventy years old, he was fit and vigorous with a full head of thick white hair.

"Lend me your ears, your eyes, your hearts and your souls. No, don't lend them to me. GIVE them to me now, for we are gathered at the greatest juncture of history since the beginning of time. What we decide tonight in this humble home . . ."

Cledith puffed up. *I don't like the sound a that. This ain't no poor-ass, humble home. Lula worked so hard to make it clean and fit for the Colonel and his high-falutin' wife. It ain't right for him to say that. Well, maybe he thinks he's a damn poet or something.* Cledith supposed he could overlook the slight. *For The Cause. Anything for The Cause.* Still, he'd be on his guard.

Colonel Hargrove's voice was resonant, rich and hypnotic. "From these humble beginnings, great deeds will grow if we seize the day and make it our own. For some time now, we have known about the federal government's plan to eliminate, or incapacitate, the white Christian man. The tactics for bringing about this heinous crime are now becoming clear to us. Let me bring you up to date on the latest techniques.

"Here's one I bet you never heard of. For years now, we've been hearing from doctors—Jews, I know I don't need to add . . ."

The gathered men laughed and nodded knowingly. Most of them never went to doctors unless they were near death. When they did, they wanted to be damn sure there weren't no Goldfarbs or Weinsteins hiding in the woodpile.

"We've been hearing for years that we all need to lower our cholesterol. Cut out the steak and pork and gravy. All that good stuff we love to eat. Oh yeah, high cholesterol will cause us to have heart attacks and strokes and God knows what else might happen.

"Well, I don't know about that, but let me tell you what I do know for a fact about cholesterol. Cholesterol is the primary substance—and I mean, the most important, bar none—the primary substance that our bodies use for making testosterone!"

There was a collective gasp in the room and a low rumbling that started near the back. Most of the men gathered knew about testosterone from the bodybuilding they had done. They knew if they took steroids, testosterone increased, and they felt meaner and stronger.

Hargrove leaned towards the men and his shadow shot across the ceiling, like a harbinger of death. "What happens when your body doesn't make enough testosterone? I'll tell you. You start to develop tits and your voice gets higher and hell, even if you could get a woman to go to bed with you looking like that, you'd be shooting with blanks, boys.

"So, tell me, why do you think those doctors want us to cut back on cholesterol?"

It was a rhetorical question, of course. Every man there knew the answer, but Colonel Hargrove drove his point home. "See, boys, the federal government wants to disarm us in any way they can. They can take away our firearms; that's easy enough. But, we'd find ways to get more. Hell, we'd fight 'em with sticks and rocks if we had to. AND, we'd win. Because we're right. We got the United States Constitution on our side, and we got God on our side too.

"But, if they take away our manhood, it won't matter whether we have guns or not. You ever see a bunch of women willing to form an army and fight for liberty? With the exception of a few like my good wife here, the answer is HELL NO! Switch off our testosterone and we'll be sitting around getting fat and watching Oprah."

The men laughed.

Hargrove dangled a limp wrist over the edge of the podium, then licked his pinkie and ran it across his left eyebrow. "Oh yeah, boys, I can see it all now. We'll be calling each other ever morning and saying, 'girl, did you see what happened on Oprah yesterday? I cried until I thought I was fittin' a die."

The Colonel did a pretty good stereotypical imitation of an urban black woman, shaking his head in a side-to-side glide and wagging his finger. His falsetto cracked on the word, "die."

"Well, that's what the World Government folks have in mind for us, brothers. Take away our manhood. Knock us into our easy chairs with a wine cooler and maybe some of them little triangle cucumber sandwiches and never let us back up again. The white man built every damn thing worth having on this earth, and now they want to take it away from us. But we're not going to let that happen! Right?!"

The men were stirred from their seats and shouted in overlapping unison, "Hell no!"

A man with a nose that had been relocated on his fierce face so many times that it practically laid sideways leapt from his seat. "Not in this country. No sir!"

"Not while I have breath in me!" shouted a pimply boy in a black cowboy hat.

The Colonel continued. "I am here with you tonight because we have strong evidence that the recent string of attacks on the manhood of Atlanta men was committed by the first Robiotic agent to be put into service by The One World Federation."

This announcement created a buzz in the room like static electricity leap-frogging from one hairy, goose pimpled arm to the next. Cledith, who had been studying Colonel Hargrove's literature for a while, could feel his stature coming up in the world. *I told that little shit, Marty. Teach him to laugh at me.*

The Colonel raised his hands to signal for the men to quiet down. "A Robiotic is a person, if you can call it that, who was genetically engineered from before conception to have the mind of a killer. It has no conscience. A Robiotic also has had structural enhancements to its body from robotic technology, like super strong artificial arms and legs. You remember the Six Million Dollar Man on TV? Like that. Only, this is real. In fact, a technician working in the early stages on the government's Robiotic program leaked the idea for that television show. The name comes from the combination of biology and Robotic technology. Robiotic. Get it?

The men nodded and mumbled that they understood, though many looked confused.

"Anyway, boys, the end result is something that looks like a real human being, but possesses superior strength and cunning. Robiotics emerged out of the experiments that the Army started in the late sixties when they were using LSD, Angel Dust, and all that other crap to fuck with the minds of soldiers. Timothy Leary really ain't dead, boys. He's somewhere else all right. But, he's on the inside now, looking out. Not the other way around like that song said."

Cledith looked around. Hargrove had lost them with the Timothy Leary reference. Most of the guys were young, barely into their twenties. They didn't remember the psychedelic drug heyday the way Hargrove did. Cledith had studied up on the Colonel. Hargrove had been in his late thirties, older than most of the other hippie dropouts, but from what Cledith could tell; the man had a ball in the sixties and seventies. Free sex and all the dope he could do. He made a small fortune selling cocaine, but most of the profits went up his own nose. He spent the last five years of the seventies in prison for his enterprise, but they turned out to be the best years of his life. For it was there he had met his mentor in the Aryan Brotherhood. Cledith read from Hargrove's own words that he had changed himself in prison from a piss-ant cokehead to a powerful revolutionary leader.

The Colonel stepped from behind the podium and walked into the center of the room. "Didn't y'all ever wonder how a woman could overpower or outsmart a strong man, especially one that's been mean enough to go to prison and live through it? Ain't no real woman could! It's an army of Robiotics. No telling how many of them are out there starting to move into place."

"Whutaya think we should do about it, Colonel?" Cledith had ventured the question.

The Colonel turned and spoke directly to Cledith. "Before

we decide on a plan, I need to tell the men here a little more about the Robiotics." Hargrove turned back to circle of enthralled listeners. "Men, these are beautiful, but dangerous creatures. Like I said before, they have no conscience. They would just as soon kill you as look at you, especially if you're a white man. It's just programmed into them. They are heavily armed and have been thoroughly schooled in guerrilla warfare. Y'all know that school over in Alabama? It ain't just Colombian drug lords training over there.

"Robiotics don't even stop and think. You boys need to know this, so listen close. You know how it is. YOU might be thinking, 'Oh, I better be careful 'cause I got the wife and kids to look after. Or, it'd sure break my mama's heart if anything happened to me.' Robiotics, they ain't got nothing or nobody on their minds but who they're supposed to attack next. So, don't fool yourself that you are dealing with just a woman and it'll be a piece of cake. Cause it won't!"

"Waycross!" Hargrove snapped back around to face Cledith. "You know the detective in charge of the investigation, I believe."

Cledith blanched under the Colonel's scrutiny. "Yes sir, I'm ashamed to say he's a cousin of mine. I already been to him to offer our services, but he flat laughed in my face. Told me he'd arrest me for terroristic threats or some such bullshit."

"It doesn't surprise me, son," Hargrove said. "He's probably World Government already. Most of the cops are. The FBI and CIA are in cahoots. It's tearing families apart, son."

Cledith was in heaven. Hargrove had dropped his military tone and was talking in a low steady voice to him alone. Not once, but twice Hargrove had called him "son." Cledith could feel all the way down to his nuts where the Colonel was going and became wild with excitement.

Hargrove patted Cledith on the shoulder. "Nevertheless, we've got to use whatever resources we have and your cousin is our best bet for finding Miss Happy Knife. We follow your cousin, keep track on police radio, and he'll lead us straight to her. The tricky part will be to make the kill before the police can step in and protect her."

Cledith shifted uncomfortably with this latest development. The idea of tracking down a woman and killing her worried him. Even if what the Colonel said was true, that she was some kind of robot, his Patriot division had never planned nor executed a killing. They had only fantasized about it.

Once again, Colonel Hargrove snapped back towards Cledith with military precision. "Waycross, I'm appointing you Commander of the Operation. Code name for it will be Samson, in honor of another man who had his power cut off from him."

Cledith was stunned. This was more than he had dared hope for, and he barely managed to croak, "I'll do my best, sir." Then, he realized he sounded as scared and weak as one of his daughters before a spanking, so he gathered himself and barked in his best imitation of a stand-up military man, "Colonel Hargrove, may I say sir that it is an honor to serve you and I will serve you with all my worldly goods and even my life, if necessary."

Hargrove shook Cledith's hand. "Thank you, Commander Waycross. Glad to have you with us. We'll talk privately and get to the details after the meeting."

Hargrove's intimate tone gave Cledith a feeling of power that he had never experienced before. He was finally on the inside with the big boys. *You'll see, Marty,* he thought. *The world is going to remember my name long after yours is forgotten.*

Colonel Hargrove returned to the podium and consulted his notes before speaking. "The rest of you men will be given your assignments within the next few days. I'm counting on you to do whatever Commander Waycross tells you to do. Remember, he will be working directly under me. Any order from him is an order from me, unless I personally tell you otherwise.

"You're dismissed, men. Before you go, take another look at the book and video table. It's got the finest, most up-to-date, information you're going to find anywhere. Remember, the best weapon in any war is reliable information about the enemy. The federal government's got all the money in the world, and when it needs more, those elected criminals in Washington just up our taxes. If we're gonna fight 'em, we need every penny and then some. Got to give 'til it hurts, men."

After a pause, an inspired glint appeared in the Colonel's eyes and he said, "Unless you ladies already been eating a diet too low in cholesterol."

FIFTEEN

"Mon, I don't know why any woman would pick you up in a bar. I don't care how crazy she is." Simone had come to watch Marty's photo shoot, and he was looking suitably skuzzy propped against the height chart in Booking.

"Yeah, well, Snippy ain't all that discriminating." Marty's mug shot was soon to be prominently displayed in the Atlanta Times.

Simone felt a giggle building up inside, and managed to choke it back down. "Didn't the Chief tell you not to use that name, Marty?" Simone was happy these days, despite their lack of success in finding Magenta Rave. Her relationship with Tina was growing, and she was giddy much of the time.

Marty shrugged and scowled at the police photographer. Marty's wife, Lyn, had dyed his sandy hair black and then streaked it with gray, giving him a grizzled salt and pepper look. His beard, fortunately, grew in darker and was already starting to gray, so it didn't have to be dyed. After a week or so, it had finally stopped itching. "We got to catch this bird whatever the hell we call her. Lyn's fussing about how much this stubble hurts when I kiss her, and my kids are scared of me. They think I'm weird."

"You are weird."

A traffic cop in the district, who had been a cosmetician prior to joining the force, had done an excellent make-up job on Marty, creating various discolorations and swellings on his face. He looked as if he had not gone willingly into custody. One eye was swollen completely shut.

Marty turned to give the photographer a profile shot. "I hope nobody from Holden County recognizes me in this picture. Lyn's got enough to do without having to explain my new look to the children's choir at church."

When the photographer had finished, Marty handed Simone a printed sheet. "Check out the newspaper article I wrote for myself." The headline read, ***Billy Cantrell Sees the Light in Prison,*** by Rose Hanks.

Simone looked up from the paper. "How'd you come up with Rose Hanks for a name?"

Marty's look was mischievous. "My two favorite hunting dogs—a couple of Bluetick hounds. One was Rosie, the other Hank."

Simone read aloud.

Billy Cantrell admits that he was an "evil man, full of the doings of the devil" fifteen years ago when he raped a ten-year-old girl. Now, even though he knows he can never make up for the harm he did, he feels he's paid his debt to society and has moved forward with his life.

"That'll get old Snippy riled up, won't it! Like a few years in prison could ever pay for raping a child." Marty turned to the photographer. "We done here?"

Simone continued reading.

Cantrell, who has been out of prison for five years and is off parole, stated that one day about a year ago, he felt the full brunt of heaven's wrath come down upon him and he was filled with shame over his evil ways. He said he got down on his knees and begged God for forgiveness. "Jesus come to me," he said, "and told me to go and sin no more. My sins are forgiven."

Cantrell has had no contact with the child or her family, out of respect, but if he could, he stated he would like to call or write them to beg for their forgiveness. But, in his own words, "the forgiveness of Jesus is the most important thing."

Cantrell is currently in a job training program with the Georgia Ex-Offenders Project. He hopes to work with computers in some way in the future. When asked what he does in his spare time, he stated that he spends most of his time praying and ministering to others to help them find the light the way he did.

Cantrell did admit to one minor vice still. He liked to have a beer or two on Saturday nights down at the Rainbow's End Tavern in his neighborhood. He said even Jesus drank wine and that a man needed something to unwind. He further stated that he had never had a problem with drinking and if it got to be one, "Jesus would let him know when to stop."

Simone looked up from the article. "That's risky, partner. You're practically advertising for Magenta Rave to drop by the Rainbow's End. She's not stupid."

Wiping the makeup from his face, Marty said, "Yeah, I know, but maybe we'll get lucky. She's bound to screw up eventually."

Simone was not so sure. "She could bolt."

"Hallelujah! She'd be somebody else's problem." Marty removed his torn, fake-blood stained shirt and slipped into a clean one.

Simone read the last paragraph.

When reminded that he could become a victim of Atlanta's serial attacker who had been targeting convicted sex offenders, Cantrell stated that he was not afraid of any crazy women who might be out there, because God was looking after him and he was looking out for himself. He further stated that "any man who lets it get cut off, don't deserve to have one (a penis) in the first place."

Simone slapped the paper down on the counter top and let out the belly laugh that had been tickling her through the last twenty minutes. "You're too much, partner. That ought to suck her in."

Marty picked up the paper, folded it and slipped it into his pocket. "Yeah, how can she resist an arrogant asshole who thinks God is on his side? They're a match made in heaven."

"More like hell," Simone said.

SIXTEEN

**Long-Lasting Effects of Childhood Sexual Abuse,
1997: A Case Study of Seven Female Survivors
Delia Whitfield, Ph.D. Clinical Psychology
Client ID #616-04
Primary Diagnosis: Dissociative Identity Disorder
(DID)
Chief Complaints: Insomnia, Lost Time, Inability to
Bond, Depression**

Catherine O'Donnell sat on the edge of the sofa, slumped forward with her elbows resting on her knees, her hands on either side of her face.

"It's been a fucking disaster today and I dread having to relive it with you."

Sitting directly across from Catherine in an upholstered rocker, Delia took a deep breath and spoke calmly and soothingly. "Take your time, Catherine. You know you don't have to talk about anything you find too disturbing."

After a moment, Catherine appeared to get her emotions under control. "I did a benefit for a women's shelter this morning. They loved it, but it was really hard to concentrate! Seems like everyone inside me got upset even before I started. Patsy Gail was crying, Preacher was ranting, Hooker kept trying to turn me on, and Cop was yelling about how he was going to throw us all in jail! I can't seem to get it through his head that if we go to jail, he will too!" She looked up at Delia. "It would be funny if it weren't so damned weird.

"The audience members had these hopeful looks on their faces. The cousins know how to deal with despair, but hope messes us up. I made them shut up at some point and managed to get through the performance. I will NOT let them stop me from being professional. It's hard enough to get gigs in Atlanta. The last thing I need to do is break down on stage."

Catherine's work ethic had never ceased to amaze Delia. Her other clients with DID would be unable to manage what Catherine was attempting—which was to allow her fragmented parts, the cousins, to continue living as separate identities. Catherine walked around with a crowd of people vying for dominance at all times, yet she somehow managed to keep everyone—including her primary personality—functioning.

"It's hope that traps you, right?" Catherine's voice was strained almost to the point of sounding strangled. "As long as you don't expect anything, you can get by. It's when you start asking, Why not me? Why can't I have this, or that? Then you get yourself into trouble."

Delia nodded her understanding, and Catherine continued.

"You know what I think, Delia? Happiness is for people who live in fictional places like Mayberry or Walnut Grove. Only fictional people have strong families, who aren't crazy, who don't hate their children, who don't hate their own lives. The cousins would live in make-believe ALL the time if I'd let them. They'd just park in front of the TV and spend every day watching Andy Griffith or Little House on the Prairie reruns. Especially Patsy Gail. She could sit for hours. She wants to live where people laugh all the time. She wants to have a mother who never leaves.

"I bet I know more about the characters on the Andy Griffith Show than members of my own family. My few happy childhood memories are of what happened to those television characters, not to me. Do you think it's possible to live a fictional life, Delia?"

Delia cocked her head to one side. She hadn't heard this from Catherine before. "What do you mean?"

"I don't know exactly. Just give in and lose my mind. Would that be so bad?" Catherine lifted her eyes and looked at Delia with such longing that she appeared to be honestly considering the idea. "I could sit before a television set every waking hour and live my life vicariously in thirty minute episodes. Do people like sitcom characters exist in real life? I've never met anybody that together. Except, maybe you."

Delia chuckled as she jotted a few notes, and then looked at Catherine. "Don't give me too much credit! Those characters don't exist in real life, Catherine. Life is messy, not predictable like a script. People are flawed and self-centered. But good people do the best they can. They try to do no harm. You weren't raised by good people."

"I'll say she wasn't!" Delia recognized the voice coming from Catherine as Hooker.

"Do you want to claim time today, Hooker?" Delia actually enjoyed hearing from this cousin. She was lively and feisty, and Delia knew that Hooker had saved Catherine's life more than once.

"Damn right I want to claim time," Hooker said.

"Is it okay with you, Catherine?" Delia asked.

Catherine's voice changed back to her normal tone and she said, "Yes."

Hooker filled Catherine's body with an electric animation. She popped up from the sofa and began pacing the room. "That's what I keep trying to tell her. Her daddy and Uncle Ted, they were evil. Both of them spouting bible verses while they do God knows what to a person. I'm the one that taught her to milk them off. Pull the pressure off their brains so they'd leave her alone. She wouldn't have to be raped if she'd milk 'em."

Delia remembered from Catherine's play that the Hooker character gave hand jobs to her johns. "You helped her when she was in great danger, didn't you, Hooker."

"Yeah, cause otherwise they'd throw her down and force something else. Something worse. Plus, they'd beat the hell out of her, poor little thing."

"You know they're gone now, don't you?" Delia studied Catherine's facial expressions, which flickered with rapid emotional shifts—worry, fear, desperation. She was prepared to intervene if necessary. "Neither you nor Catherine has to worry about them anymore. They can't hurt you now."

Hooker stomped her foot. She hacked a couple of times, and seeing no place to spit, swallowed. "I know that, but she's still awfully worried they might show up. Uncle Ted comes to her in dreams. She can't even go out on a date you know. There's a sweet boy at the theater—a lighting guy—and he's crazy about her, but she's too scared. She's filled up with hate, too. Don't trust nobody."

Delia noticed Hooker's breath becoming deeper and calmer. She was beginning to fade out. "Is there anything else you'd like to tell me before Catherine comes back?"

"Yeah. Tell her I'll protect her. She won't listen to me. I'll do the hating for both of us. I can always milk the life right out of any bastard." Hooker paused and Delia noticed a peculiar glint in Catherine's eyes. "And, if milking don't work, I've got other tricks up my sleeve."

LATER AT HOME that evening, Catherine pulled a cold Dos Equis from the refrigerator and sat cross-legged on the floor of her living room, staring at the blank walls. She had always kept her apartments nearly empty. To save money, since she often performed in other states, she would simply move out of an apartment and store her few possessions at a local storage facility. Once she returned to Atlanta, she would rent another small, cheap apartment with an open-ended lease. Of course those kinds of leases didn't exist in the safer neighborhoods of Atlanta. But, Catherine was tough and especially adept at living on the edge of violence. Violence was her real homeland, not Mayberry.

Her living room was bare except for four dining room chairs, straight backed and armless, lined against one wall. Two large beanbags were jammed into one corner of the room. Since she rarely had company except rehearsal partners, the furniture suited her needs perfectly. A small boom box that she used for studying dialect tapes sat on the floor near the beanbags. She occasionally tuned it to the local country classics station. She liked the earlier musicians best—Patsy Cline, Hank Williams, the Carter Family. They reminded her of her mother.

She had few memories of her mother, but Catherine's favorite had an accompanying soundtrack. Her father had beaten them both and then left the house. While her mother held her and rocked her in an old-fashioned, creaky rocking chair, she had said, "I'm gone fix this, darlin'. He won't hurt you no more."

If she thought about that day hard enough, she could still feel her arms around her mother's neck and her own tiny fingers idly picking straw threads from the chair's aged woven back. She could still smell the coal smoke that had settled into the house's core.

They had rocked for hours, mother and daughter, comforting each other. They'd listened to a country music station, a blasphemous and dangerous thing to do in the home of a holy-roller preacher who allowed only church music and, even that, only in church. Her mother sang along with the radio, in a high sorrowful mountain voice. Catherine's favorite was a Hank Williams song called "Settin' the Woods on Fire." She and her mother laughed and sang as loud as they could on that one. It was about a poor country couple who would get dressed up on Saturday nights and go out *jukin'*. The next day he would be "right back plowing," but oh, what a time they would have dancing to that jukebox. It was Catherine's one "Mayberry" memory, stolen from the misery of her childhood—if she could ignore the beating that preceded it.

Catherine's Atlanta bedroom contained only a twin-sized mattress and box springs on the floor, a clock radio, a cell phone, and a small black and white television sitting on a cardboard box. A few books on acting, a couple of plays, were scattered about, but Catherine usually gave books away once she'd read them. Her bed linens were crumpled and tossed haphazardly in the middle of her bed. Possessions were an unwelcome encumbrance to her. She told herself it was because of theater, but really she wanted to be able to cut and run at a moment's notice.

The kitchen came closest to revealing anything personal about her. Ten cookie jars of various sizes and shapes sat on the countertop filled with cookies that Catherine never ate, but replaced as soon as they became stale. Winnie the Pooh, Betty Boop, Mother Goose, cows, pigs and rabbits with smiling faces greeted her when she entered the kitchen. As a child, she had longed for a home with a full cookie jar and a mother waiting for her, who would ask, "How was school today, honey?" She knew the cookie jars were ridiculous; but they warmed her, just for a moment when she glanced at their stupidly animated faces and felt like she had a family.

Although the other actors Catherine had worked with over the years respected her work, she had made no real friends in the theater community. She had not been allowed to have friends growing up. Never allowed to go to pajama parties, or hang out at the local drive-in. She didn't know how to make friends, so it was a testament to her talent that she kept getting parts without the buddy relationships that so many actors relied on for casting.

Catherine hadn't quite figured out why she didn't make friends, but suspected it had to do with a great need within her. She felt it like a vacuum that sucked the energy from her core—a need to please, to constantly have her self-esteem reinforced, a need to be at the center of everything. If a director were too authoritarian, she struggled to maintain her equilibrium, to keep the cousins under control. She had given up on making friends in the theater and, since the only other work she did was through temporary agencies in order to make ends meet, or as a waitress, she was constantly breaking ties with people. She was a shy and lonely nomad.

On the wall in the kitchen, in an imposing black oval frame, hung an old sepia photograph of a large stoic family taken around the turn of the century. The people looked like a farm family, maybe even mountain folks. They were not her ancestors, but she pretended they were. She told guests elaborate stories about each person in the photograph, how they were related to each other, and to her. She described their lives. They were an heroic family, with narrow escapes and harrowing acts of courage and generosity.

In her bathroom, strips of photographs, the kind you get from an instant photo booth, covered the wall on both sides of her mirror. Some were smiling, some solemn. Some made ridiculous clown faces and some were overtly dramatic, but they were all photographs of her. Alone. The shower steam had faded and wilted the photos, causing them to curl away from the wall. She had carried them from one cheap apartment to the next, and for years had been incapable of passing a photo booth without stepping inside.

At age 16, she'd just gotten off the bus in Atlanta from High Point and was sitting on one of the wooden benches in the Greyhound station trying to decide what to do next. The ruffling of a curtain caught her eye. From behind the curtain, two little girls had stepped out of an instant photo booth. She watched as their photographs magically descended from a slot on the side of the booth. The girls tussled over the slender strip, giggling and pointing at the images, tickling each other in the ribs. As Catherine watched them, she felt safe, like she had done the same thing when she was a child—peeked from behind a protective curtain before she was lost. Patsy Gail said it had happened in her daddy's church, that the two sisters on the front pew had protected her, but Catherine had no memory of the moment.

She walked over, smiled at the two girls, and stepped inside. It was so private. No one there but her. No one would molest her in there. No one would dare open a closed curtain. There was some taboo against that, she just knew.

And the curtain! How wonderful to wait behind a curtain. A performance was about to begin and she was the star. When she sat on the hard swivel seat and stared at her reflection in the square blank screen, with the camera lens peering from the darkness behind it, she pretended she was on television. She could see the cousins looking back at her— Hooker, Patsy Gail, Cop, and Preacher Man, and more— people she didn't know. She realized at that moment what she wanted to do for the rest of her life. She would be a star! People would come from around the world to see her perform. She would be in plays and movies and no one would ever again say she wasn't good enough. No one would ever call her Patsy Gail Graves again. Greasy Graves, the hick preacher's demon seed, Gravedigger Graves, the undertaker's daughter. Everyone would know her by her real name, Catherine O'Donnell. It was the one truly happy moment she could remember having. She became obsessed with re-creating that happiness over and over, though she was never able to pull it off. For years, she stopped by the bus station just to sit inside that shabby booth for a few moments and pose for the camera.

Afterwards, she didn't know what to do with the pictures. They were not important to the experience, though she enjoyed seeing how funny or dramatic she could make herself appear. None of the cousins' images appeared behind her in the prints, but she understood their need for secrecy. She wouldn't just leave the photos in the booth or throw them away. To tear up her own image was to do to herself what her father had done so many times. She couldn't bear the idea of the photos rotting under mountains of garbage or falling into the hands of some creep, who would masturbate and fantasize her destruction while looking at her face. So she put them up on her bathroom wall and sometimes she talked to them while she brushed her hair or put on her make up. She talked to them as if they were family, not pictures of herself. In one of the photos, she looked exactly the way she remembered her mother.

"Good morning, Mother," she said to that photo, without fail, each day. When she came home in the evening, her photo mother always asked, "How was your day, Sweet Pea?" Just like Aunt Bee in Mayberry might do.

SEVENTEEN

The doctors Whitfield, Delia and her husband John, cuddled on the antique chaise lounge that graced the screened-in porch directly off their bedroom. His lean body curved against her back like a warm thought. Spooning time, they called it.

The spring daffodils, tulips and jonquils were in full bloom along the riverbank and in the mature flowerbeds that surrounded the house. From their vantage point high above an immaculately landscaped hill, the couple watched the setting sun's reflection dance atop the Chattahoochee River, which meandered along the edge of their property five hundred yards below. Beside them, on the wrought iron table once belonging to John's grandmother, sat a bottle of slightly chilled Pinot Grigio.

John had just returned home that afternoon from a speaking engagement at the University of Michigan. Over the course of their fifteen-year marriage, his career as an archeology professor at Emerson University had taken him away from home for weeks at a time on digs or, like the past week, to conduct seminars for graduate students. Spooning time was precious to them.

The past year had been especially hard. John was on a working sabbatical and had spent months away. He was leaving again at the end of the week for a month long dig in Columbia. As usual, he had invited Delia to join him, but her clients were too fragile to abandon for a month. Besides, she detested squatting in the dirt, beating off the flies and scratching around for some minuscule piece of bone or pottery. It wasn't her thing to speculate among the remains of the dead. She preferred to help the living.

John's great grandfather had built their elegant Victorian home shortly after the turn of the century. John had spent his childhood sliding down the stair banister, drinking lemonade on the wrap-around porch, and playing hide and seek among the hundreds of flowering trees and bushes that filled the landscape leading down to the river. The youngest of four children, he was the only son in a boisterous, spontaneous and extraordinarily wealthy family. Until she had met John, Delia hadn't really believed that people grew up in such houses.

It had taken her years to adjust to his family's excesses. She was still not close to John's sisters. From what Delia could tell, nothing especially difficult had happened to any of them until their parents' deaths. They couldn't relate to Delia's point of view about sexual violence or the need for cultural change, although in fairness, they did try. They supported her work through financial contributions and, if possible, supported political candidates she recommended, but had no personal experience of suffering, beyond the usual teenage struggles for grades or boyfriends. Their children were healthy and intelligent. They were, in fact, living charmed lives and appeared to experience no inner turmoil over the luck of the draw.

They did, however, adore John and wanted to be close to Delia for his sake. They invited her on shopping sprees to New York for the latest fashions, or for weekend spa retreats in California or Hawaii. Delia occasionally accepted an invitation, but not without a nagging feeling that one of her more emotionally fragile clients would pay a price for her indulgence. In truth, she did not feel comfortable with her status as the wife of a wealthy man.

Her own parents had struggled to reach middle class, and they had nurtured conformity in her as if it alone held the keys to the American dream. Each sentence her father uttered had first been measured for its effect and then doled out like government cheese. While Delia had never lacked the necessities, her only luxury had been the occasional hours she stole alone in her bedroom, thinking and reading and, most of all, planning her escape. Her family was small and closed off, afraid of calling attention to itself, afraid of public censure. As a young girl, Delia had chafed under the yoke of invisibility that had been her inheritance.

Her father's greatest fear was that Delia would get pregnant as a teenager and embarrass him. To that end, he insisted on personally chaperoning the few dates she managed to get. Her mother, a strident woman, believed marriage was to be preserved at any cost. She intended Delia to grow up strong, too, and would tolerate no messy emotions over what she considered irrelevant issues of parties and proms, or minor discomforts. This environment strengthened Delia's early conviction that emotions were important and that people, not abstract ideas, deserved nurturing.

Her parents hadn't wanted her to go to college. She realized only much later in life that they feared her intellect even more than her sexuality. In the South, particularly at that time, intellectualism in females was thought to be an anti-male aberration. It was only through her strong will that Delia had been able to break their stranglehold. Sometimes it seemed that she had grown up to be a woman who was unrelated to her child self, as if she started out to be one thing and, in the end, became another.

"Hey," John said, as he squeezed himself tighter to her. "Are you still awake?"

Delia smiled. "Pour me a little more wine, honey. Just half a glass. I don't dare drink anymore than that, but I can't bear to leave just yet."

"How's the show going?" John reached over the curve of her hip to get the wine bottle. She could've poured the wine herself, but she loved the sight and feel of his muscular arm reaching across her. John had a beautifully defined body from the long hours he spent squatting and digging small artifacts from the earth.

Catherine O'Donnell was the most challenging client Delia had ever had, and she had confided more details about Catherine's history to John than was usual. "It's been running for several weeks now. Every review I've read has been good. Catherine tells me she's had women's groups come from as far away as Savannah and Birmingham. She's getting more high school and college kids in too."

Delia shook her head in disbelief. "I don't know how she does it. She can barely talk to me about her abuse, but she gets up on stage and acts it out in front of complete strangers."

Delia took a deep breath. The evening sky was streaked with vibrant reds and yellows as the last of the warm sunshine faded away. She felt a chill in the air and shivered slightly against John. "I can't stand the thought of going back into town."

"Can't you call in sick?" he asked, knowing full well the answer.

"No, professor, I don't have one of those cushy jobs where you're on sabbatical more than you're working!"

She was lying on her back now, looking up at John. He raised her silk blouse and gently stroked her breasts. Her nipples stiffened, welcoming his touch, her breathing deepened, and she felt her energy drop into a place of ease and comfort.

John lifted himself on top of her. She could feel his semi-erect penis pressing into her pubic bone through the thickness of her skirt and his jeans. He kissed her forehead, her cheeks, her eyes; and began to slowly work his way down the length of her body. He unbuttoned her blouse and laid it open. He trailed kisses through the narrow valley between her breasts.

"I don't have time for this, John." She wrapped her legs around him and pulled his hips to her.

"Your mouth is telling me one thing, my dear, but your hips are saying something altogether different." He gently untangled himself and sat back on his ankles. He spread her legs apart, holding them wide in a v-shape. Her full skirt slid into a pile at the base of her hips. He lightly kissed her ankles, then worked his way down her left leg until he was kissing her inner thigh.

She sighed. "Sweetheart, really I . . ."

Before she could finish, he kissed her mouth, deeply and passionately, then abruptly stood up. He lifted his glass of Pinot Grigio in a toast to her, turned and walked to the edge of the porch. He leaned with his back against the screen and looked at her, teasing her with just the suggestion of a smile. The setting sun washed him in gold and pink, accentuating his lean, muscular body.

"There's a name for guys like you." She sat up and buttoned her blouse.

"Yeah, Stud." He laughed and took a slow sip of wine.

Delia laughed too. *He wants me to seduce him*, she thought. She wanted to go along with the game. They had certainly played it often enough. She would tell him how much she needed to feel him inside her. How big he was, what a great lover. How she'd missed his touch. Why did he make her wait so long? *Please come over and kiss me here,* she would say, pointing to a spot on her thigh or her neck. *I'll do anything for you my love,* she would say, stroking her own breast suggestively. *What would you like?*

John would resist as long as he could, feigning shock or indifference. Then, he would pounce, wrapping her in his arms and devouring her, covering her with kisses, sucking her breasts, her clitoris, running his hands over the length of her, squeezing and kneading, rolling her over, and over. Then, he would be inside her, thrusting and rolling, rolling, rolling, until she felt suspended, enveloped in timelessness, his occupation of her body complete. Nothing but pleasure would exist within her then. No thought, no plan, no reason for being, except to satisfy the craving that coursed through her body, surging in wave upon wave. She would scream and moan, as orgasm after orgasm connected in some sensual electrical relay, until John finally succumbed to his own need for release, and they would have one last, triumphant orgasm together. Even after all their years together, sex was still good. She knew it and was grateful.

But tonight, her mind was too full of the screams of

tortured women and girls, and she was unable to turn the sound off. This was not the first time it had happened either. Over the past couple of years, she'd had moments when she simply could not get them out of her head.

Delia straightened her skirt and slipped into her shoes. "Do you really have to go on another dig, sweetheart? I've missed you so much. I've needed you. I'm not coping as well as I used to with the stress."

"You know I have to go, Delia." A look of concern furrowed his brow. He returned and sat beside her on the chaise lounge. "The plans were made over two years ago. What do you mean you're not coping? What's wrong?"

"I don't know, really. I feel tired and agitated most of the time. Sort of overwhelmed, you know?" She gave him a knowing look. "Not my usual *carefree* disposition."

They both laughed at the last statement. Delia had always been a serious woman. "My job is taking a toll on me. Lately, it's even been bothering me during sex, John. I've got a bleak feeling—like an emotional vacuum."

"Thanks," he said.

"Sweetheart, it has nothing to do with you . . . please don't take it that way."

He took her hand. "I know that, darling. Just kidding. Why don't you check in with your peer supervisor—what's her name? Maybe she can give you some ideas."

Although Delia had never doubted John's love and commitment, he was clearly uncomfortable with the direction of their conversation. As a scientist, he preferred to leave the murky waters of emotion undisturbed. It was an unspoken agreement between them that Delia tried to honor, although she was just the opposite. Emotions, hers and everyone else's, were the real stuff of her life. Emotions were the tools she used to excavate her clients' histories, as surely as John used trowels, chisels, and brushes.

Oh, why do I bother to even bring up anything negative with him? He's an optimistic, happy man and it just makes him worried about me. Doctor, heal thyself!

But she wasn't quite sure how. Her clients' sexual feelings were laced with pain—the worst by-product of sexual violence. But, why were their memories creating problems for her? Occasionally, she had even begun to replay the day's therapy sessions while she made love to John, and when she tried to turn off her mind, it would not cooperate.

No fair, she thought. *I have a right to happiness, don't I, for heaven's sake!*

She made a mental note to see her peer supervisor about the matter. It was one of the hazards of her job. Naturally, she would experience an association between sex and violence. She was awash in it daily.

John walked back over to the corner of the porch for his wine. He took a sip and turned towards her. "Hey, you're letting a beautiful sunset go to waste here." He apparently had not given up on the idea of sex, and did a little bump and grind for Delia's benefit.

Delia snapped back to the present, and nodded appreciatively towards him. "You dance pretty good for a professor, you hunk a burning love, but duty calls. Can we make a date for later?"

"Later might be too late." He pointed to his crotch. "I may allow my semi-excited friend here to escort me elsewhere, where his talents would be more appreciated."

Delia picked up a comb from the table and ran it through her hair. "Oh, no, please don't let Moby loose on some poor deprived woman! How would she ever be satisfied by anyone else again?"

"Point well taken! Guess I'll just have to take the situation in hand." He kissed her cheek and went inside. A few minutes later, Delia heard the shower running and John singing an old Jackson Brown song.

"Looks like it's me and you again, Rosie." He sang at the top of his lungs.

Delia stretched and leaned back against the pillow. She would get up in a few minutes, and drag herself out the door. Despite her fatigue and dreading going into town for a group session, a smile tugged at her lips. She loved John's playfulness. He saw the world as a place full of amazing possibilities—a place that could be explained if we dug deeply enough. So he studied the remnants of the dead, searching for clues to our ancestors. It struck her as ironic that he was so much happier studying the dead than she was studying the living.

She reminded herself that John was one of the good guys. She had a lovely home and a good marriage. He treated her with respect. He was gentle and generous. But what did it matter that he was one of the good guys? The good guys were no more capable of stopping violence towards women than the women themselves.

She sometimes resented that he was not more affected by the violence. He could blithely go on with his research and not feel guilty or responsible for changing anything. When she became too unhappy, it only made him withdraw from her. So, she hid her feelings as much as possible. But if good men like John were unwilling or unable to involve themselves in stopping violence, would it ever end?

Her day, once again, had been tough. As part of her work as a volunteer patient advocate, she had spent the morning at Peachtree Memorial Hospital helping a woman get through a rape examination and investigation. The woman, a shy, plain widow in her fifties, had sat for hours in a beauty salon the previous day getting her hair cut and colored, her make-up done, her nails manicured and pedicured. The woman had spent a small fortune on a new outfit in anticipation of a date with a guy she'd met through a dating website. On the date, he'd raped and beaten her so badly that she needed facial reconstructive surgery. When Delia talked with her, the woman was in shock, staring off into space, trying to figure out why he had ripped her new dress to pieces.

Delia sat up abruptly. Enough of this, she thought. She shook her head and lightly tapped her forehead with her palm, as if to physically empty her mind of the rank thoughts. John was still the same loving husband he had always been, and she was perfectly fine. It was just work-related stress. She needed a vacation. That's what they would do as soon as she and John could find a mutually available date. They'd go to Aruba and lie on the beach together everyday. They'd make love, take naps, and eat massive amounts of seafood.

Delia reached for the Atlanta Times, which John had thoughtfully left beside the chaise lounge. She would take a moment to read the paper, maybe allow herself one more sip of wine before heading back into town. She needed more time to recharge her spiritual battery.

When she opened the folded newspaper, the first headline to catch her eye on the front page referred to the ongoing investigation into the recent string of sexual mutilations against men. The Chief of Police was apparently convinced the assaults were the work of a serial criminal.

Delia read the article and laid the newspaper on the table beside her. She raised her glass of wine, toasting in the general direction of the meandering Chattahoochee. "Score two more points for our side," she quipped. She took a sip of wine. Pinot Grigio had never tasted quite so good before.

EIGHTEEN

The brightly illuminated motel room reeked of artificial pine scent. It was 2:00 a.m. and the window curtains were drawn firmly shut. Magenta Rave stood beside the bed; her latest victim drugged and physically immobilized before her. Dressed in an elegant purple and gold harem costume, she wore a veil over the lower portion of her face. It was time to perform the test.

"Is your name Robert McPherson?"

The grinning man's eyes roamed the length of Rave's body, and then strayed upward to focus on something located in a far corner of the ceiling. When his wandering attention returned to Rave, he answered in the only way the drug she had given him would allow—with absolute truthfulness.

"Yes."

"Did you spend the last five years in prison?"

"Hey, Mata Hari! Yes. I surely did, Mata Hari!" He giggled as if prison were a trip to Disneyland.

"Why were you sent to prison?"

McPherson's eyes were rolling back into their sockets. "Have you ever danced through the stars and seen the Milky Way up close? That's what I'm doing right now. I'm sitting at the right hand of God. Heaven is real."

"So is hell." Rave smiled at the deliriously happy man. She didn't mind that the drug gave him pleasure. It would be the last he would know.

"Answer the question please."

McPherson frowned, as if struggling to remember. "Rape. I was sent up for rape."

"Is that all you did?" That was enough for Rave, but she wanted the whole truth.

"No."

"What else?"

"I was charged with kidnapping because I moved her from one house to another. Assault with a deadly weapon. My attorney negotiated a plea bargain. The girl was ready to testify, but her family didn't want to put her through it. I confessed and turned State's evidence against my partner in the crime. He got twenty to life. Poor sap. But it was him or me. We were just having fun."

Rave made a mental note to keep tabs on McPherson's partner. God willing, she'd look him up if he managed to get out of prison.

"How old was your victim?"

"Twelve."

"Are you sorry you did it?" *Not that it matters.*

The drug again worked it's magic. McPherson had no choice but to answer truthfully.

"I'm sorry I got caught."

Magenta Rave had heard enough. "Congratulations Mr. McPherson. I'm going to give you a night you're never going to forget!"

"Woo hoo! Take me to heaven, baby." McPherson giggled at the sight of the gleaming scalpel in Magenta Rave's hand.

NINETEEN

Marty had been at his desk for over an hour on Monday morning when Simone breezed into the station house. Her face was glowing. Strands of her still damp hair hung in wild corkscrews about her shoulders.

"How the hell do you look so fresh this early in the morning?" Marty was working on his second cup of coffee and had only just begun to feel human.

"Tole ya, partner. You need to be in the gym with me in the mornings. Make a new man of you." Simone had finished her regular light morning workout in the basement rec room and appeared to be slightly out of breath from the sprint up the stairs to the office.

Marty delicately sipped his coffee, with pinky raised. "I'm not a morning person. You had a chance to look at the McPherson file yet?"

Simone stowed her purse in her desk drawer and ambled over to Marty's cubicle. "Not yet. Same old, same old?"

"Not exactly," Marty said. "It happened on a Monday night, instead of the weekend, and she didn't pick him up in a bar this time. Waited 'til he got off work around 8:00 p.m. and struck up a casual conversation in the parking garage. They went straight to her motel room in his car."

Simone sat across from Marty and opened the case file. "How'd she explain being in a garage and not having her own car?"

Marty opened a brown paper bag and pulled out a sweet roll that he'd brought from home. "Want a bite?" It was a rhetorical question. Simone never ate that kind of crap. "McPherson said Snippy pointed out a car a few slots over and claimed the battery was dead. Said she'd call Triple A in the morning; then she asked him to give her a ride back to her hotel room. After that, everything's pretty much the same. He couldn't remember anything after having a drink with her in the room."

Simone tucked her wild strands of hair back into a ponytail. She appeared to be thinking out loud when she said, "Monday night. That's what they call dark night in the theater."

"How the hell do you know that?"

"I know a lot of couth stuff. You think I'm as unsophisticated as you are?"

Marty sniffed and once again lifted his coffee cup to his lips. "What does dark night mean?" He polished off the last crumbs of the sweet roll and washed them down with a gulp of coffee. He crumpled the paper bag and tossed it like a basketball into a waste container a few feet away. "Swish!"

Simone followed the trajectory of the balled-up paper. "Too bad you're so short. You could've been in the NBA. Dark night—Mondays and sometimes Tuesdays—are nights when live theater is closed. The other attacks have been late at night on the weekends. You doing anything Thursday night?"

"What's up?" he asked.

"My friend Tina told me about this play."

Marty grinned. He knew about Tina. Simone had sworn him to secrecy, but she'd said she would pop if she didn't tell somebody. Marty's loyalty to his partners over the years was legendary, and he would support her in whatever path her life took.

"Wipe that shit-eating grin off your face, partner. That's my girlfriend you're thinking about." She whispered on the word girlfriend. "Tina took me to this play Saturday night. One-woman show. The actress' name is Catherine O'Donnell. I've got a hunch she could be connected somehow to Snippy.

I think we should check her out."

"What, are we so desperate now we're relying on your woman's intuition?" Marty shuffled the papers on his desk and reached for the keys in his pocket. He despised going to plays.

"No way. You know me better than that. I'm telling you this woman hates men. And, she can make herself look like anybody she wants. Her voice, body, everything changes. I didn't recognize her from character to character a couple of times. And, get this—she talks all this Bible stuff. Spouting quotes from the Old Testament. In the final scene, she's a little girl, maybe about first grade, and comes out carrying a book satchel. I started thinking about the grammar school tablet Snippy leaves her notes on. It's not much, I know, but maybe she's trying to get caught. You know how arrogant Snippy is.

"Tina swore me to secrecy, but says this O'Donnell is really messed up. What they used to call multiple personality disorder. Tina's in a therapy group with O'Donnell."

Marty raised an eyebrow. He didn't like the sound of that. He wanted Simone to be with someone healthy. *Boy she can pick 'em. First, that nutty professor. Now, somebody in group therapy.*

Simone shrugged. "Tina's okay, Marty. She's just trying to straighten out a nasty childhood. Anyway, she said O'Donnell got worked up about the newspaper coverage. Couldn't wait to read it to everybody in the therapy group. O'Donnell was raving about how Snippy is a hero, like everybody should be proud of her."

"You mean I got to go watch a play?" Marty practically whined and scrunched his shoulders as if he were ten years old. He pulled the key ring from his pocket and twirled the keys slowly around his finger. Each revolution emphasized his misery. "The last time I went, Lyn dragged me to see *Les Miserables*. I'm telling you, I was the lay miserable in that theater. You wouldn't believe it, Jamaica, every song sounded like the one before it, and the songs just wouldn't end! On and on and on. And not a country tune in the mix! Monotonous as hell. These pretentious thespians up there on stage tearing their hair out. I thought I was going to pull out my gun and start shooting."

Simone laughed. "Officer Sloan, are you going to do your duty, or do I have to ask the Chief to get me a more refined partner. Somebody with class!"

"All right, I'll go." Marty slugged down the last of his coffee. "But you better hold my weapon in your purse when we get there. You remember that guy on the clock tower in Texas? Opened up on a crowd of college students? He probably just walked out of the local community theater production of *Oklahoma*."

THURSDAY NIGHT, MARTY SHOWED UP at the small Midtown theater wearing a "just go ahead and shoot me now" expression.

"C'mon Partner." Simone pushed him playfully towards the door to the theater. "It only lasts an hour and a half. I'll put you up for a special commendation if you can get through it without killing anyone."

Later that evening they shared a booth at the Highland Pub, a favorite spot for off-duty cops. Not much of a drinker, Marty stirred his weak rum and Coke. "I'll admit, I was wide awake during the whole thing. That's a first for me. I even liked her singing, except that part where the cop's getting the shit kicked out of him. Whew! You were right about her. She is one angry woman and a chameleon. Those characters seemed like different people to me."

"So, what do you think, partner? We check her out?" Simone nibbled on a celery stick that she had dipped into Bleu Cheese dressing.

Marty dipped a hunk of grilled sirloin into the dressing. "We got nothing else so far. Might as well."

Simone pulled a small notepad from her jacket pocket and flipped it open. "I did a little checking already. Her real name is Patsy Gail Graves. No prior offenses. She was brought up in one of those hell-fire, booty shaking, little churches up in the mountains. Up around Amicalola Falls. Seems like that preacher character hits pretty close to home."

"I talked to her aunt on her mother's side of the family. She said they haven't heard from O'Donnell in years. I'm driving up to meet with the aunt next weekend. She said O'Donnell's daddy, the preacher man—and I'm using her words—was 'Satan's manservant.'

Simone licked her fingertips and wiped them on her napkin before turning the page on her notepad. "Preacher man wouldn't talk to me. Said his daughter was dead as far as he was concerned. She'd taken up with the ungodly in Atlanta and he wanted nothing more to do with her. Hung up the phone on me."

Marty rolled his eyes, but before he could speak, Simone continued. "Another thing, Marty, I went by Dr. Delia Whitfield's office to see what she could tell me. That's where Tina goes to therapy. The doc got a little hinky on me. I know she can't disclose anything confidential, but she wouldn't even look me in the eye when I brought up O'Donnell. When we finally did make eye contact, there was something there. I'm not sure what it was. Fear, protectiveness, defiance of authority. I don't know. Maybe nothing. The only thing she would disclose was that she knew O'Donnell and that she'd seen the play." Simone consulted her notes. "Oh, yeah, and that she didn't think O'Donnell was capable of violence to others."

"Think we ought to bring O'Donnell in for questioning?" Marty asked.

Simone nabbed the last celery stick from their appetizer plate. "We don't have anything yet. I don't want to spook her. Why don't we tail her on the weekends for a while? See if she does anything out of the ordinary. That newspaper article we're planting in the Times is coming out next week. If she isn't getting home delivery, let's have someone send her a week's complimentary supply of the paper, starting a few days before the article. You know, like a promotional gig.

"Another theater company uses The Phoenix Theater on O'Donnell's off nights. We'll leave a copy of the newspaper lying in the backstage bathroom, like it was left by the other group, conveniently opened to that charming picture of you."

TWENTY

The Sultan's Palace sat at the rear of a weed cracked parking lot on a dead-end street a block off Stewart Avenue in south Atlanta. It was painted a dull gray, except for an old seventies style orange graphic that zigzagged across each side. The building had no windows. A large hand-lettered sign snaked its way across the front of the building in mock-Arabic undulation. *Lingerie Models. The most beautiful girls in Atlanta.* Painted near the end of the sign was a busty blonde dressed in harem pants, a spangled bra top, and a veil over her face that covered everything except her eyes. In an attempt to create a come-hither look, the billboard artist had inadvertently made her cockeyed. The girls who worked inside the building found this enormously funny, since becoming cockeyed was surely one of the hidden hazards of their business.

Immediately inside the front door was a small lobby decorated with threadbare armchairs, low wattage lamps with fringed shades, and a coffee table scattered with back issues of *Hustler, Penthouse* and *Playboy* magazines. The pseudo-Arabian theme was carried throughout the interior of the building. Faded scarves suspended from the ceiling created the look of a tented dome. An imitation Persian rug covered most of the fake brick vinyl floor.

Tina Galenski worked the day shift. She had started in the sex trade when she was eighteen, five months after graduation from Balm in Gilead. Dancing, hooking on the streets, escort services, she'd done it all before she turned twenty-one. She liked the Sultan's Palace better than anywhere else she'd worked. It was easy. She was never forced to do anything she was unwilling to do. Tina was no longer willing to be penetrated by any man. She had been penetrated her whole life by things outside herself until she really wasn't sure where the world ended and she began. She would ply the trade she had been groomed for since the age of twelve, but she dealt in fantasy now. And, she controlled the fantasy.

She had started out working the night shifts, but switched over to days shortly after starting therapy with Delia. The night shift customers were rough, dangerous men, usually drunk or loaded on something, or fired up from the strip club across Stewart Avenue where they had already spent most of their money. They expected freebies from the jack shack girls, and when they didn't get them, occasionally would attack the girls with knives and other weapons. Tina switched to days after one of her co-workers ended up in the hospital.

Her work in therapy had not yet convinced Tina to quit the sex trade altogether, but she'd made progress in that direction. Her developing self-esteem had at least limited the type and amount of degradation she was willing to endure.

The daytime customers of The Sultan's Palace were construction workers or professional men, office drones, sometimes doctors; almost always married. One of her regulars was a physician who gave her prescriptions when she got cystitis or other female complaints. They were, for the most part, just working guys taking long lunch breaks on payday, and could be dealt with quickly and effortlessly by the pros at The Sultan's Palace.

Tina and the other girls were hanging out in the employee lounge, watching television and waiting for the buzzer that would signal an arrival. Tina tried to read, but the other women had their favorite show, *Jerry Springer*, turned up loud and were screaming and cackling along with the guests. The theme for today's show, for the umpteenth time, was

"Help, my teenage daughter is out of control."

The models were fascinated by the grief stricken mothers, who with their harsh black eye liner and sagging chins, sat in chairs sobbing and wringing their hands while their daughters made their entrances swaggering like jive-talking ghetto boys, gesturing lewdly to the audience, giving their mothers the finger, or mouthing the bleeped-out words, *kiss my ass* or *fuck you, bitch.*

Most of the lingerie models had small children. Almost to a woman, they had terrible relationships with their own mothers and absent or abusive fathers, but they still had great hope for their children. They scrupulously protected them from knowing what kind of work they did. It was the only area of shame any of them admitted to about the work. They didn't want the kids to find out.

"First time my kid talked to me like that, be the last words she ever spoke," the model known as Amethyst said.

"Damn mothers sit there like they ain't nothing they can do 'bout that shit. I'd strap her little ass 'til the white meat showed," Raven said.

The women used aliases in their work, although they preferred to call them stage names. In their weekly meetings, management at the shop encouraged the girls to think of themselves as actresses; giving the customer a good show was the most important part of their business. Tina's stage name was Talon, and in addition to Raven and Amethyst, were a Revenge, Harmony, Moonglow, Tabby, Promise and Justice.

The noise from *Springer* was deafening. Tina tried to tune it out, but she was impatient for the buzzer that would signal a customer in the lobby. Her shift was nearing its end and she had made only a couple hundred bucks. She was used to taking in at least four hundred and on a good day, she could clear six. What was the point of doing this kind of work, if the money wasn't good?

In the right light, each of the women who worked at the Sultan's Palace would be considered pretty, though they had the hard look of penciled in, overly tweezed brows, from under which lurked expressions that were pasted into place and subject to dissolving under any scrutiny. None of them, including Tina, could hold eye contact for long without fueling dangerous emotions. Most of them were barely past nineteen. Tina was the oldest at thirty-two and she knew her working days were running out. Her body still looked as good as anyone's there, and she had a natural sense of style that belied her low position in life. She spent an hour each afternoon sweating through the weight machines or running on a treadmill at the tiny workout club close to her apartment, where she had met the love of her life, Simone. None of the others did a thing to preserve their natural gifts. Most of them smoked pot. The day shift girls also did pills, nothing too heavy, downers. The night shift girls; that was another story. Most of them were hooked on crack or heroin.

Tina had never smoked, but she did experiment with drugs after moving to Atlanta. For a while, she'd lived with a chemistry major, who'd spent most of her time experimenting with LSD-like compounds in a home laboratory. Tina had found the experiments fascinating, and liked the high more than she'd cared to admit, but her mother's bad end haunted her too much to continue any kind of drug use. She had known since that first encounter with the superintendent of her apartment building that sex was her ticket out of poverty, and she did everything she could to preserve her looks. Besides, the exercise helped dissipate the anger that came with the job.

Inevitably, though, the lines had begun to creep into her face. Her breasts, which had always been a source of pride, had begun to droop slightly. Her stomach was still flat, but the effort to keep it all together was becoming unbearably tedious.

Oddly enough, though, her age had also become a sort of ally in attracting certain customers. When she was younger, she had played the virgin. Let the customer think he's getting a little girl. She knew, from experience, many men who wanted to make it with children. As she aged, she had cultivated a knowing, sluttish appearance on the job, which the men seemed to like even more. Who can figure how some men think? She guessed that they were incapable of seeing women as full human beings, like themselves, so they categorized them. Virgin, Slut, Wife and Mother. She intended to work every angle until she started looking like their mothers. Hell, even then, she'd no doubt get the sick puppies who'd always wanted to make it with dear old mom.

Unbeknownst to the customers, each of the session rooms in the Sultan's Palace was equipped with a closed circuit camera. The day manager, a tough heavyset woman in her early fifties—who claimed to be writing the next great American novel—often quoted Shakespeare to the girls in an effort to educate them. At least, she told them she was quoting Shakespeare. In truth, she quoted anybody and everybody, including herself, but made it sound like it might have come out of Shakespeare's mouth. Her name was Beth, but some of the girls started calling her Lady Macbeth, and later just Lady M. The nickname stuck.

Lady M, who called the session rooms "treatment wombs," kept a close watch over the activities going on in the building from a bank of monitors in her office. If there were anything particularly freaky going on in any "womb," models who weren't busy would gather in Lady M's office to check it out.

Next to the domination freaks, the weirdest and rarest guys were the ones who wanted to make it with lactating women. The models called these customers nursers or sugar tit boys. The most recent nurser just happened to come on a slow day. He'd called ahead and asked if there were any "girls with milk." Lady M had known what he wanted, but still had made him spell it out for her.

"Whaddya mean, girls with milk? This ain't no dairy, buddy. You got the wrong number. You want the Georgia Milk Cow Association."

"You know what I mean," he'd stammered. "You know, like somebody who's got a little baby and, you know, feeds it."

"You mean gives it a bottle? You want somebody to feed you a bottle? How old are you?"

"No. Feeds it, but . . . not with a bottle."

Lady M hoped the guy would hang up on her. She didn't really care if she got his business or not. Even for her, the sugar tit boys were too weird.

"Yeah, we got somebody that's got some milk like that. You want her to spank you, too?"

The caller breathed heavily into the phone. "Maybe. I have been a bad, bad boy."

Lady M set him up with an appointment with Raven, who was still breast-feeding little Shaneequa, her third child. Raven would never let him actually nurse, but after the long dry spell of pregnancy and childbirth, she needed the money. When the caller arrived, the other models were crowded around Lady M's bank of television screens, waiting for the fun to begin.

It took Raven all of ten minutes to take care of him. The minute he saw Raven's engorged breasts, he became fully erect. Raven lifted one of her breasts, licked the tip of it, and aimed it in his direction. She squeezed the nipple and squirted, and the damn fool came all over himself the minute the breast milk hit him in the eye. The women were laughing so hard and loud, Raven had to leave the room and tell them to pipe down before the guy made the connection that they were laughing at him. Laughter doesn't come often in a place like The Sultan's Palace, but when it comes, it works magic on the women's souls.

The Jerry Springer Show had gotten to the point where somebody was about to start throwing chairs, and Tina didn't think she could handle much more of it when, mercifully, the lobby buzzer rang. Tina jumped up and practically darted for the door. Anything, even stripping naked for some fool, was preferable to watching Jerry Springer. The rest of the models reluctantly pulled themselves away from the show and trooped out to the lobby. They were dressed in mock Arabic harem costumes, without the veils, wearing the lingerie they intended to model underneath. Three open buttons at Tina's neckline gave a beguiling peek at her flawless breasts. Her naturally light auburn hair had been bleached a honey blond and fell just below her shoulders. She was the only blonde working the shift, and that's the way she liked it. Blondes definitely got more attention.

The man who had triggered the buzzer was a short pear-shaped optometrist from the nearby community of Adamsville. He was dressed in a suit that cut him across the middle, giving the impression that his buttons could pop at any time. He shifted slightly from hip to hip and smiled broadly at the women.

Tina acted as the spokeswoman for the group. The other girls instinctively deferred to her age and leadership skills. "Welcome to the Sultan's Palace, where any man can have a harem. We're your models for this afternoon, sir. Feel free to take your time and select any girls you'd like for a private modeling session. Our fees are forty dollars for twenty minutes, sixty dollars for a half hour, and a hundred for an hour. You can purchase extra services along with the modeling if you like."

The optometrist grinned when Tina said that. He slowly walked down the line of women, cautiously looking them up and down. The women mechanically produced the requisite lascivious looks. On the whole, they were a lazy group, doing only what was necessary to make a hundred bucks a day. Not Tina. Although she'd delivered the required text as if she were speaking for the whole group, she promised the little optometrist with her eyes that he would be making a big mistake if he picked anyone but her. She was practically purring when she spoke. Whatever he wanted, she could provide better than anyone there. She didn't want him to even notice the other women. Her pride was at stake. She *had* to make at least four hundred a day. She was socking away half of everything she made in solid, safe stocks and bonds, plus she had over $40,000 in her savings account. Otherwise, what was the point of being in this nasty business?

"I'll take you." He pointed to Tina, and the other women turned off the sexy vibe in unison and trooped back to catch the end of Springer.

While they were still standing in the lobby, Tina put her hand on his shoulder and said, "Baby, you want a twenty minute, half hour or one hour session?"

"Half hour ought to do it."

Oh, I think that's more than enough time! Tina took his proffered sixty dollars and led him back to the Emperor's Room. Except for the domination rooms, which contained shackles and whips, the private rooms were exactly alike and, at this time, empty. Tina led her customer back to the Emperor's Room because it had not been used that day. She hated the smell when she walked into a room where some guy just got his nut off.

The session rooms, of course, had no windows so the only fresh air she got was when she sneaked out the back door for a quick stretch. The rooms were small, no more than eight by eight. They each contained a sturdy vinyl armchair with a washable cover and a clothes tree for both the clients' and the girls' clothing. The wall across from the chair was completely covered by a mirror.

"I'll be right back, baby. Make yourself comfortable. While I'm gone, check out the poster on the back of the door. It tells you what it costs for my extra special services."

Tina winked at the man as she walked out the door. She walked to a wall safe in a closed off area of the building and dropped the sixty dollars into the slot. The up-front fee was for modeling only and went to the house. For Tina to make any money, she had to sell the customer extra services. Fortunately, it was easy to do. What man wants to look but not touch? She wrote the start time on the sign-up sheet next to the door before re-entering the session room.

In her office, Lady M sized up the optometrist with a glance at the black and white TV screen. She always remained as hidden from customers as possible to give them the illusion that it was just them and the girls in the building, but she kept a loaded shotgun beside her desk and she knew how to use it. She watched Tina's customer fold his trousers and neatly hang them on the clothes tree. He then tucked his underwear up under the trousers.

Lady M. chuckled and talked to the flickering image on the small screen. "Damn, he's like me at the gynecologist's office. He'll get bare-assed naked in front of her, but don't want her to catch a glimpse of those funky drawers. Tina can handle this boy." She yawned and turned away from the screen.

When Tina returned to the room, the optometrist was sitting naked in the easy chair. She knew then he wasn't a cop. Cops never took their clothes off.

"Did you read about the other stuff I can do for you baby, besides just model?" She slowly and deliberately unbuttoned her jacket, slipped it off, and hung it next to his suit on the coat rack. Next, while keeping steady eye contact with him, she pulled the breakaway harem pants off in one easy motion, revealing a red teddy and thong panties. She sauntered back and forth in front of the mirror in her purple stiletto heels. She turned her back to him and, placing both hands shoulder height against the mirror, she leaned towards her reflection, arching her back and jutting her buttocks towards him. She swayed her hips rhythmically and looked back at him over her shoulder. But this time she didn't look directly into his eyes. She ignored him completely, as if she were lost in her own fantasy of what might happen next. She always teased the customers by withholding her attention from them until they committed themselves for more services.

Tina understood why men were turned on by her. Sometimes when she danced before the mirror, she felt like she was looking at a stranger. The body, built for sexual pleasure, the bedroom eyes, the long sensuous legs, the full lips; everything about her was lush. Her body could be theirs, to do with as they wished.

She never became aroused during the sessions. The customers couldn't tell the difference between pretense and the real thing, nor did they care, other than to delude themselves. For Tina, it was commerce, pure and simple, and she did what she needed to do in order to make it happen. Her sexual preference, both for her emotional and physical needs, was for women.

Slow sensual music played softly in the Emperor's Room. The Sultan's Palace was always filled with music. Tina didn't know the names of many of the songs, but they were the background against which her life played itself out. Mostly it was saxophone music, sweet, melancholy, and frankly sexual.

Tina jutted her butt out further toward the customer, until it was inches from his nose, and swayed her hips in a circular motion, a move she had perfected in the strip clubs. She reached for the gold and rhinestone barrette that held her thick hair in a French knot and with one motion, released her honey blond mane, slightly shaking her head as it fell. She turned toward the customer. She could see that he already had the beginning of an erection. She wanted to slow things down a bit. He hadn't agreed to anything but the modeling, and that money belonged to the house.

"My name is Talon. What's your name, honey?"

"You can just call me Doc. Everybody calls me that." Doc was sweating noticeably.

"Okay, Doc, what can I do for you today?"

"I don't know. What are my choices?"

It never failed. Not a single one of them ever read the choices on the back of the door while they were waiting for the girls to join them. By the time they got to the session rooms, the blood had already drained from the big head and was rushing to the little one.

"If you want me to take off my clothes, that's twenty-five dollars. If you want this to be a touch session, that's where I touch you and you can touch me, that'll cost you seventy-five more. Of course, if you really like what I do, you'd want to tip me real good. 'Cause there's touching, and then there's touching, if you know what I mean."

Doc nodded. "I know what you mean, sweet thing. How long does this touching last?"

"It can last as long as you want it to, honey, but for one hundred dollars, you get thirty minutes. We start the clock as soon as you've paid the fee."

While Tina was telling Doc about the touch fee, she was bent over so as to be face to face with him and was lightly stroking his knee.

"Hand me my pants, wild thing, and let me see what I can do today." Doc's excitement showed on his face.

Tina pulled his pants from the clothes tree and Doc's jockeys fell to the floor. Both of them just looked at the faded drawers and Tina stepped over them to hand Doc his trousers. He pulled out a worn leather wallet and forked over a hundred for the nudity and touching. Tina tucked the money into a pocket in her jacket, which was still hanging on the clothes tree, and carefully noted that there was more in Doc's wallet for a tip.

She removed the teddy and thong. No dance or strip; she just slipped out of them the way she would've if she had been by herself, except by herself, the damn stilettos would have come off first. She had learned over the years how to keep her balance, but it still wasn't easy to remove her panties while balancing like a bird on one stilt.

She walked around behind Doc and reaching over his shoulders, allowed her breasts to rest on both sides of his head, while she stroked his chest. They both watched the scene in the mirror. Doc reached up to rub one of Tina's breasts, but she quickly moved away before he could touch it. She'd been pinched and punched too many times in the past to let that happen. Instead, she walked around to the front of him, just out of his reach, and ground her hips to the music, all the while stroking her own breasts and moving her hands down her belly and into the outer fringes of her pubic hair.

By this time, Doc had begun to masturbate himself. Tina knew just how to play it. He would end up doing the work and keep the mess to himself. Her job was to tease him. She moved to just within reach beside him and gently placed his non-working hand on the outside of her thigh and purred, "Oh, baby, you're so big. I've never seen a man get as hard as you."

Doc stroked the side of her thigh and began to moan.

Tina saw it was time to up the ante before Doc got too carried away. "Oh, baby, you're making me so hot. I don't know how long I can take this. I want to come too, but that costs more. I mean . . . the house won't let us throw that in for free. Oh, God, I want to come so bad."

"Just take it out of my wallet." Doc said, gasping for air. "You can have what's left, baby."

Tina emptied the wallet. At a quick glance, it looked like another fifty.

"Okay, sexy, let's see you come." Doc again reached for her

thigh, only to find her just out of reach.

Tina rubbed her vagina lightly, pretending to arouse herself. She was the Ethel Barrymore of fake orgasms. She let him see the ecstasy on her face. She moaned. She cried. She twisted and shook and tossed her golden hair. All the while, she kept her eyes open to make sure Doc didn't make any moves she wasn't expecting.

He lasted only a couple of minutes longer. With a slight shiver and a low whimper, he came into the tissue Tina had handed him earlier. She had touched him only twice during the session. She knew what most of the sex trade workers knew—for men it was a visual thing. If you distract them enough visually, you don't have to do much.

Lady M, who happened to glance at the monitor in her office, checked the time clock at fifteen minutes. "The horn, the horn, the lusty horn. Is not a thing to laugh, to scorn." Then she added her own thoughts to Shakespeare's, "And a fool from his money is quickly shorn."

AFTER EACH SESSION, IT WAS THE MODEL'S job to return to the treatment womb and clean up. Tina's clean up procedure always followed the same plan. First, she donned rubber gloves. Then, she removed the cover from the chair and deposited it into a laundry hamper in the hall near the employee lounge. She returned to the room with a clean cover and carefully tucked it in around the chair's cushion. She disposed of any soiled tissues the customer had left behind and ran a dust mop over the floor. Her final chore was the one that gave her the only satisfaction she ever felt in her job, other than receiving money. She stood before the mirror, glass cleaner and paper towels in hand, and diligently wiped away any trace of her own fingerprints. She would stand back from the mirror and move around the room, inspecting the glass from different angles until she was absolutely sure no smudge remained behind.

Tina was the only model who ever remembered to wipe the prints off the mirror. Lady M had once complimented

Tina on her thoroughness and Tina had said, "If I wipe off my fingerprints, it's like I was never here."

What Tina hadn't told Lady M was that she despised fingerprints on mirrors or windows or television screens. The appearance of fingerprints anywhere left her lonely. She could never have begun to explain why.

TWENTY-ONE

True to his word, Cledith Waycross became a loyal and dedicated servant to the Patriots, and to the cause Colonel Hargrove had named Operation Samson, in honor of the Biblical hero who had lost his manhood because of a woman.

Cledith had organized his men into two commando units, comprised of four men in each unit. The men took eight-hour shifts in pairs and were able to provide complete twenty-four hour coverage. They were young, mostly unemployed, though a few of them had willingly given up their marginal jobs for Operation Samson. They stayed awake on coffee and cigarettes, some of them on speed, and they were having a ball. It was like when they were kids hidden away in plain sight from prying adult eyes, crawling on their bellies through imaginary swamps and jumping over ditches and pointing sticks and BB guns at each other. Only now, they could lay claim to being real soldiers. They were no longer the "slow" boys who got held back in school so often that they managed to grow mustaches and beards in sixth grade. They were no longer the butt of jokes 'cause their daddies were drunks, or their mamas would screw anybody, or because they got some dumb girl pregnant at thirteen. No. Now they were important. The mission was important. It was everything.

The men of the Operation Samson corps lived with Cledith and Lula, camped out in their rotting gray barn, which

Cledith had designated command central. Even though Col. Hargrove occasionally sent money, Cledith and Lula were struggling to feed everyone and hoped for a quick end to the surveillance part of the battle. They both couldn't wait to catch and destroy the Robiotic.

Cledith had nicknamed their prey Glory, for feminist leader Gloria Steinem, whom he believed to have started the destruction of family values in America. Most of the men serving under him were too young or uneducated to have heard of Steinem, but Cledith remembered how she had stirred the females up with her lies and hatred. Got 'em to burn their bras and take jobs away from men who needed them. She was the reason men just about couldn't stand to be around women anymore. The reason they were leaving their wives and children in droves, not through any failure of their own characters, but because women were no longer the simple, kind creatures God had originally intended. Steinem had warped her own kind.

Cledith called their patrols Glory rides, which consisted mainly of monitoring police scanners and tailing Marty. The men gave Cledith detailed reports on where Marty went, how he spent his days and nights, but it was Cledith himself who discovered Marty's mug shot in the morning paper.

"Lookee here, Lula, guess who's making hisself up to be the next victim! Whoowee, we got us a date at the Rainbow's End."

Lula looked at Marty's photograph and smirked. "Well, look at ole high and mighty now."

Cledith put his arm around Lula's waist and hugged her to him. "Marty and his folks has always made theirselves out to be better than us. Maybe ole Marty'll get hisself caught in the crossfire when we shoot that Robiotic. Serve 'em right for all their airs."

Cledith pecked Lula on the cheek and hurried out to command central. Using their prearranged code, Cledith contacted his two lieutenants on their walkie-talkies for an emergency meeting. They would pass along his message to the rest of the corps. "Glory be, looks like our old dog Samson is growing back his hair, boys. Come on home."

Later that afternoon, Cledith paced in front of the men in his best Col. Hargrove imitation. "I'm proud of you, men. You done a fine job."

He broke down cackling, slapping his thigh. "Shore didn't think the Atlanta police would just announce the next location. They're dumber than I thought. Looks like Marty's gonna be hanging out at the bar ever Friday and Saturday night, so we got to be ready to nail Glory when she shows up. We might just have a minute or two, boys, before they get her in custody and under their protection, so here's the plan."

Cledith loved the look of anticipation on the men's faces, the crackle in the room. He held his pause overly long just to build up the tension. God, he loved that tension! It felt almost as good as those few seconds just before coming, when he would be riding Lula for all he was worth. There wudn't nothing in the world that felt as good as that gnawing feeling he would get just before coming. This came close.

"We gone have a different man stationed in that bar ever night that Marty's there. When Glory sits down with him, and we're real sure it's her, we'll blow up a small pipe bomb in the men's room. That'll distract the cops in the room and while they're distracted, we'll shoot her.

"Now, men, we don't want no collateral damage. We gone do everthing in our power to prevent that, but if it happens, just remember we're at war. Ever now and then, innocent people gets killed. Sometimes, it just can't be helped."

TWENTY-TWO

**Long-Lasting Effects of Childhood Sexual Abuse,
1997: A Case Study of Seven Female Survivors
Delia Whitfield, Ph.D. Clinical Psychology
Client ID #616-04
Primary Diagnosis: Dissociative Identity Disorder
(DID)
Chief Complaints: Insomnia, Lost Time, Inability to
Bond, Depression**

Dr. Delia Whitfield shuffled through the papers on her desk. Each time she tried to concentrate on Catherine O'Donnell's case file, the words would dance up from the pages and float slightly above the white background. She blinked them back into neat rows, but they didn't stay there for long. They made no sense to her anyway.

Damn, she thought, guess I'll have to start wearing bifocals like some little old lady soon. She took inordinate pride in her youthful appearance and dreaded the day she would have to take on the accouterments of old age. But, it wasn't really her eyes that were bothering her. Yesterday's visit from Detective Simone Rosenberg had left her shaky. Why would the Atlanta police be interested in Catherine?

She squirmed in her seat, trying to find a position that felt comfortable. For the third time in fifteen minutes, she looked at her watch and then at the grandfather clock standing across the room directly opposite her desk. Its ponderous pendulum swung hypnotically, with slow precision, as if it still existed in a different age and would not condescend to be brought into the chaotic present. Delia sometimes wanted to kick it over and, at other times, felt like anchoring herself against it.

It was eleven o'clock and Catherine had still not shown up for her nine-thirty appointment. Had she been arrested? Or worse, had she committed suicide? Because Catherine had attempted suicide twice in the past before coming under Delia's care, Delia had made her promise that she would call if she began to have obsessive suicidal thoughts. Delia would then have her admitted to a psych hospital for in-patient care. Delia had insisted they put their agreement in writing, signed by both of them. That agreement, as ultimately unenforceable as it was, helped Delia cope with the vast amount of time she was unable to monitor Catherine's behavior. Delia hoped the contract would instill in Catherine the understanding that suicide was not something beyond her control, but rather a deliberate act that she, alone, had the power to prevent.

Catherine had already skipped a couple of group therapy sessions and was talking about ending her private therapy. She insisted it was simply a matter of not having enough money, but when Delia offered to treat her for practically nothing, Catherine refused. She could never accept charity. The fragmented part of herself that she called Patsy Gail would have a fit. It reminded her too much of her upbringing and the pious, pitying looks she had seen on the faces of do-gooders in her daddy's church.

A childhood of beatings and sexual assaults, constant criticism, and sadistic mind games in the name of Jesus, had destroyed all but occasional glimpses of Catherine's naturally joyous spirit. In its place were self-doubt and rage. Although Delia knew there were entire chapters of Catherine's life that might never be revealed, they were making progress. Delia would lose her forever if she left now, and Catherine could very well take her own life. In fact, she might be dead already.

In order to instill more personal accountability for their treatment, Delia's policy was to insist that clients initiate the call for missed appointments. However, she could wait no longer. She dialed Catherine's number and was surprised to hear a sleepy voice say, "Hello."

"Catherine, you missed our appointment. Are you sick?"

"Oh, Delia, I got in really late last night. I just couldn't make myself get out of bed this morning. I'm sorry. I...I...I should have called you." Catherine stuttered during times of extreme stress.

Delia didn't quite know how to handle the situation. She would give any other client a mild and motherly lecture about the importance of commitment to one's own progress, about not wasting time that could be used by someone else, but Catherine's stutter was a dead giveaway that she was near the edge. Delia didn't want to scare her. She was too fragile now.

"Listen, why don't you come over to my house this evening. John is in some godforsaken place playing in the dirt for a couple of months. We can just relax a little. I'll make you dinner."

It was a dangerous idea and Delia knew it. She had never invited a patient to her home before. All those ethical warnings that were pounded into her head in school about getting overly attached to patients, or fraternizing, were churning in her mind. Still, she persisted.

"Come on, Catherine. Sometimes you need to just back off a little from therapy. We can talk about anything you want, or not talk at all. In case you haven't heard, I'm a great cook. I've heard actors rarely get home cooked meals."

Catherine chuckled politely. "You got that right." She paused for a long moment and then said, "Okay, Delia."

They agreed on seven o'clock and Delia gave Catherine directions to her house. After they hung up, Delia spent the remainder of the hour waiting for her next client and berating herself for such a reckless gesture. She knew she was asking for trouble, maybe even dangerously compromising Catherine's healing, or setting herself up for a lawsuit. Especially if the police were investigating Catherine.

What could they imagine Catherine had done? Delia had tried to reassure the detective that Catherine was harmless, but was she? Was anyone?

Delia's self-preservation instinct was battling with her therapist's instinct. In the end, her therapist self won out. It might not be proper protocol, but she would do what her heart told her in order to help Catherine.

DELIA HAD JUST POURED HER SECOND GLASS of wine when Catherine arrived at twenty minutes past seven. When Delia opened the door, she was shocked to see Catherine's hair disheveled and her clothes badly wrinkled. She was wearing no make-up.

Catherine thrust a bag of cookies towards Delia. "Sorry, I'm late. I thought we might like these for dessert. They may be a little old—I don't know."

Delia took the cookies and casually guided Catherine into the room. "Thanks. I love cookies. No problem with the time. I'm just making spaghetti. The sauce tastes better the longer it waits anyway. We just need to boil the noodles. Why don't we sit in the living room and have a glass of wine. You like white, don't you?"

After they were comfortable and sipping wine, each woman searched for a spot on the wall, or out the window, or in the flickering fire, upon which to focus her attention. The silence was murky, clouded with intimations of disaster.

"Catherine," Delia asked gently, "are you all right?"

"Sure, I'm fine, if only . . ." Catherine's voice was soft and childlike.

"What, sweetie?"

"I...I...I never sleep. Uncle Ted comes to me in dreams every night now. He's telling me things he never used to say. I mean, he's always been cruel, but . . ."

Her voice trailed off. She looked exhausted and terrified. Delia had never seen her so afraid. Catherine's way of coping with the childhood abuse had always been to be tough. She needed to appear brave whether she actually felt brave or not.

"What has he been telling you?"

"You remember how I told you a long time ago he used to quote Bible passages to me while he was raping me?" Catherine reached for a small pillow on the sofa and bunched it up into a knot.

She didn't wait for Delia's answer. This had been a major area of discussion in their therapy. Catherine could not shake the guilt she associated with the rapes. The idea of her sinfulness, reinforced by Biblical passages evidencing woman's inherent sinfulness, was so strongly tied to the act of rape that she had not been able to forgive herself for the role she thought she played in seducing her uncle.

"He comes into my bedroom while I'm sleeping, just like when I was little. He hovers over me, quoting those damn Bible passages, and nothing I do will shut him up. Last night, he told me that God directed him to kill my mother because she was a whore.

"When I was about four, I came home from visiting my aunt. Mama was gone. Disappeared without a goodbye to me, no note, nothing. Nothing! Nobody told me anything at first, but one day Daddy said she ran off 'cause she was a Jezebel, drunk on lust for other men. I was never to mention her name again. I craved to know what happened to her for most of my life. Uncle Ted told me last night. He killed her!"

"But, Catherine, these are dreams. Terrible dreams. It's not really your Uncle Ted talking to you." Delia handed Catherine a box of tissues.

"You remember I told you the rapes stopped when I was sixteen, but I wasn't able to tell you why?"

Delia nodded.

"When I was sixteen, Uncle Ted was up on the church roof making repairs and he fell off and died. Last night, when he came to me in my dream, he told me Mama's ghost was up on that roof with him. Her ghost came and, with the icy breath of the eternally damned, blew death over him like a tidal wave until he splattered on the concrete below. His soul went straight to hell, but not even Satan wanted him. He's stuck somewhere in between and it's my fault. He will never leave me alone as long as I live. He said I have to go back to church and beg God to forgive me and forgive Mama so he can enter the Kingdom of Heaven. Delia, I can't even walk into a church without feeling like I'm going to throw up."

Catherine's last words thrust from her in great choking spasms of grief. Delia fought the urge to hold her and rock her. It would have been too intrusive and may have stopped Catherine from talking. But what Catherine had needed for most of her life was a mother. Holding and rocking her is exactly what a good mother would have done.

"Catherine," Delia said softly. "Look at me."

Catherine's loud sobs gradually diminished until she was crying silently, and she looked into Delia's eyes.

"You never have to go to church again unless you want to. Never. You've done nothing wrong. Your mother's absence or death had nothing to do with you. You were a child, Catherine. Children are innocent. Like most southerners my age, I grew up in the church too and I can quote you many passages that attest to the innocence of children. Your father and Uncle Ted used their religion like a bludgeon and they perverted the teachings of the Bible. God is sometimes vengeful, but never to children. God loves children."

Delia's parents had sent her to Sunday school and vacation Bible school, through they didn't always go themselves. She knew the Bible almost as well as Catherine.

Catherine lowered her head. After a moment, she looked up at Delia. She had an odd look in her eyes that Delia recognized immediately. One of Catherine's cousins had decided to speak for her.

"That's a shit load you're telling her!" A stranger's voice that sounded somewhat like the preacher, but not exactly, came out of Catherine.

"Who are you?" Delia asked.

"Ted," the voice answered.

This threw Delia for a moment. She had never heard Catherine speak with the voice of her Uncle Ted. "Do you know who I am?"

"Course I do. Ain't I been sitting on my ass listening to your boring voice a thousand times? You're the head shrinker who's trying to convince dear little Catherine Patsy w I'm dead and buried. But, I ain't dead, am I? ain't dead by a long shot.

"Catherine's the one that pushed me off that roof, you know. Sneaked up behind me and just shoved as hard as she could. I liked to pulled her off with me, but I couldn't quite reach her. The last thing I seen before I went off the edge was her icy face staring down at me. She's been trying to blame it on her mama. Wadn't no ghost of her mama or nuthin like at. She's got hellfire coming to her, sure, if she don't make it right."

"Does she know you're here now?" Delia asked.

The entity called Ted walked over and warmed himself in front of the fire. He scratched his crotch. "Naw, the little ice princess turns deaf every time I start talking. The only time she can hear me is in her dreams. Ain't that a bitch?! Right now, she's off hiding under the bed, like always.

"How can she make it right?" Delia asked.

Ted turned and spat into the fire. "She knows what she needs to do. You tell her for me, Dr. Whitfield, that she's running out of time. If she don't confess to my murder, I'll make her sorry."

This last statement alarmed Delia. "She thinks you want her to return to church. Is that where you want her to confess?"

Ted guffawed. When he got himself under control, he said, "I don't give a flying fuck if she goes to church. Tell her she's got to contact the sheriff up in High Point and make a full confession to him. I won't settle for nuthin' less, you understand? Otherwise, she'll be double sorry she ever laid eyes on me."

"I think she already is, Ted." Delia forced civility into her voice. What could she do? Ted was living inside of Catherine. She wanted to smack him, or shoot him, but she couldn't hurt him without hurting Catherine.

At that moment Catherine shivered and lowered her head again. When she looked up, her core personality had returned. She took up the conversation with Delia exactly where they had left off, as if no time had passed.

"You know something, Delia? In my heart, I know I was

innocent. All children are. That's exactly what I would tell someone if she was sitting in my living room, melting in a puddle on my sofa." Catherine smiled, slightly, but her face was ashen. "If he would just leave me alone, I think I could get over it. He comes into my bedroom now more than he did when he was alive."

Delia was deeply conflicted. Should she inform Catherine about the new voice that had come out tonight? Ted was Catherine's tormentor and the fact that he was living inside of her was a terrible setback. Delia knew better than to try to convince Catherine he was a part of her psyche that could be integrated. Uncle Ted's ghost was haunting her and for some reason, for the time being, Catherine needed to believe that. Shattered women find many creative ways to keep their lives functioning. It was Delia's job to open their wounds gently and gradually, allowing only the parts that were ready to be exposed to the healing light.

"What do you think it will take to make him leave you alone?" Delia asked.

"Oh, God, I can't go there now, Delia. I can't do it! Please."

Catherine stood up and looked toward the front door, as if she might bolt at any moment. "You know, I'm so tired, I think I could sleep without dreams tonight. Maybe he won't wake me up"

"No problem. Let's just have some dinner and relax." Delia moved and stood between Catherine and the front door.

"I think I'll head on home," Catherine said.

Delia continued to block Catherine's exit. "Why don't you spend the night with me? I've got a spare bedroom, and I promise to let you sleep as long as you want."

"I want to. It's so quiet tonight." Catherine whispered, apparently exhausted. "Feels pretty safe. Maybe he can't find me with my therapist, right? I mean, he never shows up when you're around, right? But no therapy, okay? I can't wake up in the morning and talk about it. I've been so nervous lately, like there's a tornado whirling around me, but the sky is clear and everything looks normal. But, I can feel it coming, Delia. I can feel it on my skin, crawling. I can feel it coming." Catherine's voice dwindled to nothing.

She ate a bite or two of her dinner and afterwards, Delia laid out a toothbrush, a towel and a pair of soft pajamas for her. After Catherine had changed her clothes and was under the covers, Delia gently kissed her forehead and tucked the covers up under her chin. "I'll be just outside the door if you need me."

"I can't remember anyone ever tucking me into bed," Catherine said, as she was drifting off to sleep.

"Come here anytime you want to, honey." Delia patted Catherine's shoulder. "Sometimes all any of us needs is a little mothering."

Delia didn't sleep that night. She sat staring into the fire, occasionally getting up to throw another log on or to poke the embers into a dancing flame. She checked on Catherine throughout the night and each time, found her lying in the same position in which she had fallen asleep.

Near morning, Delia filled her deep bathtub with warm scented water and wearily lowered herself into it. She had stopped allowing herself this pleasure weeks ago. Too often lately she had begun to feel like an engine pulling a long train of obscene and overwhelmingly sad memories. Everywhere she went, the fractured lives of women she loved felt like dead weight pulling against her, threatening to derail her own life. When she slowed down, she heard the screams of children. She could see their battered bodies.

Delia's mind was racing when she first stepped into the tub, but as her body relaxed, her mind slowed until she fell asleep with her head resting against a plastic pillow that was suctioned against the tub wall. She slept for two hours. When she awoke, the water was freezing and the sun was coming up. Exhausted, there was nothing for her to do but turn on a hot shower and get ready for work. When she checked the guest bedroom, Catherine had already left.

TWENTY-THREE

Marty Sloan had been staring at the same legal pad for the past two hours. Occasionally, he crossed through a letter or moved a word from one column to the next. He had already filled several sheets that now lay wadded at his feet. He had created a list of possible combinations and, circling the last one, he slapped his forehead. "Damn!" He kicked off against the cubicle wall and rolled his chair out into the hallway. It was late Thursday, close to seven p.m. He yelled across the aisle to Simone.

"Rosenberg, you got a minute?"

"Bout that long, Partner. I'm trying to get out of town. Going up to the mountains tomorrow morning."

"Well, stop here on your way out the door and check this out."

Simone tucked the last file into her desk drawer, grabbed her purse and ambled over. "What's up?"

She peered intently over Marty's shoulder, while he excitedly tapped his pencil on a circle at the bottom of a smudged sheet filled with nonsensical words.

Marty, who had loved word games from the time he was a kid, had been noodling around with all the possible ways he could rearrange the letters.

"It's an anagram! Magenta Rave is an anagram for *Avenge Tamar*. Look. Exact same letters."

Marty tilted back in his chair and looked rapturously up at

Simone. "Tamar was the woman in the Bible who was raped and ruined by her half brother in that passage Snippy's been leaving behind at every crime scene. She was a daughter of King David, and by the time that particular little story is concluded, her good brother kills the bad one over the rape. Then, the good brother bites it in the end. The Bible's got more gore than a Stephen King movie."

"So Magenta Rave is trying to avenge the rape of some woman in the Bible? Doesn't make sense. Why would she do this?"

Marty was beaming over his discovery. "Hell's bells, ain't that something! I figured it out. Damn, I'm good! I'm thinking, it's symbolic. She ain't just trying to avenge Tamar. She's trying to avenge every last woman or kid that's ever been raped."

"Starting with her own rape, you think?"

Simone gave Marty a little pat on the back.

"Good work, country boy. See you Monday."

TWENTY-FOUR

The rear compartment of Detective Simone Rosenberg's black Ford Explorer was jammed to the roof with sleeping bags, pillows, a tent, camp stove and lanterns. Two backpacks were stuffed with clothing, including long johns and down vests. A large cooler contained steaks, chicken legs and thighs for her lethal jerk chicken, fresh fruits, vegetables for grilling, chips, cookies, chocolate, a couple of bottles of red wine, and a bottle of Courvoisier.

The weather was perfect. Seventy-two degrees and sunny. Simone and Tina had spent hours over the past week packing and planning their three-day weekend adventure and were now headed up Interstate 575 North toward the small mountain town of High Point, Georgia. With her daughter Minerva safely ensconced with Marty's family out in the country, Simone was happier than she could remember being in a long time.

The trip wasn't going to be all pleasure, though. She intended to snoop around High Point, the hometown of Catherine O'Donnell, to see if she could pull together any more clues that would point her either towards or away from O'Donnell. It had been surprisingly easy to get an appointment on Saturday with O'Donnell's aunt. The woman seemed unusually eager to speak with her. The more compelling reason for the trip, however, was personal. She couldn't wait to spend three days alone in a tent with Tina.

Both of the women were in high spirits.

They had reserved an isolated campsite in the woods within hearing distance of Amicalola Falls and the two women intended to indulge their enormous appetites for food, physical activity, and most of all, for each other.

"I ever tell you about the time I was in prison up in the mountains?" Tina teased.

"What did you do, kill somebody?" Simone checked her speed and set the cruise control to a comfortable seventy miles per hour.

Tina leaned her head against the closed passenger window and watched the undulating landscape fall away. She breathed a circle of fog onto the glass, and then quickly wiped it clean with her sleeve. "Nah. I had the audacity to go and get myself born. Got sent up here to a reform school after Granny died. They didn't call it reform school. They were much too *sensitive* for that, seeing how they were charged with the spiritual guidance of us poor fallen girls. The place was called Balm in Gilead. The buildings are still there, sitting empty, just outside the city limits. Balm in Gilead. That's a quote from the Bible. From the book of Jeremiah. Means to give comfort, something like that. It really was just a place to get us nasty girls out of sight and fuck with our heads."

Simone reached over and squeezed Tina's thigh. "They weren't too comforting, I take it."

Tina rolled her eyes. "They spent most of the time telling us how sinful we were. I did get a couple of good things out of it, though. Every Saturday, they'd haul us over to the falls and force us to take a nature hike on the trails. We'd drag our asses up Springer Mountain for five or six miles and then march back down again. It's real steep. You'll see. Springer Mountain is at the start of the Appalachian Trail. Did you know you can hike all the way to Maine on the Appalachian Trail? Amazing, huh?

"Most of the girls hated hiking and tried different ways to get out of it—you know—faking cramps and headaches, making themselves throw up. I loved it! I used to imagine hiking back to Jersey, except there wasn't nothing for me to go back to. No family, I mean.

"Oh, Simone, you won't believe how beautiful it is on the trail!" Tina turned to face Simone. "You can see for miles near the top. I thought we could go on a couple of long hikes while we're here."

"Maybe, ooman, but don't be wearin' me out in de sleepin' bag first. Me won't be gone nowhere wit chew."

Tina smiled and lightly stroked the back of Simone's neck. "I'm not too worried about your stamina."

Simone reached across the console and gently stroked Tina's breast.

"You are way too distracting." Tina playfully pushed Simone's hand away. "As I was saying, I used to look forward to those hikes so much. The hike leader was this in-the-closet old dragon who knew every kind of wild plant in the area. She knew about all the Indian legends connected to rock formations and the falls. Amicalola means 'tumbling waters' in Cherokee. Betcha didn't know that, Miss Part Cherokee, did you?"

Simone smiled. "I did not, in fact."

"So, anyway, old dragon breath would point out the names of the mountains in the distance, talk about cloud formations and annual rainfall, that sort of thing. But, a lot of the time, we just walked in silence. It's the closest I've ever come to meditation. The walking shut my mind down and I could relax and get exercise at the same time. I was so angry when my granny died. We had just found each other. Remember, I told you about her."

Simone nodded.

"Those hikes helped me keep my sanity more than anything."

"Oh, you still got your sanity?" Simone teased.

Tina pushed Simone's shoulder. "Hush."

"You said you learned two things there. What was the other one?" Simone asked.

Tina hesitated. "You can't laugh."

"I promise."

"I know this is going to sound crazy. But you already know I'm a little bonkers, don't you?"

Again, Simone stroked Tina's thigh. She was having a hard time keeping her mind on the road. "Only in the best way, likkle biscuit."

"This thing happened to me one day when I was out on the trail. One beautiful spring day—you know, one of those Georgia days when the light is strange, like at the start of a solar eclipse, and there's no breeze and no noticeable temperature. I was hiking with the group. Everyone was quiet that day and my attention was focused inside of myself. Not really seeing nothing or thinking nothing in particular. My mind became so still I could hear my heartbeats and the gushing sound of my breath, maybe what it must be like in the womb. Those sounds just took over until everything else disappeared. I was seeing the world, but not really in it—like I was just a pair of eyes floating through space. Then the heartbeats and breath sounds went away. Like that." Tina snapped her fingers. "Just vanished, and I was left in a kind of vacuum, a part of everything and yet separate. An observer.

"I walked on in that state for quite a while. It was peaceful and I wanted to hold on to it. At some point, I became aware of a humming noise. I focused my attention on that and the hum turned into a chant. Like the Gregorian monks. Have you ever heard any recordings of them?"

Simone shook her head, no.

"I hadn't either, back then, but later on when some airy-fairy guy I knew played them for me, I recognized the sounds. I had heard something like them all those years before inside my own head. It was a language I didn't recognize, but so comforting, so serene. After awhile, the chant died down to a whisper and gradually changed into a distinct voice. I know this is sounding weird, Simone."

"You can't say anything that would make me think one bad thought about you." Tenderly, Simone brushed a strand of hair away from Tina's forehead. "Remember how we say it in Jamaica 'I and I are one.' I already told you."

"Oh, keep talking Jamaican to me, my beautiful island girl. We might have to pull over. Okay, the voice was not my own. It was rich and otherworldly and powerful. Oh hell, I might as well just say it; you're going to think I'm crazy anyway. I'm absolutely convinced God was speaking to me, Simone. Now, more than ever."

Jesum Piece, Simone thought, this woman is full of surprises! "What did the voice say?"

"On that first walk, the voice kept saying *you are safe, you are safe*, over and over. Like a drum beat timed to my steps on the trail. On later walks, it told me specific courses of action to take. Like it told me to move to Atlanta and it advises me from time to time whether I should make certain decisions."

"You said you were convinced now more than ever that it was God speaking to you. Why?" Simone asked.

"Oh, I don't know. I . . . it's just that my life is finally working out. I've got you. That never would have happened if I hadn't listened to the voice and made the choices I made.

"Don't get me wrong. I don't think I AM God or anything like that. Anybody could do the same thing, you know, just listen to their inner voice. It is possible to know what God wants of us."

Simone saw that Tina's hands were shaking. She reached to reassure her, but Tina pulled her arm away. "It was a Christian reform school, okay? So, they talked a lot about Bible stuff. Back when the Bible was first written, it was nothing for God to speak to people. It happened all the time, you know? So, I was out hiking one day with the group and I heard this voice in me. At first, I thought I was losing it, but the voice was comforting. So I had this realization that here . . ."—she tapped her chest lightly—"was the real Balm in Gilead. Inside us, we got this wise voice that can help us through everything, if we ask."

"How does it work?"

Tina hesitated. "Do you think I'm crazy? I mean, people who hear voices are nuts, aren't they? But, my therapist, Delia, she said that a lot of people hear God. You know, like, they have a close relationship with Him. Nothing wrong with that, right"

Simone tried to keep her face impassive. She was a bit worried, but didn't want Tina to see it. Formal religion was pretty much superstitious hoo-ha as far as Simone was concerned. Still, it seemed to help some people.

Tina spoke again, but this time as if she were talking mostly to herself. "Maybe it's not exactly a voice. More like a strong feeling when I'm trying to make a decision. You know what I mean? Like I said, when I left Balm in Gilead, I couldn't decide if I should go back up to Jersey or down to Atlanta. If I hadn't gone to Atlanta, I wouldn't have met you. It just helps me with little choices that don't mean much to anybody else, but are important to me. Just little things, my love. Nothing much."

Simone's police training led her to believe that Tina wasn't telling her everything, but she dismissed the idea. "My father's people were religious. Always praying and carrying on with some ritual or other. Jamaica's this wild place with every kind of religion you can imagine, baby. Rasta, Catholic, Obeah, called voodoo here, Jehovah's Witness, Baptist, everything on such a small island. My grandmother was originally from Kenya, but moved to England where my father grew up, then later to Jamaica. She practiced a mix of Catholicism and Obeah.

"My mother's family was Irish and Cherokee, so you can imagine, they had a hodgepodge of beliefs too. Both sides of the family believed in the power of the natural world, that there were spirits working for and against us. Both sides loved ritual, too, baby. Couldn't wait to find an excuse to party. Weddings. Christenings. Confirmations. Solstice. Planting ceremonies. Funerals were a big cause for celebration. Homegoing celebrations they called them."

Simone smiled as she thought of her rich and colorful family. "I loved the rituals and celebrations. The music in our house was incredible. I especially loved Bob Marley and what little I know of the Rastafarian philosophy. I even had dreadlocks for a short while in college."

Simone laughed when she saw Tina's raised eyebrow. "Way ahead of my time. Now all the Trustafarians have them."

"Trustafarians?"

"Yeah. White kids with trust funds. But, no religion has

ever worked for me, my angel. I see so many things that break my heart every day and I can't figure how a wise or loving God would let them go on. I want to believe, I do. I just can't."

Tina appeared agitated. "It's not about religion, Simone. It's about God. About a pure connection. Being connected to Him so you know what's right for you. You know, a purpose for being here."

"Seems to me like you need to do your own thinking instead of looking for something outside to give you the answers." Simone managed to keep her voice level and calm. She didn't want the trip to get off to a bad start.

"But that's just it. The voice is inside me."

"Yeah, but it might not be God's voice you're hearing, biscuit. Might be some psychological phenomenon, maybe something that came from all that childhood abuse you told me about. My mama would say it could be a trickster spirit, like the rabbit in Cherokee mythology. Rabbit looks like he's trying to help you, give you good advice, but all the while he's lying and setting you up for a fall.

"I haven't mentioned this before, but you know this woman that's been going around cutting men, baby? She thinks she's following God's orders too."

"Maybe she is." Tina folded her arms against her chest and turned abruptly away from Simone.

"How can you say that? She's breaking the law."

Tina exhaled loudly, turned back toward Simone, and explained as if speaking to a child. "You're so healthy, Simone. It's what makes you easy to love. But, you didn't get the crap kicked out of you when you were little. You had people who loved you and took care of you, made sure you were fed and got a good education. Maybe the rest of the world was harder on you because of your mixed race. I wouldn't know about that. You're so damn beautiful, I can't imagine anyone ever being cruel to you for that."

Simone didn't appreciate the patronizing tone one bit. "Don't be so sure. I heard all the names when I was growing up. Nigger, Zebra, Oreo. I was too light for black kids and too dark for white kids. I felt like a freak for most of my childhood."

"Your father was a diplomat, for God's sake!" Tina smacked the dashboard. "You grew up in protected, privileged little communities all over the world, went to private schools. Besides, when you have a huge extended family that tells you how special you are, it don't matter what the world says. You get strong enough to handle it."

Simone softened her tone. Compared to Tina, her life had been a cakewalk. "You're right about that. My mother used to say, 'Worst kind of trouble starts in your own mind. Doesn't matter what anybody else says about you, long as you think good things about yourself.' She taught me to see myself as a strong, unique person. Not a freak.

"But it wears on me, my love. Racism is everywhere. An old institution. Every time a white person looks at me, I know they're sizing me up, and maybe they're thinking I'm lazy, or dangerous, or loose, instead of assuming the best about me, and I've got to prove myself over and over just to get the benefit of the doubt. I get sick of it."

Tina balled one fist and looked around, as if wanting to strike something. "It's not fair and you deserve better, my sweet girl. Just the thought of anyone hurting you makes me want to gouge their eyes out! I can understand being looked down on—I sure as hell can—but I know I get a break cause I'm white."

"And beautiful," Simone said.

Tina paused, as if weighing how Simone would respond. "But, even knowing that, I'd trade my childhood for yours any day of the week, and I wouldn't give a flying fuck what any sorry-assed white person thought."

Simone was silent for a moment. The passion in Tina's voice had moved her. She had never known a love such as this before. "I'm sorry you had such a hard time of things. I wish you could have known my mother. She would've loved you so much. Just like I do. You've got to believe in yourself, Tina."

"I'm trying to learn how to do that. Delia says I'm making progress. But, it's not that easy. Delia says when we've been abused, our own mind takes up where the abuser left off. You know, we supply the awful feedback to ourselves." Tina paused a moment, then imitated an idiotic grin. "I try to think happy thoughts."

Simone slowed the Ford Explorer into the exit lane that would put them onto the back roads leading into the park. "I think you're perfect, sweet biscuit."

At the end of the exit ramp, while they were temporarily stopped, Tina unbuckled her seat belt and stretched across to kiss Simone on the cheek.

"How did I get so lucky to find you?"

Simone turned left onto State 5 to begin the winding trip towards the National Forest. "I'm lucky, too."

Tina rebuckled her seat belt and reclined in the seat. "I bet whoever this knife-happy woman is had an awful childhood, don't you? Takes a lot to make a woman do what she's done. Besides, tell the truth, don't those guys deserve it? Aren't you secretly glad? Sure, you gotta try and catch her. Do you have to try so hard? Would it be so bad if she got away with it? From a prevention standpoint, I mean."

Simone slowed down to keep the top-heavy Explorer from swaying too much on the curvy road. "You know what Gandhi said about 'an eye for an eye and a tooth for a tooth,' don't you? Pretty soon, the whole world is toothless and blind. Besides, these molesters and rapists, a lot of them grew up in abusive families. It's a pattern, like the family china, that gets handed down from generation to generation."

"Don't tell me you are making excuses for them!" Tina snapped. "They're fucking monsters!"

"No, baby, not excuses, but if we see them as human beings, maybe we can find a way to change their behavior, not just punish them. Isn't that what we want? " Simone realized she had failed some loyalty test in Tina's eyes.

They rode the rest of the way in silence, with Simone occasionally stroking Tina's hair and asking her to check the map. The quiet settled upon them while they set up their tent and hung their food in a container on a rope between two trees to protect it from raccoons and black bears. When the campsite was organized and perfect, in the way only two obsessive neat freaks could make it, they took a short, brisk walk through the woods and sat next to each other on a platform near the top of the falls.

"You know what my partner calls the cutter?" Simone said, finally breaking the long silence. "You swear to keep it secret?"

Tina nodded.

"Snippy."

While they were laughing, Simone took Tina's hand and scooted over in order to sit as close as possible. "I don't really care whether or not Snippy gets caught. My caseload goes down every time one of these creeps gets taken out of action. As far as I'm concerned, what she's doing is just one more crazy thing in this world. But, I can't ignore it. I have to go after her with every thing I got, 'cause sooner or later, she's going to make a mistake and cut some innocent guy."

Tina sniffed audibly. "Are there innocent guys? I never met one."

"Sure, baby. My partner's great, a good father, good husband. Loyal as a puppy to the people he loves. My father was a little too strict for my taste, but he was never cruel. He was an honorable, decent man. And, what about the guy you work for? He writes books for children. You don't talk much about him, but I never hear you say anything bad."

"Let's head back to camp. I'm getting hungry," Tina said.

How could she tell Simone the truth about her job? What words would she use to justify getting men to masturbate in front of her? Simone would despise her. Deservedly, she thought.

Later that evening, the temperature dropped down into the forties. After a delicious meal of jerk chicken and pasta with grilled veggies, Tina and Simone moved into the warm tent and were fortifying themselves with Courvoisier and chocolate-dipped strawberries.

"Ooman, you de most beautiful likkle biscuit in de world." Simone delicately fed Tina a large chocolate covered strawberry. A tiny smudge of chocolate stuck to the corner of Tina's mouth. Simone licked the stubborn stain, digging in with her tongue until Tina felt desire travel within her like slow motion electricity, a strobe light that danced and tickled and pricked through her, infusing her with a mixture of pleasure and raw energy.

For as long as she could remember, Tina's body had been a product for market, a thing separate from herself. Only now was she beginning to experience the emotions that inspire poetry and music. Under the low tent canopy, Tina knelt. She unzipped her down jacket and removed her clothing one article at a time, slowly and deliberately, never taking her eyes away from Simone's eyes. This was no practiced strip tease, designed to relieve a stranger's tension. She was removing her shell and exposing the thin layers of pink skin that sheltered her beating heart. When she was completely nude, she sat back on her heels and shivered slightly.

Simone quickly removed her own clothes, and the two of them sat across from each other. Tina lightly stroked Simone's arms and legs with her fingernails and watched her lover's nipples contract into tiny pinpricks of excitement. It soon became unbearably cold, but both women were enjoying the visual feast and did not want to rush anything. They began to shiver so noticeably that they couldn't help but laugh. Soon they were laughing hysterically and scrambled into the sleeping bags they had earlier zipped together.

They held each other until the laughter and the chills subsided. Then, they made love quietly, like wood nymphs huddled beneath the canopy of an enormous mushroom, careful not to disturb the great horned owls who would be hunting for food for their newly hatched chicks, nor the sleeping foxes in their dens. Their lovemaking was equal and shared. Two souls, connected, they banished the dark forces until no thought alien to pleasure could enter. The steady escalation of their shared breath was carried on the wind like a whispered prayer of gratitude.

When they had satiated themselves, they folded into each other and slept. They were changed now, somehow, in this wild place. They had become wolves perhaps, pack sisters, and they slept deeply until the scurrying of ground squirrels and the morning songs of Brown Thrashers woke them.

TWENTY-FIVE

On the third and final day of their long weekend, Simone reluctantly left Tina behind to break camp while she kept an appointment with Catherine O'Donnell's aunt, a woman named Maebelle Hansford.

After a short trip over winding two-lane mountain roads, Simone drove a couple of miles past the quaint courthouse of High Point, Georgia, and turned onto a road that was more potholes than pavement. Another couple of bone-jarring blocks, and she spotted the address on a mailbox. She parked at the curb of a pockmarked yard that was strewn with papers and abandoned toys. A feral cat, missing clumps of fur and half its tail, darted past her on the cracked walkway that led to the front door of a sagging shotgun shack a few yards back from the road. She tapped lightly on the door. It was opened by a woman who Simone could tell had once been pretty, like her niece, but now had the haggard, lined look of someone who was deeply disappointed. Thin and angular, Maebelle Hansford wore a long-sleeved faded pink cotton tee shirt, sweat pants, and discount sneakers whose backs were folded under, exposing her cracked and swollen heels. A cigarette dangled from her right hand. Her brittle graying hair was pulled back into a ponytail.

"Good afternoon, Mrs. Hansford." Simone extended her hand. "Thank you for seeing me on such short notice. My name is Simone Rosenberg. As, I told you on the phone, I'm with the Atlanta Police Department." Simone flipped her badge open for Maebelle Hansford to inspect.

"Come on in. Everbody calls me Mae. It's short for Maebelle."

Simone stepped into the dark living room and waited for her eyes to adjust before moving forward. The house was cramped and cluttered with old newspapers, magazines and ceramic figurines. The odor of spent cigarettes and cooking oil clung to the walls and fabrics. Sleeping just inside the door on the frayed rust carpet was a small black mutt. He raised his graying chin and eyed Simone curiously for a second, flipped his stringy tail in slow motion once, then yawned disdainfully and fell back into a deep sleep. Dust motes floated in the sunlight that had etched its way through the threadbare curtain tacked across the room's only window. Lumpy, sweat-stained pillows were strewn across the couch and La-Z-Boy recliner. The cheap furniture appeared to sag under the same burden of fatigue that infused the house and it's two occupants.

"Can I get you some coffee or something?" Mae Hansford pointed to the middle of a worn plaid sofa, indicating that Simone should sit there.

"No, thank you, ma'am. I was hoping you could talk to me a little about Catherine O'Donnell?"

Mae sat across from Simone in the La-Z-Boy. "Patsy Gail, you mean? Is she in trouble?"

"No, ma'am. We're just doing an investigation, and she might be able to help us. I need to get some background on her."

"Patsy Gail is my sister's only child. My baby sister. Ann Marie Graves. Have you found out anything about her, Miz Rosenberg?"

"No ma'am," Simone said.

"Oh." Mae's shoulders drooped with disappointment. "I was hoping your visit might have something to do with Ann Marie. She disappeared on June 12, 1964. Lemme see now, Patsy Gail would a been about four. We never learned what happened to Ann. She just disappeared off the face of the earth in a instant, and we ain't heard word one from her to this day." Mae Hansford paused and propped her elbows on her knees. She held her hands over her face, as if holding back the unwanted emotions.

"Nobody ever even looked into it. The local sheriff, I mean. A few years back, I tried to contact them folks with that TV show. You know the one? *Unsolved Mysteries*? But, nothing ever come of it. I 'spect the case was too old."

"Do you have any idea what happened to her?"

"Well, I can't prove nothing, of course. But, if you ask me, it was that sorry husband she married. He had something to do with it, you mark my words. Him or that twisted brother of his'n. Ted. My sister wouldn't never in three lifetimes left her baby to fend for herself against those two sumbitches except she didn't have no choice in the matter. 'Scuse my language."

Maebelle Hansford wiped a sun-leathered hand over her lined cheek, impatiently pushing a tear away. "Patsy Gail. Sweet little angel. I can't get used to calling her Catherine. She's called a few times over the years. I tried to help when she was little, but Preacher Graves finally barred me from his house."

Mae Hansford had spat out the words "Preacher Graves," giving Simone a deeper understanding of the level of contempt with which she held him.

"Poor little thing. Left alone in that house with them two brothers. She used to cut on herself. Did she tell you that? I'd go over there sometimes and pull up her sleeves, and her little arms had slashes all the way up to the elbows. She slashed her belly, too, and . . . Lord have mercy on this evil world, I think even down in her private parts. I tried talking to her about it and she said, 'Oh, Aunt Mae, it just makes me feel better.'

Simone straightened her shoulders and jotted a note about O'Donnell's use of razors.

"Can you imagine that?" Mae Hansford shook her head. "Slicing yourself up feels better than the kind of pain you're having to deal with every day of your life? She begged me not to talk to her daddy about it, and I didn't. I called the county health department and they come out. I called Children's

Services. Nobody would do nuthin because of that old reprobate's standing in the community. Him and his family owning the only funeral parlor in town. That may not sound like much to you, but it's big stuff in a little place like this.

"You know when Patsy—I mean Catherine—was in high school, she used to do the make-up on them corpses laying up at the funeral home. Law, she could make them look so natural that you'd think they was gonna set right up and join the party any minute!" Mae's eyes danced with amusement, before her phlegmy laugh dissolved into a hacking cough. "Everbody commented on how life-like she could make them. Used to give me the willies, but Catherine said she liked doing it. I don't know how she could stand working on dead people, and her just a little bitty thing.

"Well, anyway, 'bout that cutting on herself. After awhile, when she got older, she wouldn't let me roll up her sleeves no more. Stopped talking to me pretty much. I think she give up. I wudn't no help to her no way. Me and her mama looked so much alike. Guess it just got to be too painful."

"Did Catherine ever do anything besides the cutting that seemed strange to you?" Simone shifted forward to the edge of the sofa to keep from sinking into a hole caused by the exhausted springs underneath her.

"Nothing I can remember. Like most young 'uns, she got a little wild when she was older." Mae paused and shook out a Marlboro from the box. She lit it and on the exhale said, "But now that I think on it, it was sort of odd 'cause one day, she'd be this sweet little girl like she always was—looked like a strong wind could blow her over—and the next time you'd run into her, she'd be somebody you don't even know, smoking and cussing on the street. Sort of swaggering, if you know what I mean. I bet she got the hell beat out of her three or four times a week. That and, Lord knows, what else."

"What else do you think, ma'am?"

Mae kicked one foot out towards the dog, but didn't hit him. "Plain and simple? Sex perversions! I don't know how old she was when it started, but both of them brothers was peculiar, and mean as cornered raccoons. My sister Ann just hinted at it to me, but I know it was a constant torment to her. She was making plans to leave home, and take her sweet baby with her, when she disappeared."

Mae Hansford took another deep drag on her cigarette, exhaled fully to the end of a wheeze, and then crushed the butt into an overflowing ashtray. She sat quietly for a moment, peering through the smoke that enveloped her, as if she might find clues that would answer her longing for a lost sister and niece.

"Detective, I been dirt poor all my life. I know what it's like to feel like you got no say in this world. You understand?"

Simone nodded.

"But, I tell you, I have never felt so feeble and useless as when I was trying to get some help for that child. Nobody would listen to me. It liked to eat me up."

"Yes ma'am."

"Patsy Gail quit school at sixteen. Left here and never come back. I can't blame her for that. Ain't nothing here to hold her."

Mae lit her third cigarette. "You say she might help you with some kind of investigation? What are you looking into?"

Simone stood up to leave. "She's doing a one-woman play in Atlanta right now about child abuse. We're hoping she might be able to help us understand it better."

Mae dug her two palms into the arms of the chair, pushed herself up and followed Simone to the door. "A play, huh? Well, I'll be!" A smile lit Mae's tired eyes for a moment, before fading quickly. "When she was little, she was always so shy. Well, I 'spect nobody would know more about being abused than Patsy Gail. You can take whatever she says to the bank."

Before Simone could walk out the door, Mae clutched her by the arm and held her at the threshold. "Tell Catherine I miss her, would you officer? Tell her I'm sorry too."

"Yes ma'am, I will."

Simone patted Mae's rail thin hand before gently extricating herself and walking into the fresh air—away from the billowing fog that encircled Mae Hansford's body like a shroud woven out of smoke and longing and regret.

TWENTY-SIX

Two days later, Simone showed up for her appointment with Delia Whitfield on time and rang the front doorbell at precisely 9:00 a.m.

"Thanks for working me in this morning, Dr. Whitfield. As I mentioned on the phone, we made a few inquiries and need your clarification on a couple of things."

Delia lead Simone into her private office and closed the door. "I'd be happy to help in any way I can, Detective."

"Your husband is a professor at Emerson University. Is that correct?"

"John's an archeology professor. Why do you ask?" Delia pointed to a carefully laid tray with a steaming teapot and cups, but Simone indicated she didn't want any.

"A case we're working on. The suspect is using wigs for disguise, and we noticed that your husband has bought several of them in the past year through Emerson's theater department. He's not involved in any theatrical productions, is he?"

"John? Heavens no." Delia laughed heartily. "The stage is the last place you would find my husband. You're not suggesting he had anything to do with a crime, Detective! John's a tenured professor at one of the finest schools in the country."

"Of course not, Dr. Whitfield. It's just part of the investigation. Do you have any idea why he would need wigs?"

"They're for me. I buy them using his staff discount."

"If you don't mind my asking, what use do you have for the wigs? You don't appear to be wearing one."

"I've used wigs frequently in my work for therapeutic role playing with my clients. If we can create a strong enough visual image, it helps facilitate their emotional focus. Let's see. Oh yes, I've also given wigs away to clients who need them and can't afford them. A couple of women lost their hair through radiation treatment and alopecia. One woman got a handful yanked out by her husband. And, on a happier note, I have clients who are involved in local theater productions. So, I get to support the arts in a small way." Delia paused a moment and took a sip of tea. "My husband can get great quality human hair wigs through the university at a deep discount. Why shouldn't I pass the savings along to my clients? I assume that's not against the law. Detective, you're obviously not interviewing every person in Atlanta who's bought a wig. What made you come to me?"

Simone ignored the question. "I'll need a list of clients you've given the wigs to."

"Impossible. My clients rely on me to protect their privacy. I certainly wouldn't release anyone's name without some strong evidence that she was in danger."

"Have you supplied Catherine O'Donnell with wigs in the past?"

"Just what are you investigating, Detective Rosenberg?"

Again, Simone ignored her question. "I can subpoena your records."

"Do whatever you must, Detective, but please understand that I will fight the subpoena in court."

Simone had expected as much. She moved on to the other reason she had come to speak with Delia Whitfield. "I read an article you wrote a couple of years back for the American Journal of Psychology. It was about aversion therapy."

"That's a pretty esoteric journal. How did you ever find that?"

"Cops usually can find anything they're looking for, Dr. Whitfield."

"Are you interested in psychology, Detective Rosenberg?"

"Only in how it applies to police work. From what I've read, aversion therapy's been pretty much discredited, hasn't it?"

"As a cure for homosexuality, yes. The mental health community now recognizes that homosexuality falls within the normal range of sexual behaviors and is not a psychiatric disorder. My article advocated using a form of aversion therapy, also called reparative therapy, on violent sex offenders. If you read the whole article, you will have noticed that it was to be used in a safe and controlled prison environment on incarcerated men."

"What response have you had to the idea?" Simone asked.

"Not too good, I'm afraid. Scientists feel the procedure has been tainted by misuse."

Delia walked over to get more hot water. "Are you sure I can't brew a cup for you, detective?"

"No thank you, doctor, I'm fine. How does the therapy work?"

"It's complicated, but basically, you pair an unpleasant experience with a sexually arousing stimulus. For instance, a man who is aroused by children would be allowed to watch a film showing them playing. When he reacts sexually to the film, he receives negative feedback—a terrible smell, like a decaying body or vomit, or an electric shock. Over a course of treatments, the man comes to associate inappropriate sexual behavior with a negative experience."

"Why not do a traditional talking therapy?"

"Traditional therapies usually take years, and we don't have the funding to follow these guys for the rest of their lives. They typically get released in the middle of treatment, and we never see them again. Or, they get shipped to another facility that doesn't have a treatment program. If it's done properly, aversion therapy can work rather quickly. It's the only short cut I know. I believe it's our best chance for rehabilitating sexual predators.

Will you finally answer a question for me, Detective?"

"If I can."

"What brings you to my door?"

Simone closed her notepad and stood to leave. "Just trying to better understand sexual abuse, Dr. Whitfield. You have nothing to be concerned about."

"But, why Catherine O'Donnell? Why did you ask me about her?"

"Is there anything you want to tell me?" Simone reopened her notebook and carefully observed Delia Whitfield's demeanor.

"Only that Catherine is a very talented and fragile woman. It would be devastating if you were to recklessly accuse her of something that she is incapable of doing. Please use extreme caution, Detective Rosenberg, if you are targeting *any* of my clients. Like you, I am willing to use the legal system to get what I want!"

TWENTY-SEVEN

Tina had been unable to bring herself to reveal the sorry state of her employment to Simone on their getaway weekend in the mountains. She had decided she would rather live with the lie for an entire lifetime than see the inevitable look of disgust on Simone's face for even one second. She couldn't bear it.

"Thou doest wound me, child!" Lady M protested when Tina informed her on Tuesday morning that she was leaving. "Would that I were flayed upon a spit than not see thy fair face grace these mortal digs."

Lady M tilted back in her office chair with her size ten work boots propped on the desk. It was still early, and the treatment wombs were empty.

"Got to get outta here, Lady M," Tina replied. "I'm going back to school. Someday I'll come to see you quoting Shakespeare myself."

Lady M smiled broadly. "Well, then, methinks I should stop if thou hast means to validate my speech."

She paused and looked longingly at Tina, her favorite girl, and one of her many ex-lovers. "Seriously, my dear, you know you've always got a place to land here if you need it. Long as I'm in charge." Then with a dismissal wave, she said, "Now, off with your head, wench!"

Tina was in the dressing room cleaning out her locker and thinking of Simone. God, she loved that woman, and she loved the mountains. Now the two were firmly linked together in her mind. She relished the memory of Simone curled up next to her, the two of them zipped together in their sleeping bags, their chilled toes tickling each other; laughing, the fragrance of wood smoke clinging to their clothes from the extinguished campfire outside the tent. It was too delicious. For the first time in her life, she felt deserving of kindness.

Maybe she *would* go to college. Hell, maybe she'd go on and get a masters degree. Become a therapist, like Delia, or a lawyer. Maybe she'd write a children's book about the little Buddha boy. She was still young. The lies she had believed about herself, her feelings of worthlessness, the rage that had consumed her heart and caused such reckless behavior in the past, were exposed now and withering in the heat of Simone's love. No matter what she had done, no matter how vile, she could still have a normal life, couldn't she? Let someone else be the one who . . . ."

Her thoughts were interrupted by the appearance of Lady M. "Wanna play Juliet to one more Romeo?" she asked.

"Nope," Tina said. "I told you I'm outta here."

"Fair lady, act not in haste! Thou woudst do thy mentor— meaning ME—your sweet old lover, the one who's been here for you through thick and thin . . . you know, the one who's loaned you money . . . a terrible disservice."

Tina laughed in spite of herself.

"Please, honey, you'd be doing me a huge favor. Nobody else is here yet, and sales have been really down lately. I've been catching so much grief about it. Come on, for old time's sake. Please? Then, we can call everything even."

Tina knew what she meant. Lady M had saved her ass a few times over the years, bailing her out of jail, feeding her, and later, giving her the better tippers, setting her up with a couple of generous, kindhearted, impotent old sugar daddies. Lady M had not only been her lover, she had been a surrogate mother as well.

"It's too damn early," Tina said. "I don't like the early creeps. He look like he's been up all night?"

Lady M fished a small nugget of food from between her

two front teeth with her fingernail. "Nah. He looks sane enough. What's one more, right? And, then, get thee to a nunnery!"

Tina thought for a moment. Now was the time to settle debts before she moved on, and she did owe something to Lady M. Of course, she could also sock away a little more cash, but that wasn't really the issue. She needed to test herself one last time. She listened for guidance from within, but heard nothing. Maybe if she got with this guy and felt something different, something more specific—she wasn't sure what—wouldn't that tell her something? Wouldn't that tell her that she truly had moved on and could be trusted with real love?

"Okay," she said, "what's one more?"

He was a tall, solidly built man, who smelled of cheap cologne. He gave Tina the creeps at first sight. Something about his eyes seemed unnatural, like light wasn't getting in or out, but was held compressed in those two orbs, blocking connection to other humans as effectively as an opaque window.

She considered turning him down, but her optimistic good mood overrode her instincts. She led him back to an open room, gave the usual instructions, and left him to get undressed while she deposited his upfront money.

When she returned to the room, he was fully clothed and sitting in a stiff, upright position with one hand tucked beneath his thigh. *Highly unusual for him to be dressed*, she thought. Could be a cop, but he didn't seem like a cop. Cops were friendlier and more eager to please, like they were trying too hard to make you believe they were just ordinary guys.

Tina moved seductively in front of him, slowly stripping down to her lingerie. The guy just sat there, staring at her.

"What do you want today, baby?" she asked.

He said nothing, just stared directly at her breasts.

Tina turned away from him and watched herself dance. Might as well get a little warm-up exercise before going to the gym, she thought. This guy's a dud. She braced her hands against the mirror and leaned forward slightly to give him a better view of her derriere, a view most of her customers liked. Tina suspected it was because they could imagine themselves as animals mounting the female from behind. She turned her head slightly toward him and mechanically produced a seductive smile.

He remained completely still, staring at her. Nothing seemed to affect him. Tina began to feel both angry and slightly afraid. Just slightly. She could handle men. She always had. Sure, she considered telling him to go to hell, but pride, or something, stopped her. She'd already taken his money. She had never allowed herself the luxury of giving in to her fears, not since the first encounter with the superintendent of her building when she was a child. She wasn't about to give in now.

"How do I look, baby? Am I making you hard?"

"Yeah," he said. "Why don't you come over here and let me touch you."

She paused midway through licking her lips and turned back to the mirror. She moved her hips seductively, willing him to become aroused.

"It costs more for touching. I'd do it for free, for a guy as good looking as you, but management won't let me. I really want you to touch me, baby. You got me so hot. But, it's a hundred and fifty dollars more."

She jacked up the price just because he was pissing her off.

"Figures," he muttered, barely audible, and shifted slightly in his seat, his hand pushing further under his thigh.

Tina hadn't noticed the small movement, but she felt a prickly fear that all women recognize, but can't quite name, rising up within her. She put it off, thinking it was not a fear so much of the man sitting in front of her, though he was definitely weird. She would have to watch him. She suspected the real fear came from the certainty that she had changed and would never again be the little girl who would do anything for money. How would she survive? She would have to learn to live in the straight world; she, a gay, ex-stripper, ex-hooker, about as welcome as the plague. She pushed the fear down, banished it, just like the first time she had swallowed the Super's cum. I should've just called in and quit, she thought. I didn't owe that old whorehouse madam anything. Why do I always have to do everything the hard way?

Tina looked at her customer again, and the sight and smell of him made her stomach churn. She stopped her seductive dance and turned toward the door. This is it, she thought. This is what the last guy looks like, some cold-eyed freak, more dead than alive. I don't care what I have to do for a living; I'll never do this again.

She started towards the door, confusion and hesitation evident on her face and in her walk.

"You ain't leaving are you, hot stuff?"

She said nothing. How could she speak to this trash?

I could be home cuddled up on the sofa with Simone, instead of parading around naked in front of the living dead, she thought. That vision of Simone changed her attitude immediately. She smiled. She tossed her head back and laughed out loud. She was free!

In that reckless flicker of a moment, the customer seized the opportunity to do what he had come to do. He leapt from the chair and grabbed Tina from behind, quickly wrapping one arm around her neck in a chokehold. Tina screamed and fought back with an elbow jab into his rock hard abdomen. He barely flinched. With his free arm, he stabbed Tina repeatedly in the chest and stomach with the knife he'd hidden under his thigh. He made three slashing cuts to her left cheek, leaving it shredded and bloody. Tina clawed his neck with her long fingernails, leaving two bright red streaks trailing from his jaw line to his collar. She struggled to drag him to the door and out into the hallway, where she hoped Lady M would hear her diminishing screams.

In the control room, sensing some excessive movement on one of the screens, Lady M casually glanced up from her *People Magazine* just as Tina slumped to the floor. She slammed the panic button located under her desk that would signal a 911 emergency into the nearest police station, grabbed her shotgun, and headed for the hallway. She arrived at the door to the room just as Tina's assailant bolted through it. Lady M opened fire, unloading both barrels point blank into his chest, killing him instantly. She then stepped over him to get to Tina, who lay crumpled in a pool of blood.

Lady M knelt beside her and cradled Tina's battered head.

"Tina, honey, oh God, Oh my God. Hold on, honey. Can you hear me, Tina? Speak to me."

Two other girls had come in to work and were standing outside in the hall, crying. The only other customer in the place made a beeline for the front door, zipping his pants as he went.

"Tina, baby, hold on. The ambulance is on the way."

Lady M turned to Amber and shouted, "Go call 'em again. Make sure they got my 911."

Gently, Lady M gathered Tina's body into her lap and sobbed while she rocked her back and forth. Tina opened her eyes, briefly, saw Lady M, and then closed them again. If she were dying, she would not think of anything connected to this place in her last moments. Not Lady M, not the men, not the other girls. She wanted her last thoughts to be of Simone and the mountains. She felt the mountain breeze lightly ruffle across her blood-soaked body. She heard the low sorrowful coo of mateless mourning doves circling above her, calling her to join them, to heal their mutual loneliness in the soft dying light of her being. Doves were the bearers of good tidings, she thought. She felt blessed to see them now at this hour. Perhaps they had come to escort her to a clean place, a place denied to her on earth.

But, she also felt the light kiss that Simone had planted on her forehead earlier that morning; it lingered as a reminder that there was still a promise of happiness for her on earth, however imperfect, if she could hold on. She heard once again Simone's whispered, "I love you."

Then, everything went black.

TWENTY-EIGHT

With daughter Minerva safely ensconced for a couple of nights at a girlfriend's house, Simone had spent the morning at Tina's apartment lounging in bed and then had gone to the club for a workout. Around 6:00 p.m., she was in the kitchen preparing her specialty, pepper pot stew, and anticipating Tina's return from work when she heard the news on the radio. A lingerie model had been brutally attacked at a jack shack called The Sultan's Palace. At first, she didn't think anything of it. Tina had no connection to The Sultan's Palace. But when she turned on the local television evening news, she saw a photograph of Tina, smiling. The caption under the photo read, "Lingerie model in critical condition after brutal attack on job."

Simone immediately checked with the station house and discovered that they had released Tina's name to the press after notifying Dr. Delia Whitfield. Tina had listed Dr. Whitfield with The Sultan's Palace as her nearest relative and had given Delia power of attorney for emergency situations.

Simone rushed to Peachtree Memorial Hospital, flashed her badge at anyone who tried to get in her way, and stormed into the intensive care unit, only to be stopped dead in her tracks by the appearance of Tina's brutalized face. She was unconscious with tubes and wires connecting her to a small beeping screen.

"Oh, sweet biscuit," Simone whispered. "How you get

yourself in dis fix?" She gingerly lifted Tina's hand and sat beside the bed, listening for any irregularity from the beeping machine on the wall. When she was satisfied that Tina's heartbeat was steady and that the intensive care nurses were paying proper attention, she went in search of answers.

She cornered the emergency room physician who had admitted Tina as he was exiting the nurses' station. "What can you tell me about the attack on Tina Galenski?"

The doctor consulted his notes. "She's lost a lot of blood. There was trauma to the head with brain swelling. Apparently, the guy slammed her head against the floor a couple of times. The surgery to repair damage to her liver, spleen, and a punctured lung appears to have gone well. All told, there were fifteen puncture wounds, most of which were not life threatening. We've given her blood transfusions and she's in critical, but stable, condition. We'll have to wait now to see what kind of shape she's in once she regains consciousness."

Simone wiped the tears away from her eyes with her sleeve. "She'll come out of it all right?"

The doctor patted Simone's shoulder. "Can't make any promises at this point. She's got a chance."

From the hospital, Simone headed straight to Delia Whitfield's office. Delia had cancelled her clients for the day and had just returned from the hospital herself shortly before Simone arrived around nine in the evening.

After a quick hello in the reception area of Delia's office, Simone demanded, "What can you tell me about this, Dr. Whitfield?"

"Are you here in the capacity of a police officer, or are you here as Tina's friend?" Delia asked.

Simone paced the room and raised her voice. "I think you know why I'm here. I love Tina. I'm *in love* with Tina. Except I don't know who she is anymore—stripping and doing God knows what else in some low-life jack shack. How could she keep something like that from me? I must be some kind of detective."

Delia motioned for Simone to sit. "You're angry. I don't

blame you."

Simone ignored Delia's offer. "Did she know the guy who stabbed her?"

"She never mentioned him to me," Delia said.

Simone grabbed a goddess statue from a table and looked as if she might throw it through the glass wall of the aquarium. "That piece-of-work manager over at the Sultan's Palace says he was just some scumball off the street. She'd never seen him before. I could only get a little info out of her before she gets worked up and goes into this Lady Macbeth routine, ringing her hands, like she's got blood on them. 'Out, out damn spot,' she says, shaking and bawling like a sick heifer."

"Please, sit down, Detective."

Delia lightly touched Simone's arm. "You're looking a little wobbly."

She guided Simone to a couple of chairs directly across from the aquarium, and the two women sat.

Simone glared at the swimming fish. *Nothing makes sense anymore. Why the hell does she have an aquarium this big in a therapy place? Is this marine world or something?*

"The manager told me Tina quit this morning. She was excited about going to college. I didn't even know she wanted to go to college. I thought she worked for a children's book author." Simone shrugged in disbelief.

"Tina told that old bat she was in love."

She turned her tear-streaked face towards Delia. "She was cleaning out her locker when Lady Macbeth comes in and begs her to do one more customer, for old times' sake, I guess. The old witch made Tina feel guilty because of everything they'd been through together."

Delia smiled for the first time all day. "Tina quit that job! We've been working towards that for so long now. She was finally able to do it. Thank God."

"If she loves me, how can she keep something like this from me?"

Simone's anger dug into the lining of her heart, attaching itself like a barnacle.

Delia reached across the short divide between them and

held Simone's hand. "I can't go into anything that would compromise Tina's privacy. What I will tell you—because I know Tina has told you this herself—is that she loves you. She wants to make a life with you.

"Don't you find troubled people everywhere in your line of work, Detective? Some are so damaged, there's no predicting what they might do. They seem perfectly normal, whatever that means, but inside they're bubbling with rage or confusion, sadness, emotions that overwhelm them sometimes.

"Tina's been making progress over the last few years, but she's a fragile person. She needs your love and support right now. When she regains consciousness and is well enough to handle it, you can straighten out the deception and decide what you want to do about the future."

Simone stood to leave. She reluctantly allowed Delia to give her a hug. There was no explaining any of it to her satisfaction. In retrospect, she'd been suspicious when Tina wouldn't give her a work number, but Tina had said her boss was touchy about personal phone calls. Simone should call her on her cell phone. She'd assumed Tina was afraid the boss would find out she was gay.

Simone sat in the driver's seat of her car, unwilling to crank up and go. She was parked along the street, where she watched the lights turn on as Delia Whitfield walked from the reception area to her office near the rear of the bungalow. Simone wanted to stay close to the woman whom Tina had trusted enough to list as her next of kin. She thought if she waited long enough, life would begin to make sense again.

How could I have been so blind? I guess cops are no different from anyone else, when we're in love. But, why the deception, Tina? If you'd only trusted me, I would've supported you until you found something else to do. What good am I? What good is it that I carry a gun or can kick somebody's ass? I've got a whole police force behind me, and I couldn't protect you.

TWENTY-NINE

There was nothing for Simone to do, but go on with work. She spent her off hours divided between Minerva's needs and sitting vigil in the hospital with Tina. Work was the only thing that kept her from falling apart.

While the outcome of an investigation couldn't be predicted, the procedures of police work could. Simone and a uniformed officer named Otis Bell, who had been promoted to plain clothes temporarily for the assignment, had spent the previous two weekends camped in an unmarked patrol car outside Catherine O'Donnell's apartment in the evenings, while Marty had hung out in disguise at the Rainbow's End bar. So far, Catherine's pattern had been completely predictable. On performance evenings, she left her apartment at 6:30 p.m. and returned home immediately after the shows around ten-thirty. On the nights she wasn't performing, she left for her part-time waitressing job at the trendy Gabriel's Café at around 5:30 p.m. and returned home near midnight.

On Saturday night, a week after Tina's assault, Catherine broke the pattern. Around ten o'clock in the evening, after having performed earlier in the day at a matinee, she emerged from her apartment house door in tight black leather pants and matching motorcycle jacket. She was carrying two large plastic garbage bags that appeared to be full. She looked to be in a big hurry.

"Let's go," Simone said. "I'm betting she's headed for the south side of Atlanta."

Simone had direct contact with Marty through an earpiece that he planned to remove when Catherine pulled into the parking lot of the Rainbow's End. Simone whispered to Marty, "Keep your legs crossed partner, our girl might be headed your way."

Otis Bell waited until Catherine pulled out, then cranked up and followed discretely behind her. He and Simone were both surprised when she headed toward the northwest side of town. When she turned into the winding private drive that led to Delia Whitfield's house, they pulled over to wait, once again.

THIRTY

Catherine rang Delia's doorbell once. She paused for a few seconds and then rang twice. When Delia didn't respond, she banged with her fists until the lights inside were turned on.

"Who is it?" Delia asked, her voice layered with concern.

"It's Catherine. I'm sorry to come so late, Delia. Can I come in? Please let me in."

Delia opened the door, wearing only her nightgown and bathrobe. She took one look at Catherine and blurted, "I've been trying to reach you all week! Are you all right? You've heard about Tina?"

Catherine was carrying two large plastic garbage bags that appeared to be full to the point of bursting. "Yes. Oh my God . . . I wanted to go to the hospital, but . . . Is your husband home?"

Catherine's teeth chattered and she was trembling, visibly, as if freezing.

"No, he left a week ago for Peru. He won't be back for at least a month."

Delia grabbed one of Catherine's bags and led her into the kitchen. "Do you want anything to drink? Some tea or warm milk?"

They sat down at Delia's large kitchen table. Catherine slumped forward and lightly tapped her forehead against the maple tabletop. "Oh, God, Delia. I can't stand this anymore." Her words were muffled against the wood. "I'm losing what was left of my puny mind. I keep thinking that if I work hard enough, care enough, try enough, fucking cry enough, something will make a difference." She punctuated each "enough" with a light bang of her forehead.

"But nothing matters. Not what I do, or you do with your therapy sessions, or what anybody else does to combat these demons. They're all around us. Who was that guy who tried to kill Tina? Did he even know her?"

Delia shook her head and held her palms up. She shrugged, as if to say, "Why would anyone want to kill Tina?"

"That's what I thought," said Catherine. "Probably just hated her being female. Hated what he wanted from her—her beauty and her sensuality—what he couldn't have. Maybe he despised parts of her separately like they weren't even connected to a real person. Despised her breasts or her vagina, or even her sweet, tiny hands. Remember how small her hands are?"

Catherine lifted her head back up from the table. Her face was puffy and streaked from crying. Her forehead had the beginnings of a small knot. She had been crying for days before coming to Delia's. She began to pull items out of the garbage bags. First were the ceramic cookie jars which she gently placed on the floor, handling them as if they were precious heirlooms. Next, she pulled strips of photographs and threw them up into the air. They floated briefly and landed on the table and floor.

"Look at this shit! It's like I'm trying to make a family out of crockery and scraps. I'm so damned afraid of real people that I can't stand the thought of anything I can't control. See what happens when you let anybody get too close? They die, damn it. They always die.

"I've got nothing, Delia. *I'm* nothing. Empty. When I'm not playing a role on stage, when I don't have my character fully defined and scripted, there's nobody home. Nobody but Uncle Ted and he's getting louder and louder until no matter how deafening I make the radio or TV, I can't drown him out."

She grabbed a handful of the pictures and shook them in Delia's face.

"Why would I keep taking pictures of myself? Can you answer that? I look at them all the time, too, and I can't, for the life of me, figure out what I look like. Whose face is that? Is she pretty, or even interesting looking? I don't know. Is there any character in that face? Every time I look, I see somebody different. Who is in these pictures? And, what the hell are the cookie jars about? You can't make a family out of cookie jars. I don't even like cookies."

Catherine laughed, bitterly.

"Catherine," Delia said, stroking her hand, soothing her. "What happened to Tina was horrible. I'm absolutely heart broken about it, but it didn't have anything to do with you. It was an act of violence by a demented man. You couldn't have prevented it."

"How could you let her go on working in a place like that?" Catherine accused Delia the way a child blames her mother.

Delia snapped, "I had no power to stop her from doing anything she was hell-bent on doing. You know that, Catherine. But I think she was getting closer to being able to leave it behind. Did you know she was in love? I think she was finding some peace of mind. I hope so, anyway . . ." Delia's voice trailed off. Her own sadness and helplessness were overwhelming.

Catherine sat up straighter. "No, I didn't know. I'm glad for that. Poor little thing. Maybe she had a taste of happiness before this . . . I'm sorry, Delia. I didn't mean to hurt your feelings."

Delia brushed Catherine's hair away from her sticky face and smiled gently. "Hey, we're talking about her like she's already gone. I spoke to the doctor a couple of days ago, and she's holding her own. You know how tough she is. I expect her to be back and kicking ass in group soon."

Catherine hesitated, looked around her as if expecting to find spies, then spoke. "Uncle Ted is laughing right now about it. He was there when it happened. He had something to do with it. Maybe he took over that guy's mind. He's the devil, you know."

Delia walked casually to the stove and put a kettle of water on for tea. This was the first she had heard of Catherine's uncle speaking to her in any way other than through dreams.

"Can you hear Ted when you're awake now?"

"It's just started. He's usually arguing with one of the cousins inside me. I don't know if I can stand the noise anymore! I can't hear myself think. He says he's been here all along, but I could only hear him in my dreams."

"What has he told you?"

"It doesn't matter. Everything's a lie. Get this. He's been hounding me to confess to the sheriff up in High Point. He claims I pushed him off that church roof. He said I threatened him with a knife once when he came into my room. You know, back when I was cutting myself. I did no such thing, Delia. I never threatened him, and he fell off that roof and killed himself cause he was a clumsy asshole, despite how sexy he thought he was. I did not push him off. If one of my alternate personalities did it, I would know, wouldn't I?"

Delia sat quietly for a moment. "Of course you would."

She had lied, but Catherine's mental state was at its most fragile. Delia wanted her to feel as if she had some control over her own life.

Delia felt a familiar weariness settle upon her body. Her neck and shoulders ached. She propped her elbows on the table and cradled her forehead in her hands. She felt as if she had gained a hundred pounds over the last months, and it was crammed between her ears, and throbbing. Every exhale sounded like a sigh; her inhalations were moist with tears, her throat constricted until she felt she couldn't breathe.

"What is it, Delia?" The look of alarm on Catherine's face was unmistakable.

"I'm okay," Delia's voice was high and tight. "It's just . . . it breaks my heart that you feel so unloved. I know that's not particularly helpful to you, but sometimes I feel as powerless as you, Catherine. All my expensive education and I spend half my time just trying to prevent clients from killing themselves. That's my definition of success now, you know—Oh, thank God, nobody killed herself today! If I had a magic word that would erase the memories, I'd use it. But there's no magic word. There's nothing but ordinary words glued together with hope. And I'm running out of glue."

She looked away from Catherine, but continued speaking. "I don't know why God turned his face from your suffering, but you never did anything to deserve it. My mother used to say, 'God works in mysterious ways' and we're supposed to accept everything on faith . . . and I try. But somebody should have been there to help you all those years ago. Somebody. At the very least, God could have sent an angel to comfort you. What good are angels if they don't show up when you need them most?"

The words had come out in a flood. *This isn't how it's supposed to go,* she thought. *I'm her therapist, for God's sake, and I'm acting like she's mine.* But, in truth, she didn't care anymore. It felt good to rage against the violence, the disrespect, the chaos brought about by man's eternal, damnable need to control and dominate women.

The teakettle's whistle pierced the air and shook Delia back to sensibility. She walked over and poured a cup of tea for each of them.

"Do you want milk or honey in your tea?"

"Plain is fine."

Catherine's eyes followed Delia as she moved from the stove back to the table. "Maybe we have to be angels for each other. Like that serial cutter. Do you think she's an angel, Delia?"

"I think she's trying to help. I doubt anyone would call her an angel!"

"She reminds me of you, Delia."

"Me?! How?"

"She's unorthodox. She's angry. Like you. You're both trying to help women and children. I think what she's doing is admirable. Like you."

Delia laughed. "We just use different techniques, right?"

Catherine appeared hurt by Delia's reaction. "Not everybody can get a PH.D! We have to do what we can. You know, like, I hope my show helps somebody to get out of a bad situation. We use whatever talents we have, and hers is a talent for finding these evil guys and putting them out of commission."

"She must be a pretty good actress, too," Delia said. "unless there's more than one woman involved. Do you think it's a group of women instead of just one?"

Catherine ignored the question and abruptly changed the subject.

"What made you decide to become a therapist?"

Why did she change the subject?

"Gosh, it was so long ago. Let me think. When I was an undergrad, I wanted to be a biologist specializing in indigenous cultures of the rain forests. I spent a couple of summers living in South America. It was an amazing time for me. I learned so much. But, you know, life happens. The road you're on takes a detour."

"Did anything bad happen to you? You know, like me?" Catherine asked.

Delia paused, wondering how much she should reveal about her life. "Well, you know what they say about therapists. Scratch the surface and you'll find a sick person trying to heal herself, but no, nothing so bad happened to me like what happened to you or Tina, or Mama Bea, or Janet. It was the little things that got to me over time. My high school guidance counselor telling me I shouldn't go to college, 'cause I would be taking a male student's spot. He said women quit their jobs once they have kids anyway! Boys in elementary school and high school calling me names, ganging up, and trying to corner me to pinch my breasts or my ass. College guys buying me drinks in the hopes they would get lucky. The college professors leering from behind the podium. None of them ever taking into consideration that I owned my body and sexuality the same as them.

"And, worst of all, every Sunday, until the day I left home, I was wedged between corseted adults, listening to some no-neck, sanctimonious peckerhead who had spent his whole life interpreting the Bible to fit his point of view. If women came into the discourse, it was either as whores or wives or, of course, Mary, the bearer of the Savior. All passive vessels.

"When I was a young adult, it was these little daily humiliations that were constantly surprising me. Just when I thought I was being accepted as an equal, some man would remind me that I wasn't."

"At least you've got your husband," Catherine said.

Delia shrugged. "Do you see him here tonight?"

Catherine held her steaming mug in both hands and inhaled the fragrance. "This tea is delicious. I know what you mean about the daily humiliations. You keep telling yourself they're nothing, that you're being overly sensitive, but they eat away at you, don't they?"

Delia walked to the sink and grabbed a sponge to wipe up some tea she had spilled. "The worst is when the television news report kidnaps and rapes in that breathless, pseudo-sympathetic voice, but really they're pissing in their pants because the ratings will shoot through the roof. I had a couple of friends who were assaulted. They were never the same."

Delia had become quite agitated. She rifled the sponge into the sink, then caught herself. She stopped talking and shook her head as if to clear it. "Oh, Catherine, you have enough to deal with, without me losing my objectivity. Maybe you should see another therapist."

Catherine jerked as if she'd been hit. "I don't want someone new. I can't start over with anyone else. I can't, Delia! I'm not happy that you're upset, but in a strange way, it helps me a little. It's so hard to pretend that everything is normal. That I'm normal. I want so much to get rid of Uncle Ted, but how?"

"Well, tonight we'll confront him together. I dare him to show his ugly face in this house." She turned her face toward the ceiling and yelled. "Come on out, you sanctimonious reptile."

Catherine flinched and looked around the room as if she expected Uncle Ted to walk into the room and slap Delia.

Delia continued her rant. "Picking on little girls. Raping little girls. Come on out. We're not scared of you; you rat-faced, piece of shit."

Delia knew she was behaving recklessly, but recognized that Catherine was beginning to enjoy the show. "Uncle Ted liked to drink, didn't he?"

"More than liked."

Delia leapt up from her seat and fairly skipped over to the refrigerator. She jerked the door open and yanked out a bottle of Chardonnay and waved it in the air above her head.

"Let's get drunk! Maybe we can channel his spirit if we're drunk enough. Then we'll throw salt on his mean little ghost body and shrivel him up like a snail."

"I don't think so, Delia. That's a little too spooky for me," Catherine said, laughing weakly.

"Well, let's get drunk anyway. Maybe we can channel Princess Diana. I'd like to know if it's true what they say about men with jug ears."

Catherine laughed in earnest now and accepted the wine Delia offered her. "I've never heard that. What do they say about men with jug ears?"

"Wine goes right to their heads."

LATER IN THE EVENING, after a couple of glasses of wine, both the women were in better spirits. They had forgotten, for the moment, about Uncle Ted and were singing show tunes, country ballads, and old gospel hymns. Both were excellent singers. Delia had spent many hours rehearsing with her church and school choirs back in high school, and Catherine was an experienced musical theater performer. Despite their increasing inebriation, their voices blended beautifully in traditional harmonies.

During a pause in the singing, while Delia got another bottle of wine out of the fridge, Catherine asked, "Why did you *really* decide to become a therapist, Delia?"

"I thought I told you." Delia slurred her words slightly. She carried the bottle of wine from the fridge over to the countertop, inserted the corkscrew with perfect accuracy, and popped the cork out.

"Ah, that's a satisfying sound, isn't it? I've always valued the potential I feel when I'm popping a cork."

She poured a glass for Catherine and then one for herself. They walked together back into the living room, where Delia had earlier built a small fire in the fireplace. She poked the wood with a cast iron poker and stood watching as the stirred embers danced upward and disappeared into the chimney.

"Delia, are you going to answer me?"

"I've been thinking about your question. Why did I get into this profession? I was always curious about the mind, how it works, what makes us do the things we do. That's why the indigenous people of the rain forest were so interesting. Their minds had not been corrupted by industrial life. But, that's not really why I became a therapist. Nothing dramatic ever happened to me when I was a child—that I can remember anyway. Oh, Daddy was too strict. Scared to death that I was going to get pregnant, or get a *reputation*. Mama was unhappy with the way her life turned out and took it out on us girls, blah, blah, blah. That's not enough to *wound* a person, is it?

"Nah," she said, answering her own question. "I was never raped, never seriously molested. I lost out on a couple of tenured professorships because I was a woman. That pissed me off. Like that old saying goes, I had to be twice as good at everything, in order to be considered half as good at anything. Eh, something like that."

She grinned at Catherine and downed her glass of wine.

"I didn't know you had any sisters," Catherine said.

"What?" Delia said.

"You said your mother took her unhappiness out on us girls."

"Oh," Delia hesitated, started to say something, and then paused again, looking slightly confused. "I must be getting really wasted. I meant me and my girlfriends. I could never bring anybody home with me because I couldn't trust what kind of mood Mama or Daddy were going to be in. They criticized me constantly. If I made an A minus instead of an A. If I was elected vice-president of some organization instead of president. Nothing was ever good enough for them. They'd always compare me to someone else. Yet, if I showed the least little bit of initiative or assertiveness in trying to get what I wanted, it didn't fall into their definition of what was appropriate female behavior.

"God, what a trap! You always have to be tougher and smarter than the boys, but make them think just the opposite. Them. I mean the boys. Not my parents. Got to make the boys feel good about themselves. Every fucking sentence out of your mouth has to affirm who they are!

"You know what pushed me into this line of work, Catherine? I wanted to change the world! A little megalomaniacal, don't you think." She laughed. "I wanted to open doors for myself and other women. I wanted to be valued for my intellect, not my looks or my body. That's pretty ordinary stuff, isn't if? Nothing dramatic about that.

"It was only after I had started my masters program that I understood the impact of sexism, and especially sexual violence, on our ability to sustain self esteem and a sense of personal safety. Then, I knew I was on to something I should do. Not to make myself into some sort of saint, because God knows I'm not, but how can I enjoy my success when my sisters are suffering? I mean *sisters* in the larger sense, you know? Not a blood sister."

"Sure." Catherine poked the dying embers of the fire. "Hey, do you know a song called *How Can I Miss You If You Won't Go Away*?"

Delia thought for a moment. "It's an old country song, right?"

"Yeah," Catherine said. "Let's sing it."

Then she shouted up toward the ceiling. "This one's for you, Uncle Ted!"

THIRTY-ONE

"You're starting to work my last nerve, Bell." Simone was teasing, but only a little. Otis Bell had been shifting and squirming in his seat for the past half hour like a potty-deprived four year old.

"I'm too big for this world, Rosenberg. Every time I have to sit cramped up like this, I feel like I'm going to jump out of my skin."

Simone liked Otis Bell. In fact, when the department had come up short a man, she'd requested Otis. She couldn't imagine another person, other than Marty, that she could tolerate in such close quarters for any length of time. Tina's precarious health situation had left her too vulnerable to trust herself around anyone who might want anything from her. She could do her job, she was sure of that, but the idea of small talk made her ill. Otis was a quiet, amiable man who kept his own counsel. He would do the job with a minimum of chatter.

Marty was the only person at the station who knew about her relationship with Tina, and he had been as steady in this crisis as he was in everything else. He was protective of her, but didn't overwhelm her. When the attack occurred, he had been on a romantic getaway to Branson, Missouri, with his wife Lyn. They'd stayed in a local B&B and attended a Clint Black concert. Prior to leaving for the trip, Marty had talked of nothing else for days.

After returning from the trip, Marty had said, "I never thought I'd see the day that I didn't enjoy a Clint Black show. I was so worried about you; I couldn't concentrate on a damn thing. Lyn, too. We're both so sorry. What can we do for you?"

"Nothing, partner," Simone had said, "just hang in there with me. I'll get through it."

"Just remember you don't have to go through it alone," Marty had said.

Simone smiled, sadly, at the memory of Marty's face. *Yes, I do partner*, she had thought. Marty had given her a quick hug. Over the next few days, he resumed treating her in his usual manner, but made fewer jokes. Neither of them felt like laughing. Simone had to carry on as if everything were going to work out. If she stopped to consider what she would do without Tina, she might get into her bed and never crawl out again.

Thank God, I have Minerva to look after, she thought. Minerva knew nothing of her relationship with Tina, only that a good friend was ill, and if she found Mom crying, that was the reason. At fourteen, Minerva provided plenty of distraction with her demands for privileges and clothes, her confusion about boys, grade worries, and at the same time, her irrepressible optimism and gangly forays into womanhood. For the first time ever, Simone welcomed the distraction of dealing with teenage angst! What would she do if anything happened to Minerva? Or Marty? Although Simone's profession exposed her to violence all the time, the attack on Tina had brought it home.

"You've been quiet all week, Rosenberg."

Otis had interrupted her thoughts just in time.

"Yeah. I'm enjoying the silence."

She opened the connection to Marty so that he could hear what she had to say next.

"You wouldn't believe what a chatterbox my regular partner is. Always talking your head off. Trying to tell you about the latest men's fashions, that kind of thing."

Otis laughed heartily. Marty was not known for being a snappy dresser. Once the Chief had accused him of sleeping in his clothes, falling out of bed, and coming to work. He'd cleaned up a little after that, but he had little interest in his looks, while Simone was meticulous about her appearance. Their differences in height, skin color, ethnic origins, religion and style might have made them immediately distrustful of each other, but just the opposite had happened. Because they were so markedly different, they had been able to immediately look beyond the surface and discover two kindred spirits. They were the squad's odd couple, but they felt like family to each other.

It was comforting for Simone to sit quietly in the car with Otis, a massive, dark-skinned man. He was six feet five and had to diet constantly to maintain a low enough weight to satisfy job standards. Poor Otis could never figure out why anyone had a problem with his weight. He felt good. He had plenty of energy. He could still kick just about anybody's ass that he wanted. Most criminals, at least the unarmed ones, took one look at him and decided to cooperate. Besides, his daddy had been big and his granddaddy before him. They both had lived well into their eighties. Just once, he'd like to feel that he had enough room in a seat.

Simone had always loved big men. Big men seemed more confident, more patient than the hamster-metabolism little guys. The little guys always had something to prove, fighting shadows and jumping at puffs of wind. Except Marty, of course. Her partner dispelled the stereotypes. He was a non-racist, non-sexist, highly intelligent, wiry little country guy who knew exactly who he was and what he wanted out of life.

"I bet she's not coming out tonight," Simone said, yawning deeply and stretching. "Probably inside crying on her shrink's shoulder. Why don't we . . ."

Before she could finish, they both saw the lights of an automobile moving slowly down the circular drive from Delia's house. The atmosphere in the unmarked car changed immediately.

"Well, now, looks like we might be partying tonight after all," Otis said, smiling broadly.

Catherine O'Donnell's white Honda wagon pulled past them and was illuminated for an instant by an overhead street light. Simone opened the link to Marty's ear.

"Snippy's on the move again, partner. She's a blonde tonight. Big hair."

Otis cast a quizzical glance at Simone before slipping the car into gear. "Snippy?" he asked.

Simone grinned. "It's a nickname Marty gave her, but don't let the Chief hear you use it. She don't find it too amusing."

Otis followed the Honda at a discreet distance. His adrenaline accelerated when Snippy pulled on to Interstate 285, headed squarely in the direction of the Rainbow's End.

"Marty, wake up. She's headed your way," Simone said.

Even though there were two other detectives on the way who would back Marty up inside the bar and an unmarked squad car stationed outside, anything could happen.

Simone and Otis followed the woman they believed to be Snippy to the parking lot of the Rainbow's End and watched from down the block while she pulled in, parked, and then fussed with her hair and make-up before getting out of the car. She was wearing a low-cut, tight pink sweater and a black leather mini-skirt. Her ratted blond wig hung in a cascading mass past her shoulders and bounced in sync with her swaying hips and the tapping rhythm of her stiletto heels.

"She's on the prowl for something, that's for sure," Simone said.

"Yeah, but is she a leopard or a vulture?"

"What do you mean?" Simone asked.

"She like her meat dead or alive?"

THIRTY-TWO

Inside the Rainbow's End bar, Cledith Waycross had planted two of the Patriot's best men. They had followed Marty and were waiting for the shit to hit the fan, as they had been for the past three weekends. Jimbo Clayton, who carried a small pipe bomb in his backpack, fit in seamlessly with the bar regulars. His bleached blond hair was cut short on the top and sides, but hung to his shoulders in the back. He had the perfect mullet cut—business in the front, party in the back. He wore jeans with torn knees and on the back of his tight fitting tee shirt was a large drawing of a sailboat partially capsized into a wave. Printed on the boat's protruding stern were the words, "MY DIXIE WRECKED."

The Rainbow's End had a loud jukebox, pool tables in a separate room, and one-dollar tequila shooters during happy hour. It was redneck heaven for southern rock and country musicians and blue collar types who clung to the notion that long hair kept them looking sexy, despite their protruding bellies and flabby arms. Half the men there had hair below their shoulders. Jimbo Clayton felt right at home in the bar and even danced a few times with a couple of girls, while keeping a casual eye on his backpack. At the right time, he planned to detonate the pipe bomb in the men's bathroom.

The other Patriot, Mitchell Harris, was packing a semi-automatic pistol with seven rounds and two mags holstered underneath a tailored navy sports jacket. Mitchell didn't fit the bar at all. He appeared frail, an anemic, professorial type with an occasional enigmatic smile that materialized at random, then switched back to dour as quickly as it had come. It was as if a cloud floated above him and changed the topography of his face by its shadows. Mitchell's assignment was to shoot the Robiotic as soon as the pipe bomb exploded, then dash out the emergency rear exit at the back of the building into the dark side of the parking lot and Cledith's waiting car. Cledith was counting on the cops being so concerned about Marty and the other detectives inside, they would allow a few people to escape before organizing themselves.

Oh, how Cledith had wanted to be the one to shoot the Robiotic, or at least set the bomb off. Col. Hargrove would surely award a Medal of Valor for that. He could only hope that he would get one for being Commander of the operation. No way could he hang out inside the bar without Marty recognizing him. He had played his hand with Marty, and he could kick himself for it. So he had to do the next best thing. He picked the two meanest fuckers in the outfit and went over the details until he was sure they knew what to do.

He wasn't worried about Mitchell. It wouldn't be the first time Mitchell had shot a woman. At the age of fifteen, he had blown a large hole through his mother's side. Fortunately, she had not died and never reported the assault. Took the blame for it herself. Said she was cleaning her gun. Talk around the county was that she had been too afraid to speak up. Talk also was that Mitchell was a pure, to the bone, certifiable, lunatic. Had that weird smile, and when he did talk, seemed like he was beaming himself in from a long way off. After he shot his mother, Mitchell never volunteered any information to anyone, but if asked straight out whether or not he did it, he just smiled.

To Cledith's thinking, Mitchell's history would work in favor of The Cause. If caught, he most likely wouldn't give up the others, but even if he did, who would believe him? He'd already shot his mother. Everybody in town knew it. Wouldn't be hard to pin a crackpot label on him.

Jimbo Clayton, however, was another story. The guy had

never finished anything in his life. He was almost forty, lived off his girlfriend, and smoked dope all day while watching sitcom reruns, game shows, and television evangelists. He saw himself as some kind of fine-looking gift to the ladies. Cledith wasn't sure Jimbo could even remember the simple instructions for final assembly of the pipe bomb once he was in the bathroom, though any sixth grader could probably do it. Jimbo Clayton could barely read and, with all the dope smoking, did well to remember his own address. Still, he was willing, and he was expendable. If the damn thing blew up in his hands, no big loss. Cledith secretly hoped it would. At least that was one way he could be sure Jimbo would keep his big mouth shut.

The bomb had a timer on it that would give Jimbo ten minutes to get away from the bar. Cledith told him at least twenty times to drink only soft drinks and to pay his bar tab before he went in to set the bomb, but he could never be sure Jimbo would remember. Jimbo would grin at him and say, "you betcha booties, granny!" Cledith almost decked him every time he did it, since Jimbo was supposed to salute snappily and say, "yes sir!"

In the dark of his car, alone, impatiently scanning the a.m. radio stations from one conservative rant to the next, Commander Cledith Waycross waited for the explosion and the two men who would come running out to the car. He studied the problems confronting his Patriot force, turning them over and over in his mind. He shook his head and said out loud, drowning out the pontificating Rush Limbaugh for a moment, "Citizen militia. Damn fine idea! Too bad our founding fathers didn't know half the fucking citizens would be stone cold imbeciles by the twentieth century."

THIRTY-THREE

Simone and Otis were to park outside until Marty and Snippy came out, and then follow them. The plan was that Marty would appear to be already drunk when Snippy arrived. Docile as a lamb, he would allow her to lead him out without slipping him a roofie. The bartender had already been alerted to serve Marty from a specially mixed bottle of bourbon—one that had plenty of food coloring and only a hint of alcohol. Just enough to get the smell on his breath. For good measure, Marty had splashed a little bourbon on his shirt collar.

Marty's biggest challenge for the evening wouldn't be from the suspect, but from a bad cold he'd had for a week. In the last couple of days he'd developed flu symptoms with a high spiking fever and sleepless nights. He was miserable, weak, and, unfortunately, stuck with the assignment.

When the buxom blonde walked into the bar shortly before two a.m., he couldn't be certain it was Catherine O'Donnell. He had seen her only on stage and in her publicity photo on the theater wall. She looked markedly different from any of the characters she had played. The massive wig was pouffed so far out on the sides that her face appeared to be much thinner than he remembered. She had a large black beauty mark on her right cheek. Her eyes were dark brown and smaller than he remembered, which he reasoned could have been caused by her thick false eyelashes, caked with mascara, and eye shadow. Her nose was different too. Larger, he thought. She was wearing so much make-up that her face reminded him of a mannequin, unreadable and lifeless, yet oddly compelling. It could be her. She was the right height and weight.

She sat at a table by herself and ordered a glass of white wine. That surprised him. Snippy usually drank only soft drinks. She had hardly glanced at Marty, but he could tell she had noticed him. He wanted to summon her over right away, but was afraid he would spook her, so he waited, sipping his bourbon scented water. He wasn't the only man in the bar who had noticed her. He saw a few old boys eyeballing her and wondered how long it would be before one of them made his move. Still he waited. He had to guard against entrapment on this one. He wanted her to make all the moves and, especially, to invite him to leave with her.

Marty got up from his table and stumbled over toward the jukebox. Only half of his drunken stumble was acting. His fever had kicked in. He felt light-headed and almost delirious. About halfway to the jukebox, he started swaying to the country song that was playing, swiveling and jutting his pelvis, staggering. *Glad Simone's not in here*, he thought. *She'd blow the cover laughing her ass off at me.* He winked at a gap-toothed old woman who was leaning over a half-empty glass of beer, and awkwardly threw her a kiss. He studied the jukebox selection carefully while bouncing his rear in Snippy's direction, and finally settled on three of the saddest country ballads he could find. On the way back to his table, he grinned like a satyr in Snippy's general direction.

After Marty sat down, Snippy moseyed over to his table, smiling at several of the men as she passed. "Do I know you from somewhere?" she asked, as she sat in the chair across from him. Her accent was thickly southern and slightly slurred as if she had been drinking before coming to the bar.

"I don't think so. I woulda remembered you."

He leered at her. "You wanna drink?"

"You look so familiar. I just know I've seen you before. Do you go to the New Canaan Church?"

"No ma'am. I have to confess . . . I ain't going to church

right now. I just got saved, found the Lord Jesus Christ, and he has lifted me up like I never thought I could be lifted. That was in prison, ma'am. I ain't been out long. I just ain't found the right church yet."

"Goodness. I've never known anybody that's been in prison before. What did you do?"

"Something awful, ma'am. I'd be ashamed to tell a nice lady like you what it was. But, hallelujah, the merciful Lord, through his only Son Jesus, cleansed me of my sins. Praise Jesus! Hallelujah!"

Marty raised both hands palm up into the air and shook his body in a gesture of complete, thorough, drunken surrender. Marty had grown up in the church and had watched his uncles and cousins, and even his own father, on occasion, get sloppy drunk and sentimental over the role Jesus had played in their lives.

"Yes, ma'am, He give me a new start. I ain't gone blow it. I sure wish you'd let me buy you a drink."

"All right," she said. "Just one. A glass of white wine. You ought to check out New Canaan Church. It's over on Ashley Street, near Grant Park."

Marty whistled for the waitress and ordered each of them a drink.

"You're the closest thing to an angel I ever seen." He leaned across the table and looked down her blouse. "You'll have to 'scuse me 'cause I'm pretty drunk, but I don't believe I've ever seen a better body on anybody."

The blonde rolled her eyes at him.

"Now don't get huffy on me. You ain't mad are you? I bet I ain't telling you something you don't already know. I told you I was drunk. Hey, you ever hear the expression 'built like a brick shit house?' Baby, you must be the architect's original design that everbody else just tries to copy."

The blonde stared at him, her expression a mixture of disgust and anger, veneered over with a self-effacing smile. He still couldn't tell if she was Catherine. She was definitely in the same age range, about the same size and build. Her voice was different, but hell the night he saw her, she had four completely different voices.

"What's your name, pretty lady," he said.

"Cathy," she said.

This threw Marty, as well as Simone, Otis and the other detectives listening in on Marty's rendezvous. Cathy, short for Catherine? Well, why not? Maybe she's getting cocky, he thought. Over confident, I mean. He didn't dare use the word cocky, even in his own head. He could feel the delirious hilarity of the idea bubbling up inside his fevered brain, and he coughed vigorously to keep from laughing out loud. She was getting cocky all right. Maybe she wanted to get caught. Maybe she just used her real name by accident, but that didn't seem likely. She'd been so careful up to now. Maybe it wasn't her.

"What's your name?"

"Billy."

"Can you bake a cherry pie, Billy boy, Billy boy? Can you bake a cherry pie, charming Billy?" She sang the song lightly, teasing him. She reached over and stroked the top of his hand with her finger.

"Ain't no cherries around here that I can see, but I can eat a pie, if you know what I mean," Marty said, leering.

Cathy's eyes went cold. She stood up to leave.

"Wait a minute, baby," he said, grabbing her by the wrist. "Don't be mad. I was just teasing you, like you was me. Listen I got me a bad cold and I'm probably just not thinking clear. Stay here. Come on, baby." He sniffled pitifully to try for sympathy.

She settled back down into the chair. "Don't think you can say just any old thing you please. I may be sitting alone in a bar, but I am a lady. I just like to relax and listen to the jukebox on a Saturday night, maybe meet some nice folks. That doesn't make me into any kind of loose woman. When I am invited to join someone at his table, I expect him to behave. Do you understand me, Billy?"

"Yes, ma'am, I sure do. I don't know what got into me. My mama raised me better than that. Maybe it's the pills I been taking. See, I'm taking these pills from the doctor for my nerves. They're supposed to make me relax and sleep better. On top of that, I'm taking this cold and fever medicine. You spend a little time in prison and you come out a nervous wreck, believe me. The pills don't seem to be mixing too good with all this booze. Maybe I wasn't supposed to drink with 'em. Whaddya think?"

Marty had begun to slur his words and appeared to have trouble focusing his eyes. "I ought to get on home before I get myself in too much trouble."

He rose from the table with great difficulty and staggered toward the front door.

THIRTY-FOUR

The two Patriots, Mitchell Harris and Jimbo Clayton, had been sitting close and were able to hear most of Marty's conversation. When Marty appeared to stumble while getting up from the table, Mitchell's eyes took on an otherworldly glow. The enigmatic smile flitted across his face and he leaned towards Jimbo and whispered, "Go set it off, boy. That's our Robiotic over there."

The first serious dilemma of Jimbo Clayton's forty years of life hit him. It rattled around in his head like a motorcycle racing inside a cylindrical wire cage. Round and round it spun, flinging his spare thoughts into a vast and terrible void. He had never really believed he would have to set the bomb off. He thought he would just hang out in the bar every weekend on Cledith's dime. Now that the time was here, he couldn't go through with it. What if somebody else got killed? What if she wasn't the Robiotic, but just some good-looking girl stupid enough to like Marty?

"I don't think that's her," Jimbo said. "She looks too much like a real girl."

"What the hell did you think she'd look like, fool? You ever met a real girl with a body like that?" Mitchell Harris looked ready to deck Jimbo.

"Matter of fact, I have, asshole, and don't call me no fool," Jimbo said.

"Get in the bathroom and set that thing up, or so help me

Jimbo, I'll shoot you instead of her."

Jimbo reluctantly picked up his backpack and headed for the men's room. What he hadn't told Mitchell was that the pipe bomb was a dud. He hadn't packed anything but an aluminum pipe filled with sand and ball bearings and a timer stuck on the front. Now, what was he going to do? That crazy motherfucker might really shoot him.

He checked to be sure the bathroom stalls were empty and then stood in front of the mirror. He frowned at the pimple that had recently puffed up next to his left nostril. *I was having such a good time. Why'd she have to show up?* He ran his hand through his hair and fluffed out the ends. *Better do something soon.* The only thing he could do was pretend he had planted the bomb and get the hell out of there. He would just play dumb with Mitchell and Cledith. He'd say, "I don't know why the damn thing didn't go off. Maybe somebody found it and took it apart."

He stuffed his backpack into a cabinet underneath the sink, took a piss, and then messed with his hair for a couple of minutes longer to kill enough time to make it seem like he was setting it up. He was sorry it was going to be over. Playing war in the bar every weekend was the most fun he'd had in his life—even if his playmate was old sourpuss Mitchell. When he walked back into the bar, he licked his upper lip twice, signaling Mitchell that everything was ready. Then he proceeded to stroll out the front door, down the block, and climbed into the front passenger seat of Cledith's Ford Bronco.

"How'd it go?" Cledith asked.

"It's all set up, sir. Yes sir. Mitch better get ready 'cause it's gonna go boom in about five minutes. Yep. You betcha booties, granny."

THIRTY-FIVE

Marty had gotten about halfway across the room when the woman calling herself Cathy caught up with him, put her arm around his shoulder, and carefully guided him back to the table.

"You can't drive in your condition," she said, as he plopped back down into a chair. "You'll wreck for sure. You live close by?"

"Yeah, but I'm staying with Mama 'til I can get my own place. She wouldn't take it too good if some strange lady come home with me this late at night. Even a angel like you, darling. I'll be all right."

"I'm staying at a motel not too far from here. I'll take you there. It's got a coffee maker in the room, and we can get you sobered up. Then, I'll drive you back over here to get your car. But, you've got to promise me, no funny stuff. I'm not taking you there for romance. You understand, Billy?"

"Yes ma'am. Clear as a Georgia summer sky."

Marty paused and grinned as if he was about to say a big joke. "Hey, you ain't that crazy bitch . . .er, sorry Cathy ... I mean that lady that's been . . . well, you know . . . cutting on men, are you?"

"Me? No way. I like my men with all their equipment attached. Especially their brains. That is what you guys think with, isn't it?"

Marty nodded and grinned. Snippy helped him to his feet

and together they struggled out the front door and headed in the direction of her car.

THIRTY-SIX

Mitchell Harris watched helplessly as the couple left before Jimbo's bomb went off. Should he shoot the Robiotic and just take the fall for it? Cold-blooded murder in front of a bar full of witnesses? Maybe he could explain what a Robiotic was. What a threat they were to the white man. Would Colonel Hargrove back him up? Would Cledith?

He jumped from his seat and followed the Robiotic out the door. She looked distracted having to hold Marty upright. Mitchell could blow her electronic head into a million component parts. That would prove everything. Little pieces of wire and memory chips scattered over the parking lot, blown into the walls of the building. By God, he'd be famous. The first man to expose the government's ugly plot against the rightful heirs to this country. His right hand gripped the semi-automatic butt in his pocket. He edged the gun slowly upward.

What if her head looked just like anybody else's on the inside? Maybe the government had figured a way to make computer parts out of human tissue. Maybe the electronics was in some building in Washington, remote controlling the Robiotic.

He could do it anyway. Was he willing to die for his country? Could he be a martyr like Tim McVeigh, or David Koresh down in Waco? He thought long and hard on that question while watching the Robiotic bump and wobble her way with Marty barely under control. In a flash, he had his answer. No. He could not be a martyr for one simple reason. There was no cause for which he would give up his life without a fight. He did not want to die. He wanted to kill. Simple as that. He hurried over to hook up with Cledith and Jimbo. That bomb would be going off any minute. They needed to get the hell out of there.

THIRTY-SEVEN

Simone and Otis in their unmarked car, and two other detectives in another, watched Marty's drunken struggle to situate himself into the passenger seat of Snippy's car.

"He look like he's really drunk to you, Otis?" Simone asked.

"Yeah, maybe Snippy slipped the drug in his drink somehow."

Otis worried that they had missed something. "I'll alert Albertson to check with that bartender. Make sure he was giving Marty the flavored water."

"He's been really sick for days," Simone said. "His wife tried to talk him out of working tonight. Said he was too weak."

SNIPPY PULLED OUT OF THE PARKING LOT and, shortly thereafter, the small caravan of cops pulled out behind her. Commander Cledith Waycross eased his black Ford Bronco into gear and followed the cops from a cautious distance. Jimbo Clayton rode shotgun up front and Mitchell Harris hunkered down in the back seat, glaring at the party side of Jimbo's hairdo.

"Wadn't that bomb supposed go off ten minutes ago?" Cledith's voice was doused with sarcasm.

"I don't know what happened, sir. I set it up right. Maybe the cops found it and dismantled it. Yeah, I bet that's what happened. You betcha . . ."

Before he could say "booties," Cledith snapped, "You sure as hell better hope they didn't, you moron. You probably engraved our fucking names on the pipe. You're coming over here first thing in the morning and see if it's still in there"

Jimbo's breath caught in his throat. He had thought of doing just that. Not their names, but the Patriot insignia. Just a little symbolic thing for his own amusement. It was gonna get blowed up anyway. What difference would it make? But, since he had chickened out, he was glad now he hadn't done it.

Jimbo turned away from Cledith and stared at his own simple, clueless, reflection in the passenger side window. His image flashed on and off as the car passed under the streetlights. He hoped Cledith couldn't see the flush he felt creeping up his neck into his cheeks.

Mitchell Harris leaned forward from the back seat and blew on the back of Jimbo's neck. "What did you do in the bathroom, dickhead, play with yourself?"

His whisper held a sweetness that sent terror traveling down Jimbo's spine. Startled, Jimbo yelled, "I'm telling you both. I set that bomb up just the way we practiced. I swear, man. You know me. I wouldn't do nothing to mess things up!"

"We'll see, you mullet-headed bozo. If you've fucked me up, it's the last time. You hear me?" Mitchell Harris leaned forward and twisted Jimbo's head around to the side so they were face to face. He squeezed Jimbo's cheeks together.

"Ow. Fuck man," Jimbo said, barely able to get the words out, as his mouth had been forced into the shape of a baby's impotent pucker.

"Me and you got some talkin' to do, boy."

Mitchell let go of Jimbo's face and turned his attention towards Cledith. "We gone follow the cops, Commander? Maybe see if there's a opportunity?"

"Yeah, we'll keep atter 'em for awhile. They probably ain't gone let us get nowhere near that thing, but I think we ought to stake 'em out. What's that saying? 'Luck is being ready when the opportunity strikes.' We sure spent a lot of time getting ready for this. We'll follow along and see if we can get a hit at it."

"Well, hell, ain't that what we been planning to do? Just get a shot off at the damn thing." Jimbo rubbed his still smarting cheeks.

Cledith looked sharply in Jimbo's direction. "Yeah, boy, but on our terms. Not theirs. Ain't you learned nothing from me after all the training we went through? Now, since you fucked up the bomb, we got to do it on their terms. We want to live to fight again, don't we? You want to get your ass shot up tonight 'cause we ain't ready?"

"Naw," Mitchell Harris chimed in. "Jimbo don't want to mix it up tonight, do you, boy? Jimbo wants to come out with me to my house. We'll drink us some rum and cokes in the living room while he tells me his grand theory on how come that simple, any-idiot-in-the-third-grade-coulda-made-one, bomb didn't blow up in the bathroom. Ain't that right, boy?"

"I can't tonight," Jimbo said, trying to disguise the tremor in his voice. "I got to get right home after this 'fore my girlfriend calls the police on me. She said the next time I don't show up before morning, she was gone have 'em out looking for me. I'm serious, Mitchell. The first place they'll go to is your house." Jimbo laughed nervously and stuttered. "She-she-she don't like you too much."

Mitchell's evil smile camped out on his face for all of three seconds and then dissolved. "She-she-she don't like me, huh? Well, maybe I ought to persuade her-her-her different. What you think about that, boy?"

Jimbo turned his head again to his pale reflection in the side window. He held on to the armrest and took a deep breath. He was dizzy and terrified he would throw up.

"Cut the shit out," Cledith barked. "Ya'll gone let one little setback make you lose your loyalty to each other? Hell, I want to kill this thing ever bit as much as you do, and I got a lot more to lose. If we fail, Colonel Hargrove's probably gone take my command away. My cousin Marty'll still be out there thinking he's so much smarter than me. Lula havin' to put up with them always looking down on her. I want this too, damn it.

"But you know what I say? I say to hell with 'em! That's what I say. If we miss this one and them damn Robiotics is as plentiful as the Colonel says, we can start our own branch of the movement. They's ample to go around, right? Another day—a better day—is coming for the Patriots. I know it like I know my own name, men, so don't lose heart. We got to stick together. This is just the beginning."

Maybe, thought Mitchell Harris, hunkered down in the back seat, longing for the sweet release that violence would bring him. Whether they got the Robiotic or not, Jimbo Clayton would be sorry he ruined the night. He would be sorry for the rest of his wretched life. Mitchell Harris would see to that.

THIRTY-EIGHT

In order to prevent the woman, whom he was now convinced was Snippy, from noticing the tail on them, Marty began to mutter and slowly worked himself up to barely controlled weeping.

After listening for awhile, Simone said to Otis, "We may have created a monster. Marty sounds like a country version of Dirty Harry on ludes."

"I don't know what I done to deserve such a angel with me tonight. God must be watching out for me," Marty said and blew his nose into a cotton handkerchief.

"I guess I am an angel, sort of. Who else is going to help you get relief from your urges," Snippy said.

"Whaddya mean?" Marty said. "What urges?"

"Oh, you know, the urge to drink too much. The urge to talk nasty to a woman like you were doing to me in the bar."

Snippy glared in Marty's direction.

After a short ride, when they arrived at the motel, Marty allowed her to help him into the room. The furnishings consisted of two orange vinyl chairs, a lumpy double bed, and a small television sitting on top of a three-drawer dresser. On the wall over the bed was a dust-covered print of a matador teasing a bull with a swirling red cape. A small black boom box sat beside the bed on the nightstand.

"This is a nice room," Marty said. "Is that the bathroom? I gotta take a piss."

He stumbled past Snippy before she could answer.

The bathroom looked as if it hadn't been updated since 1955, with pink and black tile and a narrow shower with a mildew-stained beige plastic curtain. Marty quickly pulled it aside to make sure no one was hiding behind it. A small window on one wall had been left open. The window was too small for him to squeeze through, but probably not for her. Someone had removed the screen.

"I'm making some coffee, Bill," Snippy yelled through the closed door. "Are you okay?"

Marty quickly flushed the toilet and ran the faucet as if he were washing his hands. He felt his stomach churning and contemplated sticking his finger down his throat, but he didn't know if that would make things worse. He knew Simone would have someone stationed outside the back of the motel by now, so he quickly waved out the window to let her know he was okay and went back into the bedroom.

The lights were low. *Probably to hide how much make up she's wearing.*

"I ain't ready to lose this nice buzz yet, baby," Marty said. "Why don't you come over here and talk to me."

"Now, I told you, Billy, I didn't bring you back here for monkey business. I'm just helping you get straightened up, and then you're on your way home." She smiled seductively and sauntered towards the bed with the coffee cup in her hand. "Why don't you take just one little sip of your coffee and tell me if you like it."

She stood directly in front of him. His eyes were level with her waist. He smiled as he looked up at her and held the cup to his lips. "Damn!" he said, spilling the drink on both of them as he jerked the cup away, "that liked to burned my lips off. I'll have to let it cool."

It wasn't that hot, she thought, and her internal dialog kicked into high gear. *Something about this guy isn't right.* Was he a cop? Once in group, Tina had described how cops behaved when they came into the jack shack. This guy was beginning to show all the signs.

She snatched the coffee away from him to save what was left in the cup. *I never got a chance to give him the roofie in the bar.* Not once did he leave his drink unattended. Cop or no, he was definitely not drunk. She'd been witness to plenty of bad acting in her life and was amazed that this twerp had managed to fool her.

Maybe this target should be left for God to handle on his own. She was getting tired of doing the work anyway. They just kept coming. Day after day after day. She was getting weary of it all.

"I think I'll call a taxi for you, Billy Boy. You're not interested in getting sober, are you?"

As she bent towards the nightstand to set the coffee cup down, he grabbed her around the waist and pulled her to him. "C'mon baby. You didn't really bring me here just to sober me up, did you? You know how long it's been since I even seen a woman like you?"

Take your fuckin' hands off me. "You're right, honey. I wanted you from the first moment I laid eyes on you in that bar. I bet you didn't know that, did you? But, you're too drunk, baby. You need to finish that coffee."

She brought the coffee cup back to his lips. He brushed it away with the back of his hand. "I don't want no damn coffee."

"Why don't you get comfortable? Take off your clothes."

He grinned lecherously. "You first."

"I won't take off my clothes, Billy Boy, but, you wait right here. I'll put on something real sexy just for you. Don't go away. I'll be right back."

While she was in the bathroom, Marty quickly unbuttoned his shirt. He jerked the tape from around his chest, pulling a little hair off with it, and removed the bug. He whispered into the microphone, "If I stop talking, get your asses in here."

Marty quickly slid the bug under the bed and left his shirt unbuttoned. He opened the front door and poured the coffee out, waving to the empty night before going back in.

"I'm drinking the coffee just like you wanted, baby. Tastes good," he yelled towards the bathroom door.

THIRTY-NINE

Fortunately for Patriots Cledith, Jimbo and Mitchell, the old motel was just off the expressway. Trees, brush, and debris lined one end of its parking lot, giving them an opportunity to hide their actions and the possibility of a fast getaway. After parking on a side street out of sight of the police and surveying the situation carefully, Mitchell exited the Bronco and crawled through the brush until he had a perfect line of fire. While the parking lot lights were far enough away to keep him in darkness, they provided enough illumination on the detectives' vehicles and the motel room where Marty and the Robiotic were apparently engaged.

Cledith and Jimbo stayed in the car, and were cranked and ready to peel off, if necessary. Mitchell would get off a shot if he could and then haul ass back through the small patch of woods, jump in, and the three of them would slip back onto the freeway before the cops knew what hit them.

Mitchell Harris lay on his stomach, waiting. The ground was damp and cold, but he barely felt it. This was his moment and he could already hear the commendation speech from Colonel Hargrove. "For his bravery in destroying the first Robiotic, my new Commander for the Southern Patriots is . . ."

FORTY

After waving out the front door, Marty quickly returned to the bed, flopped down on it, and lay with his hands crossed behind his head.

"Are you ready for me?" Cathy murmured urgently through the closed door.

"Hell, yeah, baby, I been ready. I finished my cup of coffee, and I'm clear-headed as I need to be. Come on and show me what you got."

When Snippy walked through the door, Marty burst into laughter. "Whaddya think this is, Halloween?" He sat up on the edge of the bed.

She was wearing a harem costume, complete with veil and multiple scarves, which floated around her as she twirled into the room. She hit the play button on the boom box and soft Middle Eastern music filled the room.

"How do I look? Sexy?" She moved sinuously around the room.

"Sure, baby, but why go to the trouble? You'd look hot in a potato sack."

"This outfit belongs to a friend of mine. She's in the hospital right now, and I thought it might be fun to wear it. Do I turn you on?"

"Sure baby. You move like a harem girl straight out of the desert. Why's your friend in the hospital?"

"She was just another gazelle, Billy Boy."

"What's that supposed to mean?" Marty sat up against the headboard.

"You ought to know. You're a man who likes to stalk women, aren't you, Billy?"

She danced effortlessly, as if in a trance. "You chase after them. Wait until they take a short cut through an alley. Wait until they're fumbling for their keys. Wait until they're asleep in their own homes. Life for a woman is like being a gazelle in the Serengeti, Billy Boy.

"You ever see those travel documentaries on TV? Any second, some beast can pop out and take you down by the throat. The only difference is, in the Serengeti, the gazelles don't expect another gazelle to eat them. They expect a cheetah or a lion. It's easier to smell the enemy sneaking up if it's another species. You know what I mean?"

Marty nodded. Between the music and the veil covering her mouth, he could barely understand what she was saying. She sounded as if she had marbles in her cheeks. She continued to dance a strange blend of belly dancing and plain old Southern hoochy-koo, but Marty had to admit she was incredibly sexy. She moved to within reach of him, and then waltzed away, swaying and pumping her hips provocatively. She pulled one of the scarves from her slim waist and draped it around his shoulders. Then, she pulled another from across her breasts, exposing a spangled bra beneath. Her perfume was intoxicating.

"How'd you like the coffee, baby," she asked. "Feeling better?"

"Oh, yeah," he said, pretending to nod drowsily. "How'd you make that stuff? Tasted better than anything I've ever had."

"It's my special recipe. I thought I told you to get undressed. That's a fine looking chest, you got there. Why don't you show me the rest of you?"

"I'm shy," he said, grinning.

Her heart began to pound. Her internal dialog kicked into overdrive. *This guy's a cop.* In retrospect, it seemed so obvious. A newspaper article practically inviting her to show up at the bar. *What felon advertises that he's hanging out in bars? The whole religion angle. The cops knew she was on a mandate from God. How could she have been so stupid?*

She could hear the moaning wind within her whipping up a frenzy. *Run it said, RUN.* She had known this day would come, and now that it was here, there was a relief to it. The only question was how would it end? She said nothing, but began to whirl like a dervish, around and around the room, her arms spread akimbo. *She must think! He had not swallowed the roofie. He was perfectly sober and capable of overpowering her.* Without the drug to equalize them, she was just another potential victim waiting in a seedy motel. She listened for the guidance from within. Cacophonic voices fought for dominance and she couldn't make out a word.

Do not abandon me now in my hour of need, oh God.

Marty watched with fascination. The dance was beautiful and desperate and somewhat grotesque, too. He felt she was spinning out of control and so far, he had gotten nothing from her.

"Hey, can I play too?" he asked.

She stopped spinning and slowly focused her eyes on him.

"Only if you take off your clothes. That's the only way I can take care of you."

"Whaddya gonna do to take care of me?" Marty asked.

"I could cure everything that ails you. You do want me, don't you Billy Boy?"

"Well sure I do, baby," Marty said.

She walked around and stood by the side of the bed, smiling. She stroked his arm. "Take off your shirt, Billy."

Marty complied, hoping there were no noticeable tape marks on his chest.

She sat down on the edge of the bed beside him. She gently stroked his chest and moved her hand down towards his belt buckle.

As she started to unbuckle him, Marty said, "Whoa baby, not so fast."

"I thought you wanted me," she said.

"Well, I do, but I like to do my own unzipping."

"Go ahead." She waited patiently, listening for any direction from above.

Marty reached for his zipper, thinking he would fumble with his pants to buy time. She leaned forward over him as if to give him a kiss on the neck.

"You know what, baby," he said, "I . . ."

Before he knew what was happening, Snippy jerked the veil from her face and blew a small dart into the side of his neck.

"What the hell!" Marty jerked the dart out of his neck. He tried to reach for the woman, but his arm fell lifelessly to the mattress. She appeared to float away from him in slow motion. He couldn't lift his arms. He couldn't move his head. He felt the bile of panic rising up into his throat and then, just as quickly as it had come, he found himself completely undisturbed by his new predicament. He smiled. He floated above the bed, saw himself lying on it, and smiled again, broadly. He was completely at peace.

"Wow," he said.

This was the best moment of his life. The mundane struggles and worry of his entire life . . . what had it all been about? He could just float out of the room and off into the heavens and never come back. A new reality moved around and through him in sensual waves, touching the core of his being, with a lightness he had never experienced before.

Snippy smiled back at him. He was immobilized now, as the others had been. She could finish what she had come to do, but should she? This one was a cop. He probably hadn't raped anyone or molested children.

Maybe he was a good man. Maybe. Did it really matter? They're all part of the problem. Unwilling to share power with women. Unwilling to take up the cause of sexual violence because ultimately it wasn't their problem. They were the privileged gender, with their unreasonable expectations of life-long servitude, dinner on the table, freshly washed clothes, every need handled by some subservient little woman. **There are no good ones***, her inner dialogue told her, as she unpacked her surgical supplies and looked down at the grinning, immobile Marty.*

FORTY-ONE

Out in the parking lot, Simone and Otis had watched Marty empty the coffee cup outside the front door. They had heard him remove the bug from his chest, as planned, and assumed from the shuffling noises that he had placed it under the bed. From that moment on, the sound quality had deteriorated to a low buzz of voices, indistinct and cartoonish.

"What do you think happened?" Simone asked Otis. They were straining to hear the conversation inside the room.

"Sounds like the wire's compromised," Otis said. "Those damn things break too easy. I've seen it before. Complained about it too, but nothing ever gets done."

As if in answer to the unspoken question that hung between them in the claustrophobic space of the car, Simone said, "Marty can take care of himself. No need to rush in there yet."

Otis shifted uncomfortably behind the steering wheel. "Yeah. Long as we can make out the deeper voice, we know he's talking to her."

However, the last few seconds had become uncomfortably quiet. They could hear moaning and the sound of someone rustling around on the bed, but no actual words.

"Maybe she's not Snippy. She just likes getting her freak on with the low downs."

"Yeah, and Marty's finally decided to cheat on his wife. I don't think so." Simone jerked her door open and darted for the motel room. "It's too quiet in there. Let's move."

They covered the distance from the car to the room in a matter of seconds. Otis kicked the door open on the first try. "Police!" he shouted, as he lunged through, his gun held high. Simone was close behind on his heels.

Lying before them on the bed was Marty Sloan, grinning like he was having the time of his life. Standing with her back to them beside the bed was a woman in a harem dancer's outfit. The scalpel she held poised above Marty's groin glinted in the yellow porch light that flooded the room from the open doorway.

"Drop the weapon now and put your hands behind your head," Simone said.

The woman hesitated.

"Do it now!" Simone barked.

The woman slowly opened her hand and the scalpel landed with a soft thump upon the bed next to Marty's hips. She lifted her arms straight up and then clasped them behind her head. She inhaled deeply and straightened herself to an erect, proud posture.

"Now, walk over to that wall and put your hands on it. Spread your legs and don't move." Simone frisked the woman, handcuffed her, and stepped away.

Simone glanced in Marty's direction. "Is he okay, Otis?"

After covering Marty with a blanket, Otis checked his pulse and had already radioed for an ambulance. "Yeah, but he's higher than a kite. Can't wipe that stupid grin off his face."

Simone returned her attention to the handcuffed woman facing the wall. "Turn around and don't make any sudden moves. You understand? Don't try anything. You just hurt my partner, and I might just be looking for any excuse to shoot you. You understand?"

The woman turned, without a hint of shame, and faced Simone. Her eyes blazed; her face, every facet of her bearing showed pride. She had done her job. She was the avenging angel who showed up, wherever she was needed.

At first Simone didn't recognize her. The blond wig, a prosthetic nose for sure, something odd about her cheekbones; she was a master of make-up.

"Are you Catherine O'Donnell?"

The woman didn't answer, but stared straight ahead focusing on something in the distance.

"Oh my God!" The realization hit Simone like a shock wave. "Dr. Whitfield."

FORTY-TWO

Shortly after taking Delia into custody, an ambulance arrived at the motel. Under Otis' careful supervision, the EMTs readied Marty for transport to Peachtree Memorial Hospital. Simone read Delia her rights and then manhandled her out the door towards the awaiting patrol car.

Just as Simone was about to open the back door to the squad car and shove Delia inside, she heard the distinctive crack of a discharged weapon, saw a blue puff of smoke from the trees across the parking lot, and was jerked off her feet by the dead weight that Delia Whitfield had become in a split second.

Otis, who had just stepped outside the motel room door, opened fire in the direction of the trees, aiming for the lone figure he saw scurrying through the woods. A few seconds later, he heard another shot, and after that, the unmistakable squealing of tires fishtailing at high speed.

FORTY-THREE

The Atlanta Times, September 15, 1997

PROMINENT PHYSICIAN ARRESTED FOR SERIAL ASSAULTS
By Elizabeth Reed-Monroe
Staff Writer

Shortly before six a.m. this morning, Dr. Delia Whitfield, a local psychologist specializing in the treatment of rape victims, was injured while being taken into custody for attempted assault with a deadly weapon against Atlanta detective Martin Sloan. According to a police spokesman, a bullet fired by Mitchell Harris of Holden County grazed Dr. Whitfield's head. Dr. Whitfield is currently in stable condition at Peachtree Memorial Hospital.

Seconds after Dr. Whitfield was shot, police reported hearing a second shot. They later found the body of Harris, who had been killed by an unknown assailant. The Atlanta Police Department currently has no leads on who might have shot Mitchell Harris.

In addition to the attempted assault charge against her, Dr. Whitfield is a suspect in a series of mutilations against men in the Atlanta area beginning in January of this year.

Gloria Allgood, attorney and spokeswoman for Dr.

Whitfield, stated that the doctor had been suffering from secondary posttraumatic stress disorder, (SPTSD) a relatively rare condition that occurs among emergency personnel, police officers, therapists, military spouses, and others who are intimately involved in caring for victims of physical or psychological injury. Allgood described Dr. Whitfield's condition as a "situation where the therapist had become too strongly identified with her patients and had begun to experience their traumas as her own."

Allgood further stated "Dr. Delia Whitfield is a highly respected member of the health care community in Atlanta and has been a driving force in the movement to provide better services to sexual assault victims. She simply pushed herself to the brink of exhaustion in her desire to save the lives of others. What she needs now is help, not punishment."

FORTY-FOUR

Jimbo Thorton and Cledith Waycross now had a secret that neither of them could ever share with anyone, not if they valued their freedom. After speeding away from the immediate vicinity of their crime, they had slowed down and blended into traffic on I-75. They parted company that night and were never seen together again.

Like many a scoundrel before him, Cledith went to church the next Sunday and dedicated himself to a more refined pursuit of white supremacy. Jimbo went back to hanging out on the couch, cowering and panicking whenever he heard any scratching sound, or any loud pop that could not be easily identified. No matter how the newspapers spun the story, they were both convinced that they had played an important role in shooting the first known Robiotic and would wait for the rest of the world to catch up to them.

On the night of the shooting, Mitchell Harris had come running up to the car in a state of excitement that Jimbo could see was nothing but bloodlust. He knew Mitchell would want more. My blood, he had thought, and in a split second of clarity, he had grabbed the pistol that Cledith kept underneath the passenger seat and had shot Mitchell in the head at point blank range. He watched him fall to the ground, saw the devilish light leave his eyes.

"Why the hell did you do that?" Cledith had demanded, as he slammed the car into gear and sped away.

"What was I supposed to do? Wait for him to get me drunk and kill me? Wait for him to rape my girlfriend? Cold day in hell when I do that. Yeah buddy. You betcha booties granny. I wudn't gone do that."

FORTY-FIVE

One Month Later

Simone waited anxiously beside Tina's bed, willing her to wake up. Tina was now in a private room after having been taken out of an induced coma a couple of weeks prior. She was making progress, but so far had been unable to speak. It was clear, though, that she recognized Simone and responded to her gentle caresses and soft lullabies with a lop-sided effort at smiling.

Simone had a surprise for Tina today that she knew would be just the tonic her darling needed. Outside the room, waiting for his cue to come in, was Tina's baby brother Jade. Simone had pulled every string she knew, contacted the NYPD, and had gotten the names of Jade's adoptive parents. They were happy to make the connection, since Jade had never forgotten Tina and wanted more than anything to find her.

Finally, Simone could wait no longer. She opened the door and pulled Jade into the room. The doctor had advised them to give Tina a chance to recognize Jade first. If she could remember him on her own, the prognosis for recovery would be better.

Simone patted Tina's hand. "Wake up, sweetheart," she said, softly. "There's someone here to see you."

Tina flipped Simone's hand away and groaned.

"Come on, sugar plum. This is one visitor you want to see."

Tina slowly opened her eyes. She saw her beloved Simone and struggled to focus on the small, dark haired man standing beside her. She could feel the grinding connections in her brain, cranking in this new alien rhythm. Was this someone she knew? He looked familiar, but her mind was jumping around. *Was this some ex-john? Why would Simone bring an ex-john to the hospital? She must know about the jack shack by now. Was Simone trying to punish her? Was Simone going to arrest her? No, she was legitimate now, wasn't she? She had paid her birth debt. It was okay for her to be in the world now.*

The dark haired man leaned closer to her face and whispered, "Do you know me, Teenie?"

She felt his soft breath on her skin. *Teenie? Who called her Teenie? Someone from long ago. Maybe.* She inhaled his scent. *Smells like . . . app . . . can . . . what's the freaking word?* She couldn't name his cologne. He wasn't one of the doctors. She wasn't afraid of him.

"I've missed you so much. I tried to find you."

He bent forward and rested his head lightly on her chest. He began to weep, soundlessly, small choked off sobs, careful not to hurt her, but he could no longer deny himself the embrace of the first person who had truly loved and cared for him.

She closed her eyes and the next thing she knew, she was at Coney Island riding the merry-go-round with a small Chinese king mounted proudly on the ornate pony beside her. Around and around she flew, the ponies gliding up and down, she and the tiny king in a mismatched sequence. He's up, she's down. She's up, he's down. He was laughing, staring at her, willing her to know him. A thought came to her, not quite revealing itself, just lurking somewhere behind her eyes . . . *Why it's none other than Good King . . .*

"*Good King Who?*" she thought.

She could feel the word forming, like a cloud slowly pulling itself together and squeezing through a tunnel, rushing towards her mouth.

God help me, it can't be. I'm losing my mind, she thought . . . *it's . . .*

"Ade," she whispered. Then louder, until she was shouting, "Ade, Ade, Ade!"

The spell was broken. She had found her voice again, and the first word out of her mouth was Jade.

FORTY-SIX

Later in that same week, Marty's wife Lyn called Simone. "I'm worried sick about Marty," she'd said. "Will you come out and see if you can talk some sense into him?"

Marty had been on leave since the incident with Snippy, claiming he wanted to regroup and gather his wits about him. Simone was as worried as Lyn. Over the course of his career, the man had rarely taken a day off.

When Simone arrived at his place, Marty was sitting on the steps of the old farmhouse waiting for her. A Bluetick hound lazed nearby, warming his bones in a pool of sunlight, occasionally twitching his feet and yipping. Lyn was at work; their daughters at school. Marty's beard had grown fully in and the old open, friendly, look of his face had changed. Instead, he had the look of a man used to quiet contemplation and introspection.

After they had hugged hello, he handed her a beer, and she sat beside him on the steps.

"I found Jade and took him to the hospital to see Tina," Simone said. "She recognized him and called his name. She's back to me, Marty, and I know she's gonna get well."

"Aw, that's wonderful, partner." Marty said.

"So, when are you coming back to me, country boy? I like Otis, but I'm ready for my old partner back. Me and Otis together take up too much room in the car!"

Marty spoke as if he hadn't heard her question. "I was

281

always the straight-arrow type. You know what I mean? Never caused a problem to my family. Never questioned much of anything. I just took whatever came my way and tried to do the best I could. I married the first girl I slept with and had kids. Stayed my whole life in one place. I grew up right here in this house. Can you believe it?"

"It's one of the things I've always found most charming about you, partner. The settled way you saw life. Your clarity, your strong sense of right and wrong." Simone raised her eyebrows, as if to add, *don't mess with your marriage, buddy!*

"I'm not saying there's anything wrong with that. I love Lyn and the girls just as much as I ever did, but, it's love in a bigger sort of way. Still good, maybe even better, but different—a sort of non-attachment to the specifics of my life.

"Whatever it was that freak Whitfield gave me, showed me a new way of looking at things. Reality ain't what I thought it was. Things that you think are solid can disappear or change in a flash. It was like I was really seeing for the first time, and I saw the very molecules of life rearrange themselves into different worlds. One after the other in a circular pattern— worlds within worlds within worlds."

"Man, you were trippin'. That's all. Hallucinating. You've never done that before. That drug didn't show you anything real. It made you see something that wasn't there. What you have here, partner, this is real. Your wife, your children, the life you make for yourself."

"How do you know, Jamaica? You ever feel truly ecstatic? A joy that you can't find words for. You ever feel like you are a part of something so big, so eternal, and you never want it to end?"

"Sometimes making love," she said.

"A million times more intense than that."

"Marty, you can't stay stoned. That's the trap all dopers fall into. What starts out as ecstasy becomes addiction and agony. You've seen those pitiful addicts on the streets."

Marty jumped down from the steps and walked over to scratch behind the dog's ears.

"Hey good buddy. This feel good?" The dog thumped his tail and yawned, while digging his head into Marty's fingertips.

Marty turned to Simone and addressed her, patiently, as if speaking to a child. "I ain't talking about staying stoned. I'm talking about . . ."

He searched for just the right word. "I'm talking about . . . perception. I'm talking about the nature of reality. You take five people from the same family and let something big happen. Say they get in a wreck. You talk to any one of them, and they'll all have a different perspective. They'll describe something completely different; emphasize different things, because . . . maybe the observer changes reality.

"You ever wonder why old people's skin gets like wax paper? So thin you can almost see through it? The lining of their organs, the protective fat, everything thins out. It's like the veil that separates us from the other side is our body, and it gets thinner, more transparent, the closer we get to leaving this earth.

"We want to see life as balanced, everything in opposition to a counterpart. But, somehow, in some mystifying way, what we perceive as opposites—black/white, up/down, male/female—is only part of the picture. There's more. If we can change the way we look at things, what we look at changes! That drug showed me a different way of looking at life, and I can't just forget where it took me."

Simone had never seen him this way.

"So what're you thinking you should do?"

Marty ignored her question. "Religion tries to explain this perception of duality into heaven and hell, but that ain't it, Jamaica! That's about punishment and control. That's just more 'them and us.' There ain't no them! There's just US! Everything is ONE thing."

"You're scaring me, partner."

Simone walked over, knelt down to be eye level with Marty. "Perception of duality? You been reading too many books with all this time on your hands?"

Marty laughed. "This didn't come out of a book! Well, maybe some of the language to explain it did. The rest came straight out of me."

"What's Lyn say about all this?"

"She wants me to see a shrink. The Chief wants me to see a shrink. You probably think I should see a shrink, too, don't you. Hey, maybe Delia Whitfield could fit me in. She's probably got lots of free time right about now.

"But, I'm not the first person to experience these things, Simone. You been to college. You studied philosophy, right?"

"Sure, and crazy theories about life float around. Some of them have been with us forever, but there's no proof for any of it. It's weird to hear you spouting this stuff. You got the people who love you worried. We miss the old Marty!"

Marty shrugged, as if frustrated by his inability to explain what was going on with him. "I guess you had to be there."

Simone yelled at him. "I was there, man! And the last thing I seem to remember is you grinning like a fool with that witch about to cut off your . . ."

She caught herself. "Marty, tell me what to do. You can't sit out here with your hair growing down to your ass, talking to yourself 'bout the nature of reality."

"Sometimes, when it looks like life is throwing the worst shit at you, like you're going to hell in a hand basket, it's an opportunity, Jamaica. A chance to reevaluate. That's all I'm doing. I'm still me. That drug couldn't have found anything inside me that wasn't already there. It just opened a door, and I stepped through it."

"You sound like Jim Morrison of that old rock band, The Doors, and you know what happened to him."

"Yeah," he said and winked. "I'm really more like a country cosmic Clint Black—except better looking, of course—and I can't sing worth a damn.

"Go on home, partner. I'll be all right."

Marty gave Simone one of his trademark comical looks— smugness combined with a self-effacing shrug, and for a moment she thought he was his old self again. He turned his attention back to the dog, and said, "Right boy?"

EPILOGUE

One Year Later

Simone dashed excitedly up the driveway, waving a letter she had pulled out of the mailbox. "Tina! A letter from Catherine!"

Tina looked up from the porch swing. She attempted a hand clap and tried to say, "great," but she still had not completely recovered from the damage of the knife attack at the Sultan's Palace. She'd lost so much blood during the assault that she had suffered a heart attack and a minor stroke while in intensive care.

"You've had a cardiac event," the nurse had said to her after she stabilized and was recovering.

An event, huh, Tina had thought at the time. "*Sounds like something that shoulda been catered. I wonder if they hired a band?*"

Fortunately, the only lasting damage had been motor dysfunction on her left side, and a slight speech aphasia that, thanks to Simone's loving care and a cadre of dedicated nurses, doctors, and physical therapists, was rapidly improving. Tina expected nothing less than a full recovery.

Jade, back in town for a few days, had just left to pick up a pizza for supper. Just as Simone had predicted, their reunion was the medicine Tina needed to jump-start her recovery. What Simone hadn't known and could not have predicted was how much Jade's extended family would mean to Tina. He had provided her with two nieces, a nephew, a sister-in-law she adored, and adopted parents. With Simone and Minerva, Tina's life was now filled with positive, loving relationships.

The only person she still knew from the old days was Lady M who had saved her life and, to Tina, deserved her friendship because of that. On her last visit, Lady M informed Tina that she had quit the jack shack trade and was working on a memoir called, "Out, Damned Spot!"

Simone had brought Tina home to live with her and Minerva directly from the hospital. Minerva accepted Tina and her mother's relationship, although the three of them had occasional clashes. Minerva was, after all, a teenager with the inherent mood swings. Tina was helpless for a long time, and for the first few months, Simone felt like she had two daughters instead of one.

Simone sat next to Tina on the porch swing, patted her knee and said, "Want me to read it to you, sweet biscuit?"

Tina nodded and slowly lifted her left arm up to brush away a strand of hair from Simone's face. She beamed at Simone. These moments, when she could make her arm do exactly what she intended, were victories for both of the women.

Simone tore into the letter like it was a birthday present.

Dear Tina and Simone, it began.

Mama Bea and I have been in San Francisco for three months now, and I can't tell you how happy I am here. Mama Bea is not so sure. It's WAY too chilly for her. She says she can't find any good cornbread or sweet tea! She'll stay with me for a couple more months and then go back home, but she's having a ball playing the tourist. For me, it feels like I've come home to the place where I was supposed to have been born. Do you know that feeling?

Simone stroked Tina's arm and said, "We do, don't we baby?" She kissed her lightly on the cheek and continued reading the letter.

I don't know if you've felt well enough yet to visit Delia. I went by to see her one last time before leaving Atlanta. She's still in pretty bad shape. Delusional, I guess the doctors would call it. She doesn't remember doing any of the stuff they said she did. At least that's what she's telling the shrinks. I don't know. Maybe she's got everyone fooled. She's certainly smart enough.

Simone frowned—she had made her opinion about Dr. Delia Whitfield quite clear over the past year—she could rot in hell as far as Simone was concerned. Marty had never returned to himself the way Simone wanted. He'd retired from police work and was studying a different new age philosophy every other week. He had gotten involved with peace organizations and had recently volunteered for a mission in Nigeria building an orphanage for street kids. Lyn was still with him, but the changes in him had happened at a dizzying pace. She often called Simone to complain.

Marty seemed happy enough. He still had a sense of humor, but that too had changed. His crisp edge was gone, replaced by a mushy, soft spoken, "speak no evil" streak that Simone, frankly, found dull. She missed him terribly as a partner and a friend, but every time she visited him, he had some new idea he wanted to bounce off her. She tried to understand, but just couldn't relate to him anymore.

Simone rarely refused Tina anything, but if she wanted to visit Dr. Delia Whitfield—that quack head case—someone else would have to drive her there!

Tina poked Simone. "Read!" she said.

Simone continued reading the letter.

You remember that big aquarium Delia kept in the office? Well, apparently, she minored in biology in school and did some serious study on rain forest biodiversity. I think it was a toss up which way she would go. Anyway, she also kept a small terrarium at home where she was raising poisonous frogs! (The kind the natives use for poison darts.) The last time I was there, she showed it to me. I still don't understand most of the science behind it, but she had it set up just like a real rain forest. Even supplied the poisonous ants for the frogs to eat and, with her skills in biology and chemistry, she somehow created a paralytic from the frogs' skin secretions that would freeze a person, but not stop their breathing. She synthesized this stuff and, combined with the roofie she would slip them at the bar, made her victims unable to remember exactly what had happened to them. Plus, it gave them an amazing high. Can you imagine!!? She said some big drug manufacturer is after her for the formula! I don't know if that's true. She might <u>really be</u> delusional.

She seemed so different to me when I went to see her—at peace, but not communicative. I'm used to her drawing me out, talking me through everything. Maybe she was just exhausted. I know she must have been in terrible pain to do what she did. We were together at her house just before she went out that last night. We drank too much. So much that I passed out, but before I did, she told me a horrible story that I haven't told anyone until now. Her only sister was raped, murdered, and thrown into a ravine! The cops never found the monster who did it, and Delia never got over it. Her sister was sixteen and Delia was much younger, about ten. She adored her big sis. You know how that is. Her family never would talk about it. They acted like her sister had brought shame on the family. They tried to pretend she never existed. Can you imagine?

Isn't life strange! All the time she was helping me, Delia seemed so normal. I used to wish I could just be like her. I used to imagine that her nights were filled with sleep and sweet dreams—like she never had a fearful thought.

Her husband, John, has stuck by her, even though that snooty family of his wants him to get the hell away from her. That's what he told me. Not in those words, of course. He's too classy a guy for that. But, he loves her. He's sticking by her. I'm glad for that.

During our visit, Delia's only concerns were for me and you, and Mama Bea of course, and Janet. (Who, by the way, has slipped into a really bad depression since Delia's arrest. She's gained thirty pounds. Maybe you could visit her when you feel better, Tina.)

I told Delia we were fine, and she should concentrate on getting well. She just smiled at me and said I'm not sick, darling. I've never felt better in my life.

Legally, it doesn't look too good for her. It will probably take a while before she's released, since she was found guilty but mentally ill. She'll probably have to spend time in prison after the hospital (which, by the way, is this private cushy place). John's family money and connections probably made that happen. I'm so grateful for that. I'd hate to see her warehoused in some state facility.

Oh, Simone, I almost forgot! I spoke to my Aunt Mae a couple of days ago. She said you're reopening the investigation into my mother's disappearance. How can I ever thank you enough?!! I've always believed it was my Uncle Ted, but be sure to check out Daddy too. He's probably behind it."

Simone turned to Tina. "I told Aunt Mae to keep it to herself. Probably nothing will come of it. It's been such a long time."

She returned to reading the letter, worried that she might be setting Catherine up for a huge heartbreak.

"Let me see, where was I?" she said. "Oh yeah . . .

I'm sending you this article from the Detroit Citizen. You're not going to believe it. It blew my mind.

That's about it, loves. I'm out the door for an audition. Theater is fabulous here, although no matter how well I think I've gotten rid of the southern accent, these folks think I'm from Hooterville. I've gotten a couple of small roles. Been working on my one-woman thing, but to be truthful, I don't even care right now. Besides, the cousins are getting downright lazy! Sometimes, I can't hear them at all.

Uncle Ted is still with me—wouldn't you know it!—but Mama Bea cusses him out every time he pops up. They've gone at it pretty good. For some reason, she's got him scared. I don't know what I'll do when she leaves, but like Scarlet, I'll think about it tomorrow. Besides, there's always the Golden Gate Bridge. (Just kidding. My therapist out here says I shouldn't make suicide jokes 'cause it scares people. Don't be scared. I'm just a drama queen. You know that!) I've even made a friend, a sister looney tune that I met at a workshop. (There's a workshop for everything out here!) I'll keep you posted. Enjoy the article.

Love,
Catherine and Mama Bea

Simone unfolded the enclosed article and continued reading to Tina.

Detroit, MI . . . Mr. **Juan Ramirez was admitted to Michigan Hospital this morning around 5:00 a.m. A spokesman for the hospital stated that Mr. Ramirez was apparently the victim of a penectomy by an unknown assailant. His injury was described as traumatic, but not life threatening.**

Ramirez, recently paroled after spending three years in prison for rape, was the victim of an assault similar to the serial attacks against men that occurred in Atlanta, GA, in 1997. Each of the Atlanta victims had also been recently released from prison for sex crimes.

Dr. Delia Whitfield, an Atlanta psychologist, was found guilty, but mentally ill, in the Atlanta assaults. She is currently confined to a mental institution for an indefinite period of time, to be followed by incarceration. Since Whitfield's arrest and confinement, five similar documented attacks on sex offenders have occurred all over the world, including Thailand, Germany, England, and Mexico. The recent attack against Mr. Ramirez is the first in the United States.

A spokesperson for the Detroit Police Department stated that, while they have no leads in the case at this time, the attack appears to have some connection with the assaults in those cities.

As with those incidents, a note that read II Samuel 13:14 was found at the scene of the crime. The note was signed "For Delia. The Angel Who Showed Up."

Simone put her arm around Tina and gazed across their tiny, meticulously groomed front lawn. She sighed loudly and said, "What is the world coming to, likkle biscuit? Women know better than this."

Sitting beside her, Tina's lopsided grin spoke volumes. She dug her heel against the floor and started the swing moving forward and back. She wanted to say something, but it was so damn hard! She leaned against Simone's shoulder for a moment, then clumsily turned and planted a sloppy kiss on her cheek. Here goes, she thought. The words came out slightly garbled, but they were exactly what Tina intended to say.

"Remember what you told me on that camping trip we took just before I was attacked?"

Simone gave her a puzzled look. They had talked about so many things that weekend.

Tina playfully punched her arm and said, "Remember? It's just one more crazy thing in this world, my love. One more crazy-ass thing."

ABOUT THE AUTHOR

Janna Zonder lives a few miles northwest of Atlanta, Georgia, with her husband Stu and their dog, Joni. This is her first novel.

Made in the USA
San Bernardino, CA
17 September 2013